RUST

When science unlocks the secrets of aging,
who will control the key?

A tantalizing, scientifically-based action novel

GLEN JOSHPE, M.D.

Board certified Gerontologist

"Be prepared to understand aging like never before."

© Copyright 2011, Glen Joshpe

All rights reserved

RUST

*To my firstborn grandson, Coleman Terry Joshpe,
to whom we wish eternal youth, both in body and mind.
Your Grandmother Vicki and I are preserving
your umbilical stem cells to foster that goal.*

ACKNOWLEDGEMENTS

With much gratitude to:

    My brother, Kent Joshpe,
        for the cover design and illustrations

    Franklyn Dickson and Terry Bradshaw,
        for their editing and proofreading

    Ralph Stupple, for his overall general knowledge

    Aubrey de Grey and Ray Kurzweil,
        for having the foresight to think outside of the box

    And to my wife Vicki,
        for her continuous encouragement, support, advice
        and above all, her patience

FOREWORD

When the unorthodox, free-thinking, Cornell University scientist, Alex Stein comes across a life altering finding in Africa, a series of action-packed adventures are set in motion. As the very essence of life's mysteries become unraveled, the CIA, the Russian mafia, and Stein himself fight to retain control.

The intrigue traverses Washington DC, New York, Alaska, the Arctic, Arabian Sea, Congo basin, Egypt, and Newfoundland, before reaching the site of Stein's family roots in New Hampshire.

RUST is more than just a novel. The reader will be confronted with thought-provoking dialogue in the fields of religion, philosophy, morality, history, mathematics, chemistry, medicine, pharmacology, psychology, and science, as well as poetry. In addition, one will not only comprehend the process and science of aging, but will learn what scientists have discovered to alter it as well, findings that will surely affect you and your family.

Animal studies have successfully proven that we now have the ability to extend life to new horizons. Currently, we can manipulate yeast into behaving as if they are in a state of caloric reduction—the only proven method of extending life in humans—enabling them to produce the gene that can significantly prolong life. A similar gene also exists in people. It will not be long before these scientific advances become clinically available to mankind. Techniques such as gene manipulation, stem cell research, bone marrow transplantation, and nanotechnology, as well as other findings, have already yielded great success. The relationship between diabetes and the acceleration of the aging process will be clarified so that the non-scientist can comprehend the intricacies involved.

The stealing of electrons from our mitochondrial proteins by free radicals alters their ability to function effectively. Such alterations and mutations cause the loss of flexibility and viability, which we refer to as aging. Through nanotechnology, we can now transform powerful light energy into electrical energy and supply it directly to the cell where these proteins exist. Hopefully the electrons supplied by this electrical energy can stop free radicals from stealing electrons from our proteins. Some futurists believe that if we can survive for another fifteen years, then our life expectancy will continue to increase at a greater rate than our biological age.

Such advances will not only prolong life, but will restore vitality and flexibility to our heart, blood vessels, skin and other organs, thus enhancing the quality of lives as well. Utilizing this very same approach, many cancers, metabolic degenerative diseases, as well as inherited disorders, will no longer be considered the threat that they are today.

My hope is that the reader will be able to personally reap these benefits, but if not you, surely your children and grandchildren will, and their bodies will be insulated from oxidation, as they may look forward to the day when they are no longer faced with the reality of death by rust.

I
Washington, DC

*I don't want to achieve immortality through my work,
I want to achieve immortality by not dying.* — Woody Allen

Sally Bears gazed out the window, focused on the Washington monument. Although it appeared the same as the last time she had looked at it, she still found it more intriguing than the reams of data being spit out of her printer. She was convinced that she possessed the world's easiest job, and all of her friends were in envy of her status. She redecorated her home often, drove a nice car, and took frequent vacations. Only Sally knew that she was *bored to death*.

On her desk, the plastic sign read, U.S. Census Bureau-International Data Base-Statistical Analysis Division. Sally had started with the Census Bureau directly out of college, thanks to Uncle Harry's relationship with Senator Bradly. Now, 30 years later, she thought about packing it in, but with her $80,000 salary and great benefit package, she concedes, "Just one more year." Sally was preparing the *World Population Data Sheet,* which is readily available to anyone at www.prb.org.

As she sat staring out the window, her printer worked tirelessly, providing lists of demographic statistics from around the world: mid-year populations, growth rates, fertility rates, crude birth rates, neonatal mortality rates, life expectancy rates, crude death rates per thousand, percentage of resident over the age of 65, etc. As her printer fired away, Sally seemed more concerned about the alignment of the paper than the flow of data. Here comes one on the Central African Republic, as she reflected on what country that used to be. Sally's mind began to drift again. This time she wondered about the true cost of employing tens of thousands throughout the world, with jobs such as hers, to digest all of the useless data the Census Bureau had collected. Surely it was enough to house, feed, clothe, and educate every child from the Central African Republic, wherever that might be. Sally's mind again began to wonder, for it was now 11:45. *What would I be ordering for lunch?*

Once a month, Sally would focus on an apparent deviation from expected criteria, print off a duplicate, and waddle down the hall, passing several dozen other small cubicles, to the Office of the Assistant Director of the U.S. Census Bureau-International Division. She would pretend to be concerned about the data, only to give her boss James Hall the impression that she was doing her job.

Today was different. Sally didn't just waddle, but all of her two hundred plus pounds motorized down the hall with her hips swinging wildly. As she knocked on Mr. Hall's door, he quickly shoved the Washington Post Crossword puzzle into his desk draw, and turned on his laptop. "Look at these figures from Central African Republic, Mr. Hall. They don't make any sense!"

" Obviously a typo, can't be, check it out Sally."

"I already have, sir. I had Justin call over to the African Bureau. They had the same concern, but they verified the numbers as well, and insist it's not a typo."

"Today is March thirtieth, correct?" Hall asked.

"Why do you ask?"

"Just want to be sure that no one is playing an April fool's joke on us. How can this be, Sally? Something is way out of whack. This is not what either one of us needs this close to retirement. If I take this to the Director, I better not wind up with shit on my face."

The two-dozen or so data entry clerks at the bureau didn't need to be told that a crisis was ensuing. For starters, no one saw Sally propel herself down the hall so quickly, with hips cranking and desktops shaking. Looking through the glass partition of Hall's office, they could sense the heated discussion as phone extensions began to light up and start ringing. Twenty minutes later, Hall buzzed his secretary. "Brenda, call the Director and tell him we need to meet ASAP. And Brenda, we're going to a Code RED." Brenda dropped her sandwich instantly. In the past 35 years, the division had gone to a Code RED only once. That was when six Pakistani census workers were kidnapped by the Taliban and executed in full view over the Internet. "And by the way, Brenda," Hall said, "you better cancel my dental appointment."

2

The conference room at the Office of the Director of the Census Bureau was a large sterile appearing room devoid of pictures, with the exception of a second grader's interpretation of a Census Bureau enumerator at work. A stick figure character, pencil in hand, was seen counting a group of five people, each standing in front of a house. The caption read, *"Let's get the count right."*

Mr. Troy Roberts, Director of the Bureau, sat at the end of a twenty-foot table. He was flanked by four of his deputies. Roberts was 68 years old. He wore a tweed suit, white shirt, and a bow tie. He appeared pale, with thinning gray hair, and Coke-bottle spectacles. He gave the appearance of an about-to-be-retired high school superintendent. Roberts disliked meetings, and he despised emergency meetings. Hall knew this, and he certainly didn't want to enter the arena unprepared. His staff of four had neatly spread out all of the relevant data on the easel.

"The focus target is the Central African Republic," Hall said. "We are focusing on the percentage of population over the age of 65. The figure has always come in around 3.4 %, but recently it has jumped to 3.7%. It has changed only in Lobaye Province where that number is now 3.9%. Now get this, all of the changes come from a region in the Lobaye Province called Bongele, where the number has reached an astonishing 30%. These figures have now been verified three times by their census takers and we are assured that there is no error. All of the figures were reviewed again, and again. The data seems to be real, but quite disturbing; I have never seen deviation from expected criteria like this before," stated Roberts." We need to get to the bottom of this quickly, and find out why folks just stopped dying in Bongele of the Central African Republic."

3

With all of his years in public service Troy Roberts never anticipated that he would have difficulty in locating CIA Headquarters. History however, had proven him to be wrong. For in 1719, Thomas Lee purchased a tract of land from the sixth Lord Fairfax and he named it *Langley* after his ancestral home in England. Many wealthy settlers from Europe subsequently moved there and many large plantations were established in the region. During the War of 1812, President James Madison and his wife Dolley fled the British invasion of Washington to the safety of friends at Langley. Langley was a Union stronghold during the Civil War, and had two forts, Camp Griffin and Camp Pierpont, which housed soldiers to protect Washington.

With the development of the Great Falls and Old Dominion Railroad in 1903, the area began to grow, as those working in Washington were able to live outside the city. In 1910, a new post office was constructed and officially named McLean, rather than Langley. In 1947, President Harry S. Truman signed the National Security Act, creating the Central Intelligence Agency for the purpose of combating communist aggressiveness by the USSR, and in 1959 the CIA headquarters was built at this site. Despite the official name of McLean, the name Langley still lives to describe the neighborhood where the CIA Headquarters is located. So Troy Roberts tried to hide his embarrassment from his deputy James Hall, as he needed directions at a service station to find CIA Headquarters, when the GPS in his Lexus seemed confused.

4

Dr. Ronald Brenner, Director of the Technical Targeting Division of the Central Intelligence Agency sat silently awaiting the presence of Roberts and Hall in the first floor conference room. Dr. Brenner was 59 years old. He was 5' 9", bald, pleasant looking and immaculately dressed. He wore a black suit, white shirt and had a black and white striped tie to match. He usually said very little, but always tried to give the impression that he was engrossed in deep thought. It was difficult for anyone to know if he truly was or whether he simply tried to give that impression. In reality, his subordinates had very little knowledge of what he actually did. When the two gentlemen entered, three minutes late with apologies about the Capital-area traffic, Brenner gave them a look of discontent. There were a total of twelve officials in the room, including representatives of Homeland Security, the State Department, and the NSA (National Security Agency), as well as a number of staff from the CIA.

After brief introductions, a technician wearing a headset said, "Ten seconds, Sir." A massive twelve-foot by four-foot screen began to flicker and then focused on a robust black man wearing a military uniform bearing an abundance of medals. General Salagi was an imposing heavyset man with a huge head and a mouth overcrowded with pearly white teeth. The General was flanked by a half-dozen soldiers wearing khakis and shouldering automatic weapons.

"Thank you, General Salagi, for agreeing to this meeting on such short notice," said Director Brenner. "Naturally, we are all quite concerned about the recent findings that have emerged from your country. The way things are in the world today, I'm sure that you would agree with me that no one likes surprises. Your people have assured us that the data is not faulty. If so, such a drastic change in mortality rates would not only have a dramatic impact on the Central African Republic, but on everyone else as well." "First of all, Dr. Brenner, I can assure you that our data is reliable. In fact, we can attribute the findings to a very remote area in the southwest jungle, which the locals refer to as Bongele. We subsequently sent some of our troops back in with the census takers. You may not believe what they found."

"Go on, we're listening."

"They found several thousand natives who claimed to be between 110 and 118 years old, and some as old as 120. They certainly didn't look it and we suspected someone was trying to pull a fast one. However, their papers all checked out: birth certificates, medical and other governmental papers. They had the proof. It was no joke. Those who died prior to reaching one hundred were predominantly from HIV, accidents, malaria, snake bites, and animal attacks. We even checked out the cemeteries and the headstones. It was rare to be able to find someone who recently died between the ages of 75 to 95."

"And the explanation General?" "I should be asking you Dr. Brenner. This whole thing began when one of your Americans first arrived here."

5

"Tell me more about this American of ours, General; tell me everything."

General Salagi began, "We have examined our old immigration records when this gentleman entered our country and I can now recall some of the details. Thirty years ago we had a small band of Catholic missionaries and along with them was an American named Alex Stein. We are faxing over his visa photo. We became suspicious of him right off the bat."

"Why's that?" Brenner interrupted.

"First of all he was an atheist, so we assumed he wasn't tagging along to preach the gospel. Secondly, he brought along four natives just to carry his equipment, and with all that he had brought along he had only one single change of clothing. The rest of his stuff was scientific and laboratory equipment. Naturally we suspected he was up to no good, perhaps going to start up a meth lab or something of that sort. Perhaps start some type of cult and get all the natives off, like that guy with the Kool-Aid you folks had back then. The missionaries, however, confirmed that he was indeed a medical caregiver.

We were still skeptical, so we detained him. Kept him for the good part of a week. Very strange man as I recall. Wouldn't make eye contact, didn't have much to say to us, but when he did, we could make little sense of it. We even considered torturing him, although I doubt if we would have gotten anything out of him. We couldn't find anything illegal about him, so eventually we just let him go, and the guides proceeded to bring him to Bongele. Never thought much about him again but all that changed yesterday."

"What all changed General Salagi? ""You already know. Folks in Bongele are no longer dying. We reached Stein yesterday via satellite, and once again couldn't get a straight answer out of him on anything. When I mentioned that the American CIA was asking questions about him, he became very upset, and pretended that we had a bad connection. He was clear about one thing only."

"And that was?"

"If we came looking for him, we wouldn't find him."

"Very, very strange," Brenner said.

"Surely you people, with all of your resources, must have something on your fellow American."

"Never heard of him before," stated Director Brenner, "But you can be sure that's going to change real soon."

6

Carlton Terry had been a CIA field operator for six years. He was young, ambitious, and apparently bright. He had long, dirty-blond hair, blue eyes, a straight nose and attractive features to go along with his 6' 3" frame. Carlton was born and raised on Cape Cod, where he attended high school. He did well there, and had his choice of several Ivies to attend. He selected Brown in Providence, Rhode Island as his first choice, because Brown was one of the few Universities that allowed students to be totally creative in selecting their courses. He despised the study of foreign languages, and in high school he had promised himself he would never study another language again, especially after Professor Naimark's French class. After Carlton was asked to read out loud, the Professor said, *"Monsieur Terry, zat was not too bad, except for one ting, I swear I did not understand a single woord zat you said."* Carlton was humiliated as his classmates burst into uncontrollable laughter. Subsequently, he was asked to read aloud each day of class. When asked by a fellow classmate why his dialect was so poor, Carlton responded, "I don't get it. Why would anyone want to place a perfectly good consonant at the end of a word and then decide not to pronounce it? And furthermore, when someone says that word, how are they supposed to guess which consonant they meant, if they didn't pronounce it?" At Brown, Carlton would have no language requirement, and that suited him just fine.

    Carlton had majored in Psychology at Brown. His mother's mental illness as well as his father's addictive personality had sparked his interest in learning what made the human mind tick. Upon graduating, Carlton was uncertain of a career path. He liked science and was fascinated by psychology, but did not want to enroll in med school. Research had no appeal for him since it wasn't fast moving or exciting. He considered teaching college, but would need to continue his own education first. He just happened to attend a career opportunity day at Brown where he met a recruiter from the CIA. Although he found the discussion exhilarating, he doubted if he would ever qualify as a candidate. First, he had committed some indiscretions in his youth. He was also aware of the thorough screening process that included polygraph testing, and he believed his history of smoking pot in his first two years of college would eliminate him, along with his lack of foreign language skills.

When Carlton was eleven years old, his parents were having serious problems. Shortly afterwards, Carlton began to misbehave. He broke a neighbor's window with his BB gun and when caught shoplifting a baseball he was arrested. Eventually he found his way to the principal's office. Mr. Beck knew Carlton was bright and believed he had potential. During the course of discussions Carlton admitted to feeling sorry for himself. He resented the fact that his dad never came to any of his Little League games and was out of town for most of his school extra-curricular activities. In addition his mom was unstable. Mr. Beck listened attentively without interruption.

When he finally spoke, he said, "Carlton, life is unfair. Some kids are born with a golden spoon in their mouths. Apparently, you are not one of them. Some folks start life on a high rung of the ladder. You are starting near the bottom, and have a lot higher to climb. You have a right to be angry and feel sorry for yourself. The big question is where do you go from here? Are you going to be a failure and blame it on others, which may be justifiable, or are you going to start climbing the ladder?"

"The true greatness of this country is that regardless of where you begin, there is opportunity to advance. So here is my advice to you: Go home and lock yourself in the bathroom and stare at yourself in the mirror. Ask yourself, am I going to continue to feel sorry for myself at the risk of becoming a failure or will I make something of myself, something of which I can be proud? You can be *bitter* or you can be *better*, it is your choice. Stay in school! Study! Go to college! The worst part of not getting an education is the risk of having to take orders from someone who isn't as smart as you for the remainder of your life."

Carlton did not utter a word. That simple advice from Mr. Beck turned out to be the defining point in his life. From that day on, he never complained, never acted out and became an outstanding student.

So in spite of Carlton's apprehensions, he decided to go online and check out the requirements for the CIA. To his surprise, he learned that anyone using illicit drugs in the past twelve months only should not apply. After further consideration, he realized that it would be difficult to find any eligible college students if the regs were more stringent.

Carlton's other apprehension revolved around the problems of his parents. His dad, Herbert, was a traveling salesman who sold pencils to large department stores. He was on the road all of the time and had developed a serious drinking problem. His mom, Anna, had suffered from frequent bouts of depression. Ironically, her case wasn't correctly diagnosed until she was started on the anti-depressant Prozac. Prozac was a selective re-uptake serotonin inhibitor (SSRI) that slowed the breakdown of serotonin in the brain, and by raising the serotonin levels, helped those with depression. Prozac has been shown to be extremely effective in cases of ordinary depression, but can actually make matters worse in patients with bipolar disorder. Failure to distinguish between ordinary depression and bipolar disease could be disastrous. The drug triggered a full-blown manic episode, for which she was hospitalized, and the correct diagnosis was eventually revealed.

Anna suffered from Type I bipolar disorder, the most serious of the several variants. At times, she would spend most of the day in bed. She would neglect housework, have difficulty in concentrating, and display feelings of anxiety, guilt and depression. After months of such apathy and listlessness she would emerge into a manic phase. Suddenly she would display excessive energy, become extremely talkative, start many projects while completing none as many thoughts raced through her head. During these periods she would require little sleep and her attention span and judgment were impaired. She often went on shopping sprees and charged items that she was unable to afford.

Similar to other patients with this disorder, she would never seek medical attention during this phase, as she might during the depressive phases, thus making the correct diagnosis difficult to detect. Unable to effectively communicate, Herbert and Anna divorced when Carlton was eleven years old.

When Anna was placed on the mood stabilizing drugs lithium and Depakote her mood swings were less dramatic and she was able to return home. Her disease played a significant role in inspiring Carlton to major in Psychology at Brown. He read extensively about bipolar disorder, and developed a genuine empathy for anyone who was afflicted with it. As he learned, there is a strong inherited component to this disorder. These patients suffer from a chemical imbalance in the brain that makes them feel that *things just aren't right.* They cannot put a finger on the problem, but suffer from a general sense of uneasiness. Rarely do they see themselves as the source of the problem. It is the job, the spouse, the kids, the neighbors, the school, the government. Everyone is to blame except themselves.

When they are in the excitable stage, it is often similar to the stages of one who has had too much to drink. Initially they are up and outgoing, then very talkative; even feeling a bit tipsy. Next they make inappropriate accusations and make an ass of themselves. Often this is followed by a period of guilt, which the mind often converts to depression. In severe cases suicide can follow, which occurs in up to fifteen percent of cases of bipolar disease.

Without proper mood-stabilizing medication, such as lithium, tegretol, Depakote as well as the newer atypical anti-psychotics, such as Seroquel, Abilify, Geodon, Risperdal, Zyprexa and others, these individuals will have difficulty adjusting to the stresses of life. They have trouble holding down a job, sustaining a marriage or meaningful long-term productive relationships with others.

Knowing all of this, Carlton was somewhat anxious about his own future. If one parent has bipolar disorder, there is approximately a twenty five percent chance that the offspring will. When both parents are affected the risk increases to 50 to 75%. The disorder, which previously was named manic-depressive syndrome, is not uncommon. Over three million Americans are affected, or one out of every 83 Americans. Most cases first appear in the 15-to-24-year-old age group, so when Carlton approached thirty, and showed no excessive mood swings, his anxiety dissipated. His father's alcohol addiction also had a potential genetic component; however, that too seemed to spare Carlton. This left him with the conclusion that for any and all problems and faults he possessed, he would have no one to blame but himself.

7

The career opportunities website for the CIA stated that they received more than 10,000 résumés per month. Applications were accepted only online, and if one did not receive a response in 45 days, you were not being considered. After reviewing the extensive list of positions, he discovered the Science, Technology, and Weapons section, and within that, the Technical/Targeting Analysis Division. The hype stated, "Be part of a dynamic team that unites three disciplines; analysis, development, and operations. The work is extremely complex and we are looking for high-energy, intelligent, curious individuals who thrive on tackling the most difficult problems." Carlton felt there was little chance that he would be considered, but with nothing to lose, he decided to apply nonetheless.

Three weeks later, he received an email stating that he should report to Langley for a screening interview. He was reminded that only a small percentage of those given an interview are ultimately accepted. Over the next six weeks, he found himself undergoing a wide array of interviews and tests. There were IQ tests, psychological evaluations, and polygraph testing. There were also personality tests to evaluate career strengths and weaknesses, such as the Minnesota Multiphasic Personality Inventory. He was subject to medical tests, including stress testing, along with blood, urine, and hair analysis.

He noticed that as the process continued there were fewer and fewer applicants still standing. Next he was presented with a number of situational problems and asked how he would respond to hypothetical scenarios.

There was one particular question that intrigued him. "Different individuals come up to a house where a dog resides; some of those are welcomed by the dog, as the dog wags its tail. Others, such as the mailman, come by on a daily basis, and yet the dog always barks or growls at them. Why?" Carlton immediately knew that the answer would not be as simple as the dog sees the mailman wears a uniform. In order to arrive at the correct answer, he would need to think like a dog. After a moment of silence he responded: "The dog sees his job as protecting the house. There are some folks who come up to the door and are welcomed into the home. These are friends. Another group may approach the house daily, but they are never invited in. They are repelled. The dog sees his role as reminding these folks that they are not welcome."

"How could you prove such a theory?" asked the examiner.

"Invite the mailman into the home and have him sit down at the table with the home owner, and the dog will no longer bark at him."

"Mr. Carlton, you are the first candidate all week to give the correct response," the examiner said.

One week later, Carlton was notified that he had been accepted to an entry position with the CIA with a starting salary of $42,209 plus a full benefit package. He would spend the next year in training, but at least this time, someone other than himself would be paying for his education. "It's a dog's world!" Carlton shouted out as he read the letter.

Carlton received excellent evaluations from all of his assignments over the next several years. His salary rose to $120,000 and he was being given more important assignments. He seemed to be on the fast track at Langley after recovering an Exxon tanker from Somali pirates. He was anxiously awaiting his next big case and thought he may have hit pay dirt when he received orders to report directly to Director Brenner, Chief of the Technical Analysis Division of the CIA.

Carlton was expecting to see Director Brenner in person, but when he arrived he was greeted by Deputy Johnson. Jerry Johnson had been an employee of the Technical/Targeting Analysis Division of the CIA for nearly twenty years. He received his undergraduate and Master's degrees at Emery University, and had worked his way up to number three in the chain of command within his section, as well as the highest position ever held by an African American.

Johnson possessed a keenly logical mind accompanied by an excellent memory. On one occasion, when his superiors were unavailable, he was called upon to testify before a Senate committee on CIA matters. It was an experience he vowed never to repeat again. One of his colleagues estimated that he lost a good five pounds in perspiration. So Johnson's superiors were comforted knowing that he had no desire to rise any higher in the department.

Johnson was a master strategist. He dominated opponents in both bridge and chess, and possessed an uncanny ability to anticipate his opponent's next moves. As a psychology major, he thrived on the challenge of getting into the minds of others, particularly if they had a reputation of having a superior mind.

"Terry, the Director wants you to fly up to Fairbanks, catch the Alaskan Rails, and interview a guy named Steve Hinden down in Wasilla. He roomed with a fellow named Alex Stein about 50 years ago at Cornell University in Ithaca, NY. This fellow Stein may have found a way to keep some African tribesmen from aging. Find out everything about the guy. I mean, I want to know what brand of toothpaste he uses." Carlton had never felt more disappointed, and it showed on his face. Here he was expecting to be given a major assignment, but instead he found himself checking out old frat buddies at Cornell. *Whose toes had he stepped on*, he wondered?

"Your file has all the pertinent information, Terry. Believe it or not, this investigation started at the Census Bureau, of all places. FBI says it's overseas, and not their jurisdiction. Homeland isn't interested, and so State has dumped it on us. Apparently this gal over at Census has connections with old retired Senator Bradly. He called State and asked the Secretary to look into this as a personal favor. Perhaps he is hoping that they have found some fountain of youth to rejuvenate him at ninety. I guess his Viagra® just isn't doing it for him any longer. Anyway, State contacted Brenner who wants us to check it out. You should know how this town works by now, Terry; if you don't keep greasing the higher ups you'll never last more than four years around here.

"Usually we would send a Probbie on an assignment such as this, but Brenner has a feeling that there could be something big here, so he specifically requested you. This fellow Stein is up to something, and before we confront him, I want to know what we're dealing with. You know the old adage: *No surprises.* "We're sending Chris Hogan to Africa to pick up Stein. Don't need much to charge him with at this juncture; after all, his visa expired 30 years ago. Before we interrogate him we want to know what he is really thinking. We are just like good lawyers here Terry: never want to ask a question for which you don't already know the answer. Remember what we learned from the Simpson case: *if it doesn't fit, then you have to acquit.* We don't expect any trouble with Hinden; after all, he is about 70 now, so you will not be in need of any back-up. Take as long as you need, but be thorough. This Hinden guy may be a nut job as well. Perhaps we have a real *folle à deux*. Excuse me, I forgot about your lack of French skills. That's two nut cases, sharing similar psychotic delusions. I want instantaneous updates, so take the Dragon software along so you don't have to type the interview. And Terry, don't look so disappointed; you're not the one who may be contracting malaria in the jungles of Africa. Hogan had to get shots and meds not only for malaria, but yellow fever, typhoid, and hepatitis as well. All you're going to need is a hot water bottle."

Rust   15

8

As he rode the Alaskan Railroad, Carlton wondered whom he pissed off to get this assignment. Was there any more of a god-forsaken place in the entire US of A? There were only three interesting facts about Wasilla, Alaska. First, it was the hometown of Sarah Palin. Secondly, it was the site where the Iditarod dogsled race was actually held. Since so few reporters could even get to Wasilla to cover the world's longest race, they had to hold a fake ceremonial start in Anchorage, and then move the actual race to Wasilla. The final earth-shattering fact about Wasilla is that if you spelled it backwards, it reads, *All I Saw*.

Carlton shook his head, "Yes indeed; "All I saw. Right! All I saw was snow!"

Steve Hinden's cabin was a good eight miles from the train station. When Carlton summoned a taxi, he had no idea that he was going to get two dogs, a sled, and a musher. The outdoor temperature was 4 degrees F, not exactly what Carlton had anticipated for early April. Carlton was thrilled when he saw the roof of Steve Hinden's subterranean cabin. As the door opened, there stood a thin elderly man, who appeared years older than his true age of seventy. Hinden was untidy, his hair gray and matted down, his teeth poorly maintained. He wore an old torn flannel shirt with mismatched plaid pajama bottoms and wore sandals without socks. One thing was for sure. Hinden didn't get much company.

Hinden's cabin was actually quite cozy in spite of the fact that Wasilla apparently didn't seem to offer house cleaning services. The log home consisted of only one room, approximately 40 by 24 feet. A large fieldstone fireplace was located at one end, and a Vermont Castings stove was at the opposite end, near where the bed rested. A large oak table was the focal point of the room, with two kerosene lanterns hanging from the beams. The table was cluttered with books and stacks of papers; two Adirondack chairs were present along the side of the long table.

"Thank you for agreeing to speak to me, Mr. Hinden, about your old friend, Alex Stein," said Carlton, as he helped himself to one of the two chairs.

"Well, you did make it sound like a matter of life and death. I haven't seen or spoken to Alex in over fifty years now. Did the ol' buzzard finally kick the bucket?" Before Carlton could reply, Hinden chimed in. "Let me guess, you're here to tell me that Stein left me all of his worldly possessions? Actually, it doesn't surprise me that he hasn't made any new friends in the past fifty years. By the way, please excuse my manners, Mr. Terry; would you care for something to drink? How about a glass of iced tea? I guess I'm not used to getting a lot of company. You know that's why I came to Wasilla. Since my work is funded by the NIH, they require me to live in the USA. I'm not very fond of a lot of people and so this is about as far away as I can get from civilization."

"If it's not too much trouble, I can go for a cup of hot tea. That trip up here was a bit chilly," Carlton said. "To answer your question, Mr. Hinden, we believe Mr. Stein is still very much alive. And we believe he is in a remote area of Africa."

"Then what brings you all the way out here?"

"We are conducting a thorough background check on Alex Stein, and we are going to need your help."

"Did Alex do something bad?"

"No, just routine matters, and all of our leads to date have said the same thing: If you want to know what Alex Stein was really like, you need to speak with Steve Hinden. So here we are."

"I appreciate the compliment, Mr. Terry, but I haven't seen Stein since gasoline was twenty cents a gallon. I don't think I can be of much help. Besides, I have some really important work that I am conducting myself. Perhaps the folks back in town have mentioned it? I'm studying the alteration of the migration patterns of the Alaskan Salmon. It may not sound very important to you, but it is to the Eskimos and the Alaskans; their entire economy is dependent on those salmon. If you want to know about Alex so badly why don't you just go see him instead? Now if you don't mind, I have to get back to my own work."

"We do plan on paying Mr. Stein a visit, but before we do so, we were hoping you could tell us what to expect. In our line of work, we really don't like surprises."

"Well, I wish you lots of luck, but as I said, I need to get back to my own work. Sorry, I can't help you."

"The information we need to gather on Stein is a matter of national security, Mr. Hinden, I'm afraid that we can compel you to cooperate with us."

"Compel me! You have got to be kidding! You can't compel me to do anything! I'm an American citizen!"

"That may be so. However in accordance with the Intelligence Reform and Terrorism Prevention Act of 2004, the National Security Act was amended to provide for a Director of National Intelligence who may assume many of the roles formerly fulfilled by the Director of Central Intelligence, under a separate Director of the Central Intelligence Agency."

" What in the world is all that hogwash about?"

"It means that I can compel you to cooperate."

"See, there's the reason I ran away from the mainland. I knew this kind of crap would come about some day. Should have gone over to Europe when I had the chance. Perhaps they would appreciate having someone save their salmon."

"Listen Mr. Hinden, there's one of two ways we can do this. I can summon the U.S. Marshall Service in Anchorage and have you escorted back to Langley for interrogation as a hostile combatant under the Homeland Security Act, or you can select choice number two".

"Which is?"

"We consider you a cooperating testifier, and reimburse you $750 per day for your time."

"Why didn't you just say that in the first place? I'll make some hot tea and let's get started."

9

Carlton began speaking into the microphone, "Carlton Terry recording interview with Steve Hinden at his home in Wasilla, Alaska, on April 7, at 1:15 PM. Data to be simultaneously transcribed by Dragon with wireless transfer to Operator 7, Conference room 103, at Langley, Virginia. Are you ready to begin, Mr. Hinden?"

"Sure, but wouldn't it be easier for you to just tell me what you already know, and I can just fill in the blanks? After all, you have agreed to pay me $750 a day, and time is money." Hinden was now taking precautions to document his arrangement with Carlton on tape.

"We prefer to do it this way so that we don't prejudice or influence your responses; besides we know very little about Mr. Stein. May we proceed?"

"Just one more question if you don't mind?"

"Is that going to be your personal check or a business check?"

"Mr. Hinden, the check will come from the same place as your NIH consulting check and your Social Security check."

"That being?"

"The Treasury of the United States of America. Is that acceptable?"

"Yes, very acceptable."

"Let's begin then."

Carlton's comment that the CIA knew little about Stein at this point was untrue. The agency had already gathered a considerable amount of background information. Alex Stein was born and raised in the Bronx. His father was a second-generation electrical engineer of German descent, who died of a heart attack shortly after Alex moved off to Cornell. His mom was a bookkeeper for a regional bank; she died after being involved in a motor vehicle accident with a suspected drunken driver. Hinden was sketchy on these details himself, since Alex didn't speak much about his family, or much about anything else. Although Hinden added little new information, Carlton did not interrupt or interject until Steve Hinden had reached the crucial Cornell years. "Before we get to your first meeting with Stein, let me ask if you recognize this photo of him? I apologize for the quality of it, but it was taken by satellite and it is the only recent photo available. Is that Stein?" Carlton asked

"Yes, it is, but it's very strange. He hasn't aged a day since Cornell. I look like his grandfather." Hinden then showed Carlton a photo he had hanging on his wall of the two of them together back in Cornell. Hinden was right—except for a receding hairline, Stein hadn't aged a bit.

10

Steve Hinden resumed. "We met as freshman roommates at Cornell. The first few days he hardly looked up from his books to even say hello. He didn't socialize at all, but he gradually warmed up to me. He was definitely the weirdest guy in the dorm, and I was probably runner-up. I guess that's why they stuck us together. After all, he was a geek and I was no Don Juan. Alex had a different manner of thinking than most people."

"Could you elaborate, please?"

"For example, we would be walking past the TV lounge, headed for dinner, and he would glimpse at a show about spiders, and he would just stop in his tracks and stand there for forty-five minutes. Now who in their right mind would miss a nice chicken dinner just to watch a couple of spiders? Once he started focusing on a subject he would not stop until he reached a satisfactory conclusion. He was able to block everything else out. Sometimes he would just sit on his bed in the dark and not say a word. He was quite an impressive guy."

"How's that impressive?"

"Well, to quote the Dalai Lama, "Sometimes one creates a dynamic impression by saying something and sometimes one creates an impression by remaining silent." If I asked what he was doing, he would respond, 'binary reasoning.'"

"Did he ever say anything when he was in one of those states?"

"One day he just sat there saying, *'I got it. It's all the same.'* Here is another example of Alex's logic. We were sitting in the cafeteria one afternoon with another one of the students, and one of the physician instructors from the graduate school was at the next table. The student had a rash on his arm and he asked the physician if he knew what was causing it? The physician tersely replied, 'Why don't you see me in my office, and I'll look into it.' I commented to Alex that perhaps the physician didn't care to hand out any free advice. Alex then became very short with me. He said, 'You don't understand. Physicians don't use magic. There is a logical process that needs to be applied before one can arrive at the correct diagnosis. It's called the SOAP method. S stands for subjective. What did you eat? Where did you travel? Did you wear any new clothing? Did you

Rust 21

change soaps or detergents? Did you receive any tick bites? O stands for objective findings. What is the texture of the rash? Is it bilateral? Are other areas of the body involved? Does the patient have a fever? Does the patient have a murmur? A stands for assessment. What are all of the possible diagnoses that are to be considered: Allergy, infection, Lyme's disease, bacterial endocarditis? And P stands for plan. What tests need to be done to verify the diagnosis? Blood counts, cultures, tests for Lupus, syphilis, rheumatoid arthritis?'

"Alex pointed out that patients insist on the correct diagnosis when they see a physician, but most do not comprehend that there is a logical process that needs to be followed when encountering any problem." He would say, 'One can't just give casual responses when complex logical problems come into play.'"

"Would you say that he had a photographic memory?"

"I'm not really sure what that means. Everyone's memory works differently. We had this one guy on our dorm, named Gary Elinoff. He could read something a half a dozen times, and yet he still *CRS*. That's short for *couldn't remember shit*. He could never find his keys or his glasses. But if he took notes in his own hand, at exam time, he could see his notes as if he was looking directly at them. Go figure? Could Stein just look at a page and instantaneously read it back? No, but if he was interested in something and gave it his attention, he would retain it forever.

"Alex was fascinated by the powers of the human mind, more specifically the cerebral cortex, of which he would say, 'Here lay millions of complex, neurological pathways, both stimulatory as well as inhibitory, with an entangled network of self-regulatory control via a number of nerves and neurotransmitters. This massive protoplasm of gray matter has the ability to build itself, nourish itself from within, translate a chemical message into innumerable languages, requires no additional parts, never shuts down, makes its own repairs, regulates itself by utilizing electrical energy, needs no external power supply, has unlimited memory storage, needs no software updating, is completely mobile, weighs merely a few pounds and lasts for the major part of a century. If one counted the neurons in the cerebral cortex at a rate of one per second, it is estimated that it would take 32 million years to count all 100 billion nerve cells with over 100,000 connections. This is the marvel of the human brain.'"

"That was quite impressive, Mr. Hinden, you seem to have a pretty good memory yourself."

"Believe it or not, when I came to Cornell, I didn't really know how to study and my memory wasn't anything special. Rooming with Alex made me want to try and emulate his ways. He was a terrific student.

"Alex would say that we now have two substrates in which to conduct reasoning. There's the one that uses organic matter, carbon, and the inorganic substrate of the computer chip, silica. And in spite of his fascination with the human brain he believed that the silica substrate was superior and faster, and that man ought to start thinking like the computer if he wanted to catch up, and so Alex attempted to use binary reasoning. He would select the two most logical options, accept one and reject the other, and then proceed to the next switch. On occasion he would go through hundreds of switches at a single sitting. If you dared to interrupt him, he became very upset. The strangest part of it all was that he never wrote anything down. It was all in his head.

"Take the chess club story, for example. When Alex lost the chess championship match at Cornell he became very upset. He blamed it all on the distractions: the lights, the crowd, everything. After that he would only play by phone or mail and he never lost another match. The real crazy part was that he never even looked at the board. He said the red and black checker boxes distracted him from focusing. He had all 64 spaces pictured in his head.

"Here's another example of how Stein thought and how he over analyzed simple matters. How could anyone begin a discussion about a cat on marijuana, and conclude by saying that one of man's greatest virtues, the ability to love, is simply just another defense mechanism? Allow me to elaborate. One of the guys in the dorm named Charlie was asked by a friend to watch his cat Bernice while he was out of town. Charlie transported the cat in a cardboard box to his frat house, and when the box was opened Bernice hightailed it behind the couch and hid. In spite of an exhaustive search, Bernice was nowhere to be found. After several days we all thought that someone must have left the door open and Bernice took off for better accommodations.

"Seven days later someone lit up a joint, and guess what? Out came Bernice. She sat on Charlie's lap and just purred, as mellow as any pussycat could be. Everyone thought it was a riot, except for Alex. He decided that this was a case for which to apply his binary reasoning."

"What did he mean by that? I don't follow."

"I'll try and give you the abridged version of how Alex might think. Humans and cats have similar neurotransmitters and cell physiology. Yes

Rust   23

or no, he would select yes. Human and cat therefore respond similarly to similar stimuli. Yes or no, he would select yes. The cat hid because she missed her master or she was scared shitless. Correct response, scared shitless from anxiety. Why did cat emerge from hiding? Cat was hungry, or cat was no longer anxious since defense mechanisms were broken down by being high. Correct response; when defense mechanisms are muted, anxiety dissipates, and cat becomes friendly. I'm sure I can't explain this the way Alex did, but then again, no one really thinks like Alex.

"From here, Alex goes on to postulate that all responses that humans make are related to their desire to minimize anxiety. He adheres to the theory that the human mind could be looked upon as a sphere. The deeper inner core contains your innermost feelings, wishes, fears, and desires. They are often difficult to elicit, since they make one vulnerable. As we move out towards the outer portions of the sphere we are confronted with additional feelings and protective defenses. We resist having anyone probe too quickly or too deeply into our true emotions and feelings. On the surface of the sphere we find those normal defense mechanisms that we all utilize every day to ward off anxiety and enhance our self-esteem, i.e. rationalization: 'I didn't get that job, but it's for the better. I didn't really want to drive that far anyway.'

"Alex supported the belief that mental illness developed when these normal defense mechanisms designed to minimize anxiety, began to decompensate. Those of us who have a need to over utilize these mechanisms in order to control anxiety develop impairment in the ability to function. Alex would say it's all relative, but too much of one thing can be bad, and that is what we refer to as neuroses. It's one thing to desire a neat desk before sitting down to a difficult task, but if your anxiety is such that you can't get started for 45 minutes until every pencil is sharpened and all the pens stacked in size order, your ability to function is now impaired and you have been given the label as being neurotic.

"The psychotic takes it one step further, one very big step further. Here the anxiety has reached such outrageous levels that simply utilizing or even over-utilizing rational defense mechanisms are an inadequate means of controlling symptoms. The psychotic now needs to distort reality in one's thinking. The psychotic develops an illogical thought disorder by either employing unrealistic delusional thoughts or hallucinations. Such delusions or hallucinations appear to be bizarre to the non-psychotic, but once accepted by the psychotic, these unrealistic intrusions of the mind are actually anxiety relieving. Psychotics cannot understand why they are unable to develop meaningful lasting personal relationships; they cannot comprehend why they are unable to hold on to a job; they do not understand why people snicker when they pass by. However, once they become convinced of something, like 'my neighbor is trying to poison me,' suddenly it all becomes clear and less anxiety producing to the mind. Alex would say that regardless of the coping mechanism, the goal of all individuals is to minimize anxiety. The technique used is simply a matter of degree. As anxiety progresses, the need and desire to increase compensatory mechanisms will increase as well.

"In the 1960s most psychiatrists adhered to the belief that regardless of the stress, a neurotic would not become psychotic, since the neurotic had better inherent coping mechanisms. The old adage was a neurotic remains neurotic, and the psychotic stays psychotic. Today that theory no longer holds water, for under the right amount of stress; just about anyone can be turned psychotic. It's all the same: just a matter of degree, as Alex would say."

"Many of the things that he had to say are now considered accepted psychiatric findings," Carlton interjected.

"But wait, I'm not done! Alex, now utilizing his binary method of thinking, goes on to state that each and everything we say and do, is motivated and guided by our desire and need to minimize anxiety. I tried arguing with him but I don't believe I was able to change his position. In order to negate his argument, I asked, 'What about *love?*' We don't love someone because it makes us feel good or less anxious. We love because we enjoy giving and supporting others. It is a true virtue in itself, as opposed to a defense mechanism."

"What did he have to say to that?"

"First of all, don't ever expect to win an argument in logic against Alex. He said, 'A man claims to love his wife. When asked why he works so hard, he responds that it is to make his wife happy, to give her what she wants. He speaks not of what he receives from the relationship, only how much he enjoys giving. He now comes home from work and finds his wife in bed with another man. He becomes enraged. What has happened to his love? Where did that giving, loving attitude go? He said he wanted his wife to be happy, didn't he? Obviously, it made her happy to sleep with someone other than her husband. Didn't he also say he wanted to give his wife everything she wanted? How then, did his love turn to hate so quickly? What did he really love? Perhaps it was having a good-looking wife to compensate for his feelings of inadequacy? Perhaps he loved being loved? Certainly, there were more factors in play then saying he simply wanted his wife to be happy?' So according to Alex, love is simply just one more defense mechanism which man evokes to minimize anxiety.

"Next I asked him about the love people have for their children. I thought I had trapped him with that one. However, Alex said that we perceive our children as an extension of ourselves. We live our lives vicariously through them. When two kids are playing Little League and one kid is the pitcher and the other is the batter, why are we so focused and preoccupied on our kid being the successful one? Alex said it was because the success of our children enhances our own feelings of self-esteem, which reduces ones anxiety."

"There's a lot to digest in that one, Mr. Hinden. I'm going to have to give that some more thought, besides the very thought of this is making me anxious," Carlton added.

Hinden, however, went on, "Alex even had a theory for why so many folks were overwhelmed with anxiety in their everyday routine lives."

"And his response?"

"He illustrated his answer with a simple story. A woman leaves on an overnight trip leaving her husband to care for their three kids. Not being the usual primary care giver he decides to plan a special evening. Miniature golf followed by a burger and fries goes as anticipated. He now gets them ready for bed, lying down with them for a bedtime story. His hopes of their little eyes slowly beginning to close are disrupted by the six-year-old now jumping on the bed. His words of 'settle down' go unnoticed. Within minutes the eight-year-old joins in. Dad's request for order falls on deaf ears as the twelve-year-old smacks her sister in the face with a pillow. The free-for-all is in full swing as all bedlam breaks out. Dad now loses it as he shouts out, 'That does it! Lights out! End of story!'

"How did this perfect evening go astray? What went wrong? Alex would say it was because events didn't turn out as *anticipated*. That is the reason why so many of us feel overwhelmed. We did not anticipate the traffic jam that made us late for work. We did not anticipate misplacing our keys. We did not anticipate a flat tire. When our imaginary plans do not unfold in the manner in which we anticipate, anxiety emerges."

Hinden now stated, "Let's take a break for some lunch. Hope you like salmon, because that's about all I eat. We have salmon and eggs, salmon and lox, salmon and cheese, salmon and macaroni, and even salmon with tuna fish. Which will it be?"

"Isn't salmon and lox really just salmon and salmon?"

"True, but I like a bit of variety."

"I'll just have some salmon, thank you."

I I

After lunch Carlton went on to ask, "Did Stein have any special interest in human biology or pharmacology?"

Hinden responded, "Alex was very intrigued by the mysteries of life. Furthermore, he also had an incredible ability to digest and explain the most complex of problems in the most simplified ways and with the fewest words possible. After freshman biology, Alex felt the he completely understood the basic principles of pharmacology. The course he took didn't even talk about pharmacology, that was a course for second-year med students, not college freshmen. He said it was all so simple, that he could even explain it to me."

"*I have got to hear this*," thought Carlton to himself. He recalled how his brother Brad, who was a pharmacist, had to study into the wee hours of the night memorizing the names of hundreds of drugs, their actions and side effects. Very complicated stuff!

"At the risk of oversimplification, Mr. Terry, why don't you just sit back and relax, and see if I can uncomplicate this for you?" Steve Hinden walked over to a bookshelf and pulled out an old wrinkled spiral notebook. On the front cover was a red circular logo with a coat of arms within— *Cornell University, founded A.D. 1865*. Beneath that was a hand written note which read, *Alex Stein's writings*. Hinden turned to the pages marked *Pharmacology*, and then began to speak:

> Imagine a water pump in a closed system where there is just so much water. As you can see from Stein's notes, the water is pumped into a pipe that then splits into two smaller branches, in a Y shape, and each of those two branches has a valve that can control the amount of water running through each branch. Now assume that the valves on both branches, A and B, are open only half way, and you now want to increase the flow to branch A only. This can be accomplished in one of two ways. You can either open the valve on branch A completely, or you can close the valve on branch B. That is how simple pharmacology is.

"Look at this diagram from Alex's notebook."

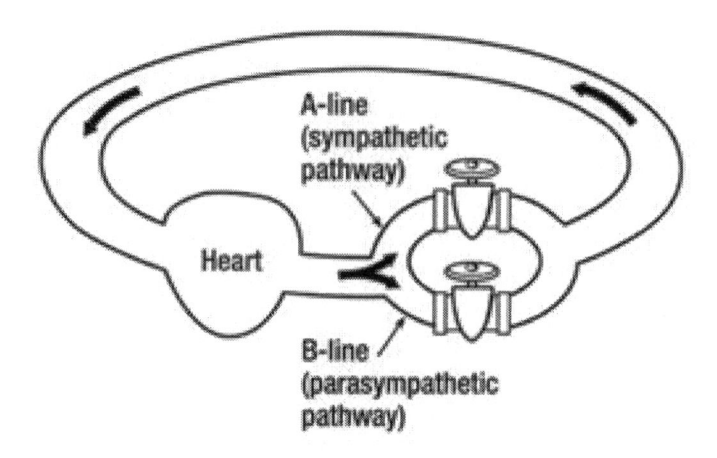

Diagram: A closed loop labeled with "Heart" on the left, "A-line (sympathetic pathway)" on the upper branch, and "B-line (parasympathetic pathway)" on the lower branch, with valve-like structures on the right.

The body has only so much blood, and therefore acts as a closed system, and through the autonomic (automatic) nervous system, it can shunt that blood to areas of high priority. It accomplishes this through specific chemicals or neurotransmitters, that act on specific nerves to stimulate certain muscles which surround the blood vessels to either open (dilate) or contract (close), thus acting like valves. By either contracting or dilating select muscles, they apply a valve like effect and either increase or decrease blood flow to the organs involved, thus sending blood to where it is needed.

The small circular muscles surrounding the blood vessels act as valves. Assume that line A, represents the blood vessels which supply the organs of the sympathetic system; which sends blood to the heart, brain, muscles, and the pupil of the eye, in preparation for fight or flight. Line B, supplies the organs of the parasympathetic system; sending blood to the gut, liver, pancreas, and urinary systems.

One can now increase the blood flow to the sympathetic system (line A),

Figure 2

A-line (sympathetic pathway)

Heart

B-line (parasympathetic pathway)

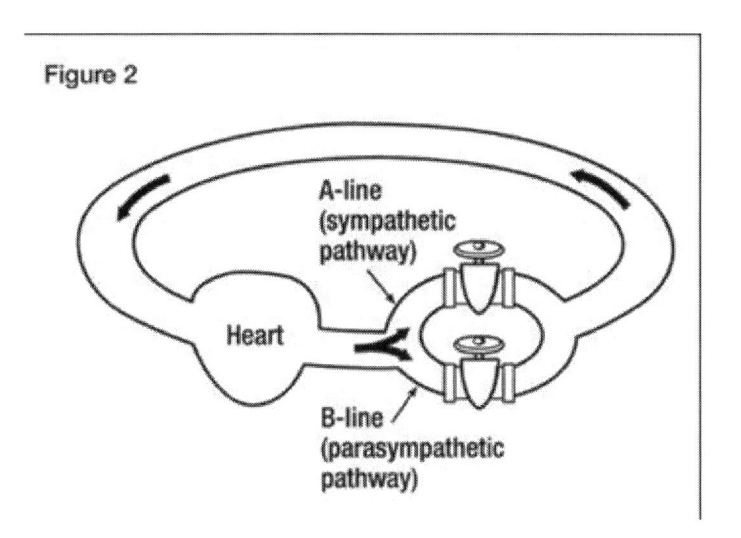

(as seen in Figure 2) in one of two ways. Either dilate or relax the muscles surrounding the sympathetic system (line A), or contract or close the muscles of the parasympathetic system (line B). Similarly, to increase the blood supply to the parasympathetic system, either open or stimulate line B, or contract or inhibit line A.

At this point Hinden digressed from the notebook and went on as if he were presenting the lecture. "Are you still with me on this, Terry?" Hinden said. "Because now comes the pharmacology. Alex pointed something out to me, to which I had never given any thought. When a person takes a drug, it doesn't do anything unique or magical within the body. All it does is speed up, slow down, or block a pathway that already exists. The drug mimics the role of the previously mentioned neurotransmitters. One cannot invent new pathways that do not already exist, but only modify the ones that are already present. That is why med students spend the first two years of schooling studying the body's basic physiology.

"The autonomic (automatic) nervous system is able to perform these duties without any decisions by the conscious thought portion of the brain, the cerebral cortex. The sympathetic pathways are those that are activated during the *fight or flight* response when an animal is either hunting or being hunted. Whether it be a lion chasing a deer, or a deer fleeing from a lion, both will have the same chemical response. Their adrenal glands will pump excessive amounts of norepinephrine, which is chemically similar to epinephrine, also known as adrenaline, into the blood stream. This prepares the animal for the classical *fight or flight* response.

The nerve endings which supply or innervate the blood vessels to these organ receptors, cause those vessels to dilate, increasing the blood flow to the needed areas only; the heart speeds up in preparation for flight, the muscles receive more oxygen for running, the brain receives more oxygen and blood to make better decisions, the bronchi of the lungs open wider to allow for more oxygen, and the pupil dilates for greater visibility. Remember, there is only so much blood to go around. Therefore, this is all accomplished at the expense of blood flow to the organs of the parasympathetic pathways; that being the gut, the liver, the kidneys, resulting in slowing of digestion and urine flow.

"In a similar fashion, when the nerves of the parasympathetic system are stimulated by releasing their chemical substance, acetylcholine, the organs innervated by them, such as the gut and the urinary system, receive an increase in their blood supply. These pathways are typically activated during the digestive process. This is the reason that our mothers always told us not to go swimming right after we have eaten. During this period, most of our blood goes to our gut, at the expense of our muscles. Now if your muscles are exerting themselves, they can't get enough blood and oxygen and therefore they are prone to developing a cramp. The autonomic nervous system can only send extra blood to one of these two systems at any given time, never to both.

"Now in addition to the drugs that can stimulate each of the two systems, both sympathetic and parasympathetic, we may also use drugs which can block or decrease blood to these systems. As previously described, we can increase the blood to branch A by opening the line on branch A fully, or we can also increase the flow to line A, by closing the valve to branch B. The same holds true in our bodies. In essence, we have sympathetic stimulators, and we have sympathetic blockers, which can slow blood to those organs. Similarly, we have parasympathetic stimulators and we have parasympathetic blockers. In other words we can accomplish the exact same thing with two different types of drugs. It's a simple box diagram; allow me to draw it for you.

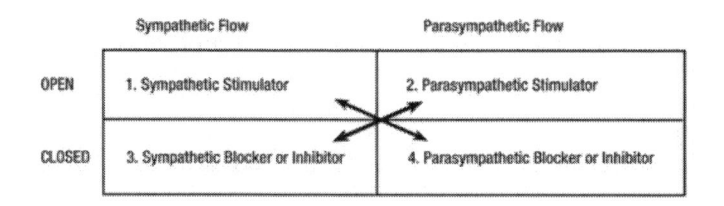

	Sympathetic Flow	Parasympathetic Flow
OPEN	1. Sympathetic Stimulator	2. Parasympathetic Stimulator
CLOSED	3. Sympathetic Blocker or Inhibitor	4. Parasympathetic Blocker or Inhibitor

"At the top of the diagram we have sympathetic vs. parasympathetic. Along the side of the box we list open and closed. If you now draw a diagonal arrow from box 1 to box 3 and another from box 2 to box 4, it shows how one can get the same exact results using two completely different classes of drug. One can speed up the heart by using a sympathetic stimulator i.e.; epinephrine (which opens valve A) or a parasympathetic blocker (i.e.; atropine (which closes valve B). One can slow the heart by administering a parasympathic stimulator (i.e.; probanthine) or by using a sympathetic blocker (i.e.; Inderal).

"The side effects likewise aren't that difficult to figure out, once you know what box you are in. A sympathetic stimulator will produce the side effects one would expect to see in blocking the parasympathetic system. The side effect of a sympathetic stimulator or a parasympathetic blocker may cause urinary retention or constipation. Parasympathetic stimulators or sympathetic blockers may slow the heart excessively, drop blood pressure or cause diarrhea."

The clarity by which Hinden regurgitated the lecture he had heard from Alex Stein fifty years ago astonished Carlton. "Did you get that entirely, Terry?"

"Every incredible word!" uttered Carlton. Carlton's reaction was similar to that expressed by Aldous Huxley, when Charles Darwin explained his theory of evolution in the *Origin of Species*. "How simple, why didn't I think of that?"

12

After 15 days Terry felt that he had drained Hinden dry, and that next to Hinden, no one understood the status of Alex Stein's Cornell mind better than he did. Terry had asked about Stein's political, social, and economic viewpoints. He had asked about his suspicions and anxieties.

"Did you ever hear Stein show any interest in the aging process?" Carlton inquired.

"It's strange that you mention that, since aging was one of those topics that simply fascinated him."

"Did he ever get into any specifics on the subject?"

"No, I don't believe so, in fact that's one of the times when he would simply say, '*It's all the same.*' Do you think he may have come up with something?"

"Please, Mr. Hinden, I'm the one asking the questions here."

Hinden was not a fool, and based on Carlton's interest in Stein and the nature of his questions, it became apparent to him that his old friend Alex Stein had come across something big: *Big enough to send a CIA agent to visit him in the middle of nowhere.*

When it became apparent that Hinden had nothing further to add, Carlton decided that it was time to say good-bye. "Mr. Hinden, thank you for your assistance. I would also appreciate if I could borrow that notebook on Stein from Cornell. Here is your voucher for $11,250, signed by me. Simply sign, date, and place in the self-addressed envelope and the funds should be wired to your account very shortly. You do understand by the terms of this agreement that you are absolutely forbidden to discuss or mention to anyone the nature of our conversations."

"You're not bullshitting about the check now, are you?"

"Mr. Hinden, Good day."

13

As Carlton sat in the train on the first leg of the journey back to Langley, a plethora of thoughts flowed through his mind. To begin with, he remained astonished how anyone could summarize the field of pharmacology so succinctly. Carlton's parents would always brag that Brad was the real genius in the family. "After all, he was a pharmacist who had to memorize thousands of drugs and their actions." I guess that Brad failed to mention that all he needed to do was place those drugs into one of four boxes; two of which were the same. "Shit, I could have done that," he thought. "Just imagine, they almost had me convinced that he was the real brains of the family." Now it was time for Carlton to use his brain, and find out what Alex Stein was planning to do with his!

14

Students who participated in the summer research program at Cornell University were required to maintain diaries and by reviewing them, Carlton had some insight into Alex Stein's thinking when he traveled to the Arctic at age twenty-five. He was one of two-dozen students, instructors, and Professors who volunteered for the STAR program (Students in Arctic Research summer program). It was here that Alex would develop his fascination with diabetes and its sequella: accelerated aging.

The trip from Cornell in Ithaca, New York, was an arduous one. The initial flight was from Binghamton to Pittsburgh, then Seattle, next Anchorage, followed by a stopover in Fairbanks Alaska. In Fairbanks, the group paid a visit to CRREL (Cold Region Research and Engineering Laboratory) to view the 360-foot-long Permafrost Tunnel being constructed by the U.S. Army Corps of Engineers. During the summer months it was necessary to refrigerate the tunnel to protect it from damage. The reason given for its construction was to study methods of frozen soil extraction and mining. Its true purpose was to study the possibility of building missile silos. At Fairbanks, they also visited the old gold mining ghost town of Utica in the tundra and witnessed wild musk oxen roaming the plains.

From Fairbanks, they flew to the northernmost tip of the U.S., Barrow, Alaska. Alex was anticipating bitter weather conditions when he arrived at the Arctic Circle in mid-July, but he was pleasantly surprised to see folks in shirtsleeves. And finally, from Barrow, they flew via Alaskan Airways to their final destination, a gravel airstrip in Deering, Alaska.

Deering was situated in Kotzebue Sound, of the Arctic Ocean. It displayed high cliffs with sea caves, beautiful beaches, and rolling plush green hills. Beyond the cliffs, one could watch the sun setting at midnight over Siberia. During July there were over twenty hours of sunlight each day. With the exception of swarming mosquitoes and very cold water, it was a remarkably delightful place.

Deering was the perfect site for archeological digs, as it contained thousand year old artifacts ready to be unearthed. There was Pleistocene ivory, wooly mammoth tusks, antler tools, Eskimo pottery, and bones from all sorts of creatures, including walrus, caribou, and of course, humans.

During the digs, most participants were engaged in conversation and exchanging stories, although Alex was content to simply dig quietly and mostly listen. There was one other graduate student, Rose, who wasn't a big fan of small talk, and she and Alex took a liking to each other. In time, she managed to get Alex to speak up more, and she enjoyed listening to his style of reasoning.

Furthermore, when Rose spoke, she had something of interest to say. Alex overheard one of the students refer to Rose as being shy. "Why do you think she is shy?" Alex asked.

"Because she doesn't say much," was the reply.

Alex rebutted, "That doesn't make one shy. Shy is being quiet because of a lack of self-confidence. People who talk too much, often lack self-confidence as well. Being quiet and having confidence is to feel secure with oneself, and that isn't being shy." During evenings, Alex and Rose would keep each other company in either conversation or by simply reading together.

Alex and Rose found the Eskimo natives to be extremely hospitable. They were down to earth, sincere, respectful, and always willing to offer a helping hand. One Eskimo couple they befriended in particular were the two cooks for the summer program. Nanuq and Shila lived in Barrow and worked in the medical field; they enlisted as cooks for the expedition for their summer vacation. Both worked in a Diabetic Clinic, where Nanuq was a medical assistant and Shila was a R.N.

The four of them got along fabulously and spent evenings together conversing about the States, Alaska, cooking, and Alex's favorite subject, the changes of aging, particularly in diabetes. As the program approached termination, they all expressed sadness about the thought of parting. Shila's mother had recently passed, and being that they had an extra bedroom, they decided to offer to rent it to Alex and Rose, who initially considered the possibility farfetched, but with each passing day the subject resurfaced. They carefully reweighed all of the pros and cons. The straw that broke the camel's back was Shila's caribou stew. They would remain in Alaska.

15

Alex was excited about remaining in Alaska for other reasons as well. He was always fascinated by the physiological similarities between diabetes and accelerated aging. Worldwide epidemiology studies on diabetes revealed a marked difference in diabetes prevalence rates between various ethnic groups. The Alaskan Eskimo had a particularly low rate of diabetes when compared to other groups, and this fact, stimulated Alex's desire to determine why.

Initially, all went well. Nanuq and Shila were able to land Alex a job as a medical assistant in their clinic. They taught Rose their culinary skills as she became the key homemaker. When Rose found out that she was pregnant, she and Alex decided to marry. All was well until the baby arrived, and along with the baby came an unwelcome intruder: winter.

There were no short sleeve shirts to be found in the Arctic in the month of April. Often the temperature ranged from -20 to -40F, with the wind howling. The Arctic Ocean was one solid block of ice. Even with thick insulated gloves, heated handlebars and throttles on the snowmobiles, insulated Sorrel rubber boots, a Siberian polar bear hat, and the *Titan* coat, insulated with Northern down feathers, your fingers, toes and nose felt like icicles. Whenever you did venture to journey out, you had better take a shotgun with you, for the polar bear is the only animal on the planet known to track human as prey. Alex stated, "But I don't own a shot gun. Can a man outrun a polar bear?"

"No way. That's why we Alaskans say that if you don't own a shot gun then you need to take a friend along who is a slower runner than you are."

When the couple's son was born, Rose felt that the Arctic was no place to raise a child, and so she decided to head back to her home state of New Hampshire. Alex tried unsuccessfully to convince her that New Hampshire wasn't that much different from the Arctic during the winter. It was a difficult parting, but Alex was deeply involved in his work at the time, as he read everything ever published about diabetes. In spite of the fact that he lacked an M.D. degree, within two years he was considered an authority on the subject, such that the University of Alaska in Fairbanks, invited him to be the keynote speaker at its annual biochemistry seminar.

Alex had an intense distaste for public speaking and refused the invitation, but submitted his presentation in writing instead. A paper that he never dreamed would be reviewed and discussed, in conference room 103 at Langley 45 years later.

16

It was 30 years ago when Alex Stein first learned about the plight of the inhabitants in the Central Africa Republic from an article in the *New York Times*, pointing out the terrible hardships of its natives and the paucity of medical care. He was frustrated with the events in his own life at the time, the red tape of the FDA, the lack of grant money because of his refusal to meet publication deadlines, and his inability to help the indigent, particularly since he did not have a medical degree. He was now forty years old and felt that he had not yet accomplished anything meaningful with his life. When he heard that the Catholic missionaries were planning a visit to CAR and that medical personnel were needed, he was quick to enlist. He had six weeks to obtain a visa, gather up all of his books, along with all the medical equipment he could beg, borrow or steal.

Alex knew little about where he was heading or what his role would be when he got there. The missionary was headed to the Lobaye province in the Southwestern portion of CAR. A quarter of a million natives resided in that Province, but the missionary group of eighteen was headed to a remote jungle village north of Mlbaiki, known as Bongele.CAR was a landlocked country located in the geographic center of Africa, approximately the size of the state of Texas. It was formerly a French colony, named Ubangi-Shari, which declared independence in 1960.

In the 30 years since Alex first arrived, a civilian government was established in 1993 to replace the years of military rule, but that lasted only a decade. In 2003, General Francois Boziza took over in a military coup, and Presidential elections were held in 2005, and the General was elected as the country's President, although many pockets of lawlessness still persisted.

The country was one of the poorest in the world. It was plagued by civil unrest, as well as attacks of ethnic cleansing from neighboring Sudan. In 2002, more than 30,000 refugees had to flee the country for safety. Many families were slaughtered mercilessly. Others had since fled to the forests to avoid being murdered and crime was rampant. More than 75% of the population resided in outlying areas that were still not under the control of the government. Most natives live in small huts made from vines with roofs made of leaves. The majority of the country has no running water, and medical facilities are severely limited. Malaria, Hepatitis A, bacterial diarrhea, typhoid fever, and pneumococcal meningitis are all endemic. More than 13% of the population suffers from HIV/AIDS.

If conditions were horrifying in CAR nowadays, they were considerably worse when Alex Stein and his entourage arrived years ago. Murder, robberies and corrupt police were ubiquitous.

In spite of its poor infrastructure, the wild life is second to none, with elephants, lions, leopards, rhinos, and inland gorillas seen often. The scenery, with its rain forest, waterfalls and mountains, is breathtaking, along with the majestic Mt. Kayangangira with an altitude of 4,660 feet.

The official language of CAR is French, although there are over 80 ethnic groups, each with its own language. Many of the natives are Moslems, and outsiders are warned not to photograph anyone without asking permission first. The photographing of all government and military buildings is strictly forbidden and illicit drugs and homosexuality is dealt with by very harsh penalties. Visitors are reminded to eat with their hands as the natives do, but only with the right hand.

In the 1880's the local Pygmy population was decimated by the slave trade, but then the French stepped in to put a stop to slavery. The wet season in CAR runs from May to October, with flooding being extremely prevalent. In the central and southern provinces, one sees a series of forested rolling hills, and a dense tropical rain forest, which the Ubangi River meanders through. The Ubangi is a tributary of the Congo River, which collectively drains a greater area than any other in the world with the exception of the Amazon. The countries of Angola, Cameron, Chad, Democratic Republic of the Congo, the Republic of the Congo, Equatorial Guinea, and CAR all drain into this basin. The main agricultural products are cotton, coffee, tobacco, corn, and bananas. Gold, diamonds and uranium are also mined, but one cannot remove them from the country without governmental commercial permits. Estimates state that the population in 2015 will reach five million, with merely 15 people per square mile, and much of the east remains virtually uninhabited.

17

The British government strongly urged travelers to avoid CAR. "There is no embassy in CAR and all but absolute essential travel should be restricted. The North and West, the areas bordering on Cameroon, Sudan and Chad are especially dangerous and should be avoided. It is no longer safe to travel any of the roads without a military/police escort. Rebel forces are active in the northeast country, particularly in the Vakagsa Province and around Birao. Incidents of robbery occur regularly and armed gangs are known to operate in the outlying areas of Bangui, where several World Health Organization physicians were murdered by unidentified assailants. We strongly recommend that one obtain medical and comprehensive medical insurance. All immunizations need to be up to date. One should take anti-malarial medication and take precautions against mosquito bites. All water needs to be filtered or boiled or brought in brand bottles with unbroken seals. Food obtained from local vendors may not meet adequate hygiene standards. In an emergency the French Embassy in Bangui may be able to offer assistance. For further information, check with your Department of Health." Alex thought to himself, *sounds like a great vacation spot.*

18

Thirty years later. CIA Headquarters, Langley, Virginia.

"Deputy Johnson, summation conference at 10 a.m. on Stein; I hear that Brenner will be watching the feed personally from upstairs, so do a thorough job ol' chap," stated Deputy Chief Myers, as he patted Johnson on the back. Johnson himself wasn't sure if it was a back pat or a back stab, but he knew that he better be prepared for what was to come.

The first floor conference room, 103, held about 15 participants comfortably. Exactly how many individuals the CIA employed was a mystery to all, and if one asked the question, you were basically told that such information was on *a need to know basis and you didn't need to* know, a polite way of saying that's none of your business. Today, room 103 was packed to capacity.

"No idea where this one may take us, but let's be thorough, "said Deputy Chief Johnson. "You have all had the opportunity to digest Terry's field report from the Hinden interview. I know it's long and it has lots of rambling, but there should be some helpful info in those 925 pages, so once again, let's not miss anything. Obviously this fellow Alex Stein has a brain. You all read Hinden's comments regarding his talents as a chess player. There aren't many folks out there who can play on that level and not have the board in front of them." Johnson's appetite for probing into the mind of Alex Stein had intensified more than ever. He thrived on a good chess opponent and Alex Stein was right up his alley. "Okay folks, let's get started. Family history, you're up, Debbie."

"Alex Stein, no middle name by the way, grew up in the Bronx. His father, Victor Stein, was an electrical engineer, worked for GE for a while, and was of German descent. Before becoming an engineer he briefly joined the IWO (International Worker's Organization), a socialistic union to which he and many of his co-workers joined for the health and funeral benefits. Never attended any meetings. Totally apolitical, no radical group or religious ties. Two pack a day Camel smoker. Yes, he did inhale, and no alcohol. He died during Stein's freshman year at Cornell. Death certificate; massive heart attack or acute myocardial infarction. Mom, maiden name, Sophia Schultz, homemaker, worked part time as a bookkeeper for a regional bank. Negative background check. Died of an MVA, hit and run, during Stein's junior year at Cornell. Driver never located. No siblings.

"After graduating from Cornell, Stein was selected as a research assistant by one of his professors, and spent the next three years doing research in the biochem department. Eventually, they gave him his own lab. Did some poorly understood work with yeast and gene manipulation. Never published a thing, so he lost his funding and then he became involved in the STAR program at Cornell. This was a program for instructors and students to attend the Arctic during the summers and do scientific research near Barrow, Alaska. At the end of the summer he refused to return to the mainland. That's when Cornell cut him off. He remained up there for several years working with the Eskimos, doing some research on diabetes. He did write one paper for the University of Alaska and they have agreed to track it down and fax it to us. I suppose there wasn't much to do in the Arctic, so he hooked up with another grad student, named Rose, who also stayed behind. They married and had one son, named Ralph.

"Rose moved back to her home state of New Hampshire after the baby was born. Didn't feel Alaska was a suitable place to raise a child. She passed away at the young age of 42 from breast cancer, and the son stayed on to farm the land. He married a local and had one daughter named Abigail. She still lives on the family farm. Her dad also died of a myocardial infarction in his fifties. Her mom passed away a few years ago. That's about it."

"Well with all these premature deaths in the family, perhaps that explains Stein's fascination with prolonging life," Johnson added. "Becky, you're up."

"Stein went to P.S. 50 in the Southeast section of the Bronx. No discipline problems. Very strong math grades. Reading just average or even below. I found one interesting comment by his first grade teacher, Miss Cuba. Stein was involved in a class play in the auditorium. It was entitled *Skidoo, Ka Chu*. Its purpose was to encourage kids to cover their mouths after sneezing. Stein had two lines in the play, and in both cases, his two lines followed Nancy Bartodietz's lines. They both gave their first lines flawlessly near the onset of the play, but when it came time for Nancy's second line she inadvertently repeated her first line again. Now Stein had to make a quick decision. Does he repeat his first line again, taking the play back to the beginning, or does he go with his second line, which is completely out of context but sparing the audience from any additional pain, and bring the ten-minute presentation to a near end. Tough decision for a five year old!"

"What did he do?" inquired Johnson.

"Logical reasoning told him to go with the *mercy rule,* and so he ended it."

"Good decision!" Johnson again chimed in.

"I mention this in my report because of the sequella. After the play, his teacher noticed a precipitous change in behavior. He stated he would never go on a stage again, and he became more withdrawn. Refused any type of group activities. The only other standouts I found were his grades in third grade Arithmetic: SO (outstanding), Reading: S (satisfactory), and Works and Plays well with others: NR (not responding). Jr. High and High school were pretty much of the same. Nothing to add, it's all in my written report."

"Cornell years, Betty?"

"I don't really have a lot to add beyond Terry's notes which are quite detailed. The routine jargon is enclosed in my written report. Just a few interesting comments. Stein's cum at Cornell was a 4.1. All his electives were in science, with the exception of one course on the history of religion—no literature, no political science or anything like that. Lots of A pluses in science and math. In four years he had only two grades less than an A. One was in Introduction to Debate for which he received a C. Apparently he couldn't speak when standing in front of an audience, and he also pulled a C in Phys Ed."

"Ann, post-college."

"One year after his wife left Alaska, Stein followed suit. He then moved back to New York City. Lived in a 12 by 8 foot room in the YMHA on Lexington off 92nd. His rent was $80 a month. His hope was to be able to land a job as a research assistant at New York Hospital, but when that didn't materialize he found a job at the main branch of the New York City library, on Fifth Avenue and 42nd St. He was assigned to the nonfiction stacks. Spent most of his time reading before and after work. Worked there for a good seven years. One interesting comment by his supervisor: When asked what he would do if he won the lottery, he replied, 'I'd lock myself up in the basement of the library and just read my way through.' No arrests, he didn't have a car or even a driver's license for that matter. No known social contacts. Zippo on political, although he apparently despised bureaucrats.

"I found only one minor scuffle at the Y. The rule was lights out after ten, and the fellow across the hall from Stein would blast his stereo every night, right up until ten. Stein had difficulty with his reading, and one night Stein confronted the guy in the hallway and asked him to lower the stereo. The chap, with cigarette hanging from his mouth, responded by saying 'I have until ten o'clock, if you don't like it, report me.' Stein then slapped the cigarette out of the guy's mouth and said, 'I don't have time to report you, so now *you* can report me.'"

Johnson now nodded to the next speaker, "Steve?"

"We used Terry's report and Googled all the key words in it in conjunction with Alex Stein. Does anyone here realize just how many Alex Steins are out there? We came up with very little. Stein never published, never had his name in a newspaper, and never applied for a gun permit or even a fishing license. The guy is off the radar screen."

Johnson again kicked in, "Come on people, give me something, we're the CIA, not the City Council meeting. We have a lot of manpower tied up here. Let's get something."

"I do have more, sir," added Steve. We made contact with a doctor named Charles Goodnough. Attended New York Medical College-Flower Fifth Avenue Hospital. States he knew Alex from med school."

"We have no records that Stein was ever enrolled in med school," Johnson remarked.

"That's just it, sir; he never was enrolled. The lecture classes at New York Medical College held 128 students. No one ever bothered to check the attendance. Stein showed up on day one with the other freshman, and just sat down. Goodnough started to get suspicious when he observed that Stein never took any notes. This was unheard of in med school. In fact, there's the tale that there was this professor who lectured to both the dental and medical students, and the way he would differentiate them was by saying *Good morning*. The dental students responded with *Good morning* as well, but the med students simply wrote it down. Also, Goodnough never saw Stein taking any exams, never asked any questions, and Dr. Speers never called upon him during Clinical Pathology class. When Goodnough confronted him, Stein 'fessed up. He said that he wasn't called upon, because he wasn't actually registered. He said that he didn't desire a degree, never planned on treating patients and was just *auditing* the first two years of med school."

"Unbelievable!" exclaimed Johnson, "Do you mean to say that someone can just sneak into medical school?"

"Apparently so, sir, and even if they did take attendance, they would be trying to catch the folks that were sneaking out as opposed to trying to sneak in."

"What the hell is this country coming to," Johnson asked.

"After his two years of sitting in at medical school, he found a job as a research assistant, working on gene manipulation in yeast, and after that he simply took off for Africa. One final thing, sir. I was able to find some exchanges between Stein and the NIH just prior to his departing for Africa. He requested approval to conduct some clinical trials to increase life span in yeast."

"Was he approved?"

"No sir. The NIH responded by saying that aging was not classified as a disease, and therefore did not qualify for any clinical trials or any attempts to modify it."

"Are you saying that if one wants to conduct research that may enable us to live longer that the government will not consider funding it? You have got to be kidding! If it isn't a disease, then why are we all dying from it? What a government!" Johnson exclaimed. "Don, what did we get from the Africans?"

"As you know, we have both his visa and satellite photo. We are getting an operative to infiltrate Bongele and interview the natives to find out what's going on, but we don't want to spook Stein just yet. We were also able to retrieve two pieces of mail from their unclaimed postal division. They have been lying around for some time, incorrectly addressed, but both addressed to Stein. One was from his granddaughter, just saying that she hoped he was well and that she missed him and hoped they could get together in the future. The good news is we know where to find her by the return address.

"The other piece is of much greater interest and is a copy of a scientific paper that Stein apparently requested from the US National Library of Medicine at the National Institute of Health. The paper came out of the Buck Institute for Age Research and was written by a Dr. S. Melov et al, in 2000. The title is 'The extension of life span with superoxide dismutase /catalase." The authors were able to improve life expectancy of worms by 44% by feeding them a synthetic antioxidant known as EUK-8."

"Now we're getting somewhere," stated Johnson.

"Dr.Rickett, I'm sure we are all very interested in your psych eval."

"Stein appears to be an Asperger's. For those of you who are unfamiliar with Asperger's syndrome allow me to explain. Asperger's is one of those disorders classified under the autistic spectrum of diseases or pervasive developmental disorders (PDD). Asperger's was first recognized in 1944 by an Austrian pediatrician, named Hans Asperger. It affects predominantly boys who have normal intelligence and language skills, although some can be highly intelligent. They have severely impaired social skills, are unable to communicate effectively with others and have poor coordination. They also have impaired abstract thinking and interpret metaphors literally, displaying impairment in abstract thinking."

"Can you give us an example of that, Victor?"

"Sure. If you ask, what it mean when one says, 'People in glass houses shouldn't throw stones,' a person with Asperger's syndrome might say, 'Well, if you throw stones, you might break something in the house.' So getting back to Stein: father was an engineer. Having an engineer for a father is very common in Asperger's. He also shows poor social skills, no eye contact, and difficulty in communicating. He obviously is very high functioning in many areas: math, recall retention, chess. Lots of savant traits. Possibly some PTSD (Post traumatic stress disorder) from his early school years. Pre-morbid personality, typical schizoid, but I haven't heard anything to cause me to believe that he is schizophrenic. Pretty suspicious of others, but can't really call him paranoid at this junction."

"Why not?" asked Deputy Johnson.

"First of all, he has some very good reasons to be suspicious, especially of us. After all, it doesn't take a genius to realize that we are going to come looking for him real soon. Paranoia is unjustified fear. His fear is justifiable. Many folks confuse the terms anxiety and fear. There is a difference; anxiety is unjustified, whereas fear is justified. Furthermore, I haven't been convinced of any psychotic thinking at this point. And so far there hasn't been a fixation on any obvious delusions, and no hallucinations that I know of. Sure, the guy is nutty as a fruit cake, but every university in the country has a bunch of those."

It was now time for Deputy Johnson to speak. "What I'm really concerned about here is what Alex Stein's motives are? From what we have learned today they don't appear to be either economic or political. And I don't think he is seeking publicity, since the paparazzi haven't reached Bongele yet. It also doesn't seem as if he is working on anything in the bioterrorism sphere. It does appear that he has hit upon some very powerful information and no one here has as of yet given me a clue as to what he intends to do with it. I am convinced of three things. First, we are dealing with a real *weirdo* here. And second, there's a lot we can learn from him. Third, whatever it is that he has hit upon; we need to get our hands on it before anyone else.

"I'm going to ask Professor Rothberg to join us for our next meeting. If we are going to figure out exactly what this fellow Stein is up to then we better know his language and get an update on the science of aging. Also, since the only family that he currently has is his granddaughter up in New Hampshire, and he may just try and reach her, I have just the right person to give her a visit. Let's all reconvene in 48. Stamp the minutes, Classified report-Technical Analysis Division, CIA EYES ONLY."

19

Bongele, CAR, Thirty years ago.

Alex and the missionary group had to travel by air, boat, and foot in order to reach Bongele. After the flight to CAR, they boarded two large flat-bottomed motorized boats on a two-day trip through one of the tributaries of the Ugandi River. Next, the group, along with native guides, had to trek through fifteen miles of heavy jungle. The trip was delayed after one of the guides inadvertently stepped on a snake and was bitten on the foot. Even in Africa, most snakes are non-poisonous and tend to avoid humans. Even when poisonous snakes bite, they rarely inject a full load of venom. However, the native guide did not step on just any snake. He stepped on a *dendoaspis polyepis,* more commonly known as the Black Mamba.

The Black Mamba is the largest venomous snake in Africa and the most deadly. Their average length is eight feet long, and their color is actually olive brown with a jet black mouth. Although they are most often found in shrubs and tree hollows, they are often found within homes of natives. When one encounters prey it can strike up to twelve times in a minute, delivering enough neuro and cardio toxin to kill a dozen men. Without anti-toxin, the mortality rate is one hundred percent. Even with anti-toxin, to step on a Black Mamba could result in a death sentence. Alex had carried anti-toxin amongst his supplies and immediately injected the victim. However, his foot had already appeared swollen and gangrenous and his prognosis guarded. It would be impossible for him to travel and another native remained behind with him. Alex considered leaving him with an ampule of morphine to comfort him, but his supply was limited and he knew the prognosis was bleak. He most likely would not survive the night and so a pint of Blackberry brandy was issued instead. Alex had a severe phobia of snakes and this was not how he had hoped to begin his African experience. *Perhaps this mission was not such a good idea.*

When they finally came within a mile of the village, the jungle became sparser and several native huts came into view. They were of various sizes, but each was made from vines with roofs made of leaves and had just a single room. As they approached the center of the village a circular clearing appeared with a diameter of two kilometers. Three log structures stood in the center of the village. One served as the general supply store and post office. The second was for schooling and also served as the infirmary and the third was the chapel for prayer services. Eight tents of various sizes were also used for the missionaries. On the edge of the clearing one could see hundreds, if not thousands, of native huts extending back into the forest. The village had no running water, but was fortunate to have a small stream that came from a tributary of the Ugandi; a rubber hose drained water from the stream down to the village. The power was supplied by generator. Alex was hoping there would be at least one real physician in the village. Instead, he found a self-trained midwife, an herbal tribal medicine man and his wife, and that was it. Before too long, it became apparent that Alex had the most modern medical knowledge and so within a very short span of time, he became in charge of the medical care. His first major contribution was to obtain mosquito nets for the natives, which drastically diminished the incidence of malaria.

When a teen-aged orphaned boy named Kiros, which translates to "the king," developed a life threatening staph infection, Alex cured him with a shot of penicillin. After that, the natives all referred to him as *Atta Jeune*, which in the local dialect meant *Young Father*, although he had the wisdom and experience of an elder. Kiros was so grateful for his recovery that he pledged the remainder of his life to be a loyal servant and follower to his healer. Alex taught him sterile technique, showed him how to change dressings, sterilize the instruments, and even administer injections. For Alex, Kiros became not only a loyal friend, but his nurse, and one whom he also looked upon as his own son.

After a two-month stay in Bongele, their visitors' visas were about to expire and the missionaries prepared for departure. Alex, however, had decided to remain in Bongele. Although he would remain in the country illegally, he didn't let that discourage him. After all, everything that Alex was doing in CAR was illegal, including practicing medicine without a license. He doubted if the authorities would ever bother coming to Bongele to find him, as they had many more challenging matters to deal with, and so his decision was made. Alex would disappear.

20

Just about everyone considered it a nasty April day in the nation's capital with one exception: Carlton couldn't be happier to get back to the 38 degree weather of Washington. Deputy Johnson greeted him as he entered Johnson's office. "Hope your trip back was uneventful, Terry. Nice thorough reporting, some helpful info there. Looks like you got a bit of a bug, Terry."

"Just a little bit under the weather from the trip, sir."

"Well you better get better real soon, because we're sending you right back into the field."

"Well, it can't be any worse than Alaska, sir."

"Perhaps not, but its real close."

Carlton reviewed his briefing on the plane from Dulles to Dartmouth, New Hampshire. He was to use the alias Chad Jay and contact Alex Stein's granddaughter in New Hampshire. Her file stated that she was 30 years old, single, self-employed as a horseback riding instructor on her family farm in Grafton, New Hampshire. She had attended Syracuse University, received her B.A. and got a job with Google in their media division. Apparently, office and computer work was not her thing, and so she reverted to her true passion: horses.

Carlton's assignment was to get up there ASAP and pump her for information. Had she heard from her grandfather recently? Was she aware of the nature of his work? What he planned to do with his findings? Carlton's cover was that he was going to be taking graduate courses in the spring at Dartmouth, and he needed riding lessons to impress some babe he met on campus who was into horses.

In her twelve-year-old yearbook photo, Abigail Stein was pretty hot looking, but Carlton was well aware how a gal that age could go downhill quickly. Carlton was suspicious of why he was the one selected for this operation, and when it was Johnson handing out the mission, even more so: *First Alaska, and now New Hampshire, what next, the Arctic?* He knew the way Johnson thought, and he was aware of his own assets. If she were a real dog, Johnson would assume that Carlton would be able to extract any vital information quickly, knowing Carlton's charm and good looks. Carlton began to ruminate on whether someone in CIA Headquarters was out to get him, or more specifically, out to get him out.

21

Alex's medical facility and laboratory would never comply with the standards of the regulatory agencies of the States. But Alex wasn't in the States; he was in Africa, and the FDA and OSHA and Health Department were nowhere to be found. Although less than ideal, he considered the facilities to be adequate. The missionaries had given him a budget of $10,000 for the purchase of equipment and supplies. With these funds he purchased used equipment, including a refrigerator, incubator, centrifuge, test tube racks, and glassware. Many of the supplies were donated by the Red Cross, Rotary International, and many physicians from New York who gave drug samples and old equipment, such as an ECG machine, stethoscopes, ophthalmoscope and an Otto scope, fans, and blood pressure cuffs. Expired medications which could not be sold in the States would still be very beneficial in since they still retained 90 to 95% efficacy, and were a blessing to the Africans.

His medical facility was a 30 by 20 foot tent, which had side flaps that could be used during inclement weather. His medical equipment was scarcely basic and it wasn't until years later that he was able to attain his most indispensable asset, that being a laptop and a Hughes International satellite dish. It was this that enabled Alex to communicate and interact with scientists around the globe. In spite of the paucity of his facilities, Alex was not alone.

During their first year at Bongele, Alex and Kiros worked seven days a week. Undoubtedly, they had made significant improvements in the lives of its residents. In spite of this, Alex was deeply moved by the fact that less than 4% of the inhabitants at Bongele lived past the age of 65. Alex realized that there were many factors contributing to such a high death rate and that he had little or no control over many of them. He did, however, always have a special interest in the events that caused and accelerated aging and so he decided to devote more of his energy to the problem. His research with the Eskimos, observing the acceleration of the aging process in diabetics, and his experience with gene therapy, gave him an early insight into the problem. Before the missionaries had left Bongele, they were so impressed with what Alex had accomplished, that they handed him an additional $12,000 to continue his work.

Years later Alex would use some of these funds to obtain internet access. Alex would spend approximately an hour each evening surfing the net. He would enter chat groups with other physicians, scientists and even futurists to discuss his interests in aging. However, it wasn't until the website www.DIYbio came about that Alex's knowledge and theories began to develop exponentially. For www.DIYbio was a free website used by many of the world's greatest minds. The time had now come for Alex to test some of his theories and he selected a dozen chimps to work with. His first thought was appreciating how nice it was, not to have to file a mountain of paper work with the FDA, and then need to wait a year or more to receive a response. For the first time in his life, Alex Stein not only had his own lab, but also his own patients, and no one to answer to, or so he thought.

22

Steve Hinden couldn't miss the roaring sound of the snowmobile that pulled up to his front door, "Hello Mr. Hinden, my name is Nicholi and this is my associate Andrei, we understand that you may have some information for us," said Nicholi as the Russians stepped forward.

"Yes, I was hoping we could do some business together as I believe I have some useful information to sell."

"Yes, we're listening."

"First, shouldn't we discuss what it's worth to you? I have just spent two weeks with the CIA and if you find what they are looking for before they do, there can be an enormous profit in it."

"Why don't you just tell us what you know first, and then we can decide what it's worth?"

"Do you folks think I look like a fool?"

"How much are you asking for?"

"Fifty K, which is about one-millionth of what you will get. I am going to give you the name of the man who has found the way to slow the aging process. Do you have any idea what that is worth on the open market?"

"If the information is as good as you say, then we have a deal, except we only brought $25,000 American dollars with us, but we can give you an IOU for the balance."

"Can you fellows be trusted?"

"Mr. Hinden, we are businessmen. We have a reputation to uphold. We are not as you Americans like to say, *welchers*. As soon as we have this man in our possession, we will forward the balance of the funds into the account of your choice. After all, we don't want any collection agency coming to look for us, and we are confident that our mutual friend, Mr. DeMiceli, can vouch for our reputation."

"Very well then. There is a man named Alex Stein who . . ."

23

At 7 p.m. Carlton got a call from Deputy Johnson. Immediately, he suspected the news was not good.

"We have some real bad news for you Terry. Steve Hinden is dead, murdered."

"What happened?" Carlton asked in shock.

"We got a call from the bank in Wasilla. They felt that something wasn't right. Hinden had been calling twice a day to see if his check came in yet. When it finally came, they called him, but he never came in to pick it up. Very atypical for Hinden. Didn't even answer his calls. They sent the Sheriff up to his place to check it out. The door was wide open, blood all over the place and no Hinden. They got the State CSI people in. They feel from the blood spatter that someone cut his throat. Arterial spray on the wall at five feet, then gravitational droplets and evidence of drag marks on the flooring, much too much blood loss for him to have possibly survived. The local Sheriff said it was a real coincidence that Stein was murdered shortly after you spoke with him."

"Did you tell him we don't believe in coincidence?" Carlton asked. "Was anything missing?"

"Just a throw carpet that they probably wrapped him in, and possibly a photo from the wall. Several other photos present, but there's one picture hanger without a photo. CSI has faxed me the other photos and I'm looking at them right now."

"Is there a photo of two college kids in front of the Cornell clock tower?" Carleton asked.

"No, don't see anything like that."

"Deputy Johnson, we have ourselves a big problem. Better get our folks up to Bongele and locate Stein before we're too late."

Rust 55

24

Two days after the committee first met, they were all re-summoned into the first floor conference room at Langley. "Thank-you all for inviting me to address you this morning. It's always a special honor for me to address the Agency, and of course to get out of the lecture hall," said Shelly Rothberg, as he peered over his spectacles. Professor Rothberg had been a full professor at Georgetown for the past fifteen years. When the Agency was confronted with an attempt to vaporize anthrax so that it could by spread as an airborne agent, he was one of those called in on consultation. Rothberg's specialty was metabolic disorders and the Agency had decided to retain him as a consultant thereafter. He was close to sixty, short, stocky, and a good forty pounds overweight with most of his weight excess being in his belly. He wore an open tweed sports jacket and corduroy pants with a blue button-down shirt collar. He was full faced and had salty gray hair with a matching goatee.

"It is my understanding that you are investigating an individual who has either attempted or has succeeded in modifying the aging process, and so I have been asked to make you aware of what is currently understood about the subject so that as Deputy Johnson likes to say: *There will be no surprises.* Also, I have received a copy of the lecture that Mr. Stein presented to the University of Alaska 45 years ago, so we know of his interest in diabetes and aging. Although we have learned a great deal about diabetes since then, I must admit that this gentleman was way ahead of his time back then. Many of his postulations are only coming to fruition right now. So not only will I attempt to summarize his paper, but I will try and bring you up to date on all of today's knowledge as well.

"I have already received some of your questions by email, such as what are free radicals and how do they come into play, and another very astute question about the role of inflammation; hopefully, in the next hour or so, we will be able to address them. In order to understand the aging process, one first needs to comprehend the body's normal physiological functions. From there, we can see what goes wrong and most importantly, at what rate, and then try to determine if that rate can be altered or delayed in any manner.

"Let's begin by discussing diabetes, since diabetes is nothing more than accelerated aging, as Alex Stein discovered many years ago. If you understand diabetes, then you will have a good start on comprehending the aging process. Diabetes is actually two separate and distinct diseases. There is diabetes mellitus 1, which formerly was known as juvenile diabetes, and now is referred to as insulin-dependent diabetes. That name is an improvement, but still not perfect. By naming things improperly it only makes it more difficult to understand. The proper name should be deficient-insulin-level diabetes. Type 2 diabetes previously was referred to as adult onset diabetes, and is now referred to as non-insulin-dependent diabetes. A more accurate name would be elevated-insulin-level diabetes. They both do have one thing in common, in that the end result is an elevation of the blood sugar level, but by completely different mechanisms. To refer to them by the same name would be analogous to stating that pneumonia and measles are the same because both give you an elevated fever.

"In order to better understand the two types of diabetes, let us make an analogy to your car. Your car needs gasoline to run. Without gas there is no go. This is the problem in Type I diabetes. The pancreas cannot make insulin and without it the cells cannot get sugar into them to make energy. In Type II diabetes the problem is completely different. There is plenty of gasoline but it can't effectively get into the engine to be utilized. "Insulin is a hormone that is made in the beta cells within the islets of Langerhans in the pancreas. It is secreted into the blood stream and acts on the surface of cells, such as muscle cells, at receptor sites near the cell membrane to allow glucose to enter the cell where it is needed to generate energy. Before Banting and Best successfully discovered and isolated insulin at the University of Toronto in 1929, if you were unfortunate enough to have insulin-dependent diabetes, you simply died.

"**Slide I** shows a schematic of the action of insulin in normal individuals. Insulin is made in the pancreas, and secreted into the blood stream. It then acts on the receptor, or door, on the muscle cell surface, to allow glucose, or sugar, to enter into the cell. Without insulin, glucose cannot get into the muscle cell for energy. Think of insulin as the lubricant that allows the revolving door to turn.

Slide 1

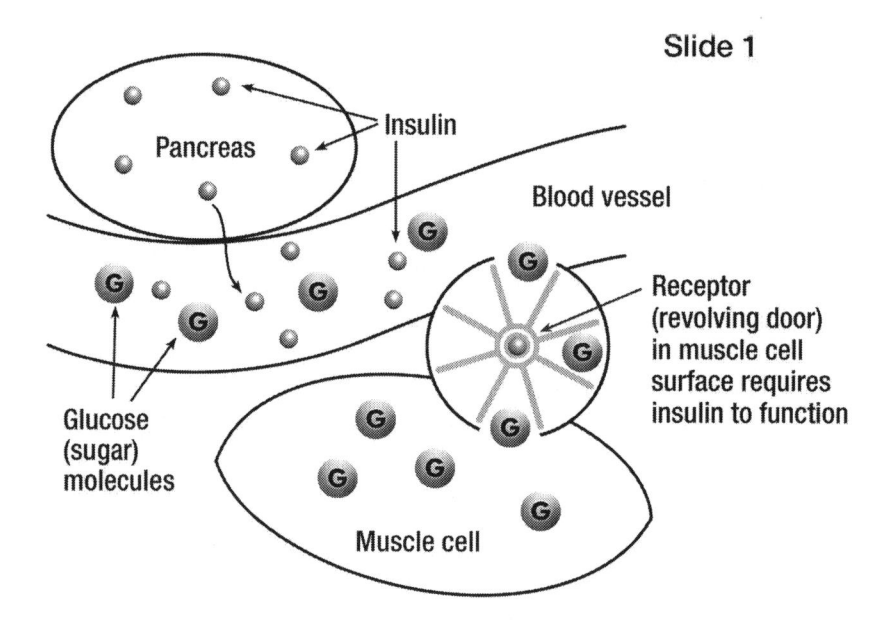

"Take a look at **Slide 2**. The abnormality is in the pancreas, which is unable to produce insulin. Without insulin, glucose cannot enter the cells, and therefore high abnormal levels of glucose build up in the blood.

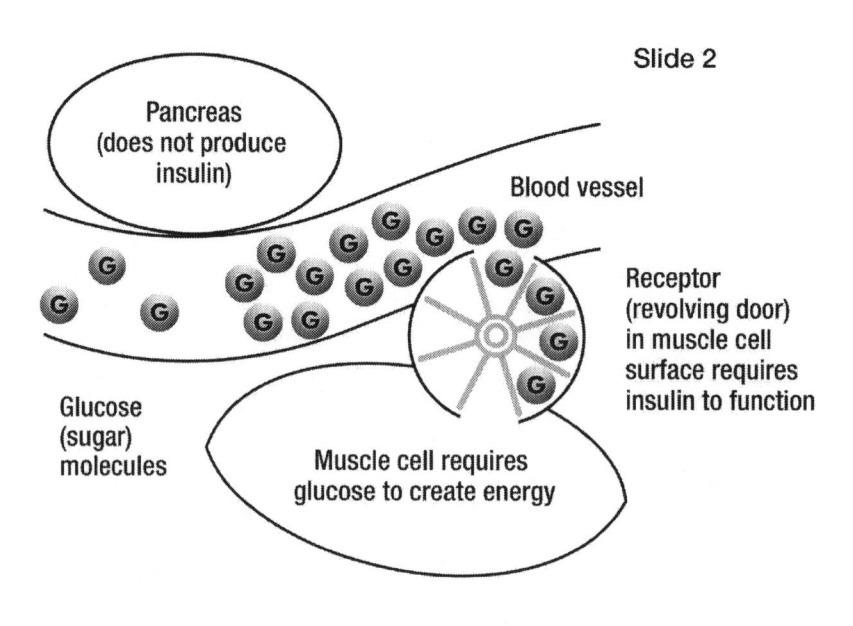

Slide 2

"As one can see in slide 3, the story is quite different in type 2, or non-insulin-dependent diabetes. As I mentioned previously, here the insulin levels found in the blood are elevated rather than absent or depressed. You may ask how can that be? How can you have elevated insulin levels and an elevated blood sugar, when the job of insulin is to lower the blood sugar?

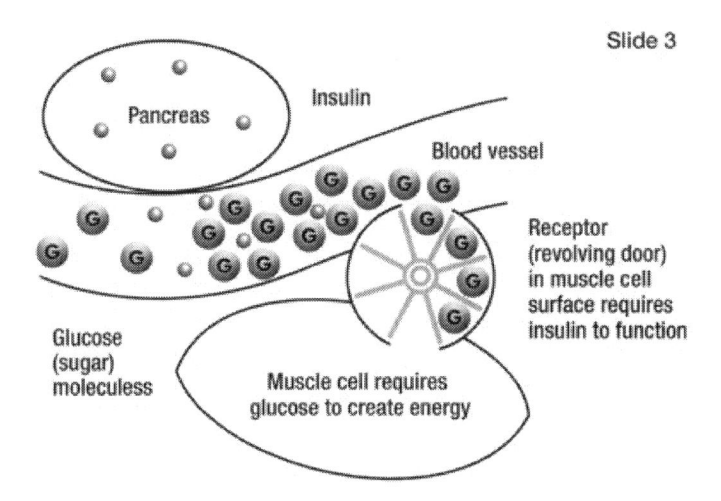

Slide 3

Pancreas — Insulin — Blood vessel — Receptor (revolving door) in muscle cell surface requires insulin to function — Glucose (sugar) moleculess — Muscle cell requires glucose to create energy

"The answer is that in non-insulin diabetes, the abnormality is not in the pancreas, but at the site of the peripheral receptor, or the door into the muscle cell, where the insulin exerts its effect. There is plenty of gasoline, but it cannot efficiently get into the engine. In spite of the fact that insulin is present, it cannot effectively drive glucose into the muscle cell because the door or receptor "sticks." Imagine the receptor where insulin exerts its effect on the cell membrane to allow glucose into the cell as the revolving door one might find in a department store. Think of insulin as the lubricant or grease that allows the door to rotate. Therefore, in order to allow glucose into the cell, the pancreas needs to compensate by turning out extra insulin, to lubricate the "sticky" or faulty receptor.

"Glucose eventually is able to enter the cell; however, the extra insulin remains in the blood stream hours later, causing the blood sugar levels to drop below normal, and that stimulates hunger. Thus a vicious cycle occurs; faulty receptor, extra insulin secreted by the pancreas, low blood sugar (hypoglycemia), hunger, excessive eating, and so forth."I hope you folks are still with me, because if you don't understand diabetes, then you can't possibly comprehend aging. In summary, in Type I diabetes there is no insulin and so glucose cannot get through the door of the muscle cell. In type 2 diabetes, there is insulin but the door isn't working properly.

"Now, there is a very common, yet poorly understood condition known as Metabolic Syndrome. It was recognized only a few decades ago and was first called Syndrome X, and subsequently Dysmetabolic Syndrome. Many endocrinologists say that it affects one out of every eight men; others say it can be as high as one in four, to some degree. A better name for this entity would be to call it: insulin resistant pre-diabetes. It is one of those conditions that you can probably accurately diagnose by simply looking at someone's appearance.

"In Metabolic Syndrome, as in Type 2 diabetes, the receptor is defective (There is plenty of gas but it cannot get into the engine). In these individuals, the blood sugar has not reached diabetic levels as of yet. In order to drive the glucose past this sticky receptor (insulin resistance) the pancreas needs to secrete *excessive* amounts of insulin, which eventually manages to drive the glucose into the cells. These individuals now have the same problem as the type 2 diabetic. Over the next several hours, that extra insulin in the blood continues to exert its effect. The pancreas normally secretes insulin after meals but between meals the levels drop. In the patient with Metabolic Syndrome the prolonged but delayed action of insulin, now continues to act and drive sugar from the blood vessels and into the cells beyond the normal duration. The result is reactive hypoglycemia, or a lower than baseline blood sugar. What happens to folks when their blood sugar drops?"

"They get hungry and want to eat," said Steve.

"Exactly, one needs to protect the brain from the damage caused by low sugar and therefore one seeks out food. Now the vicious cycle continues to perpetrate itself. Glucose load with food, faulty receptor, insulin overshot, reactive hypoglycemia, and so on. Such individuals have a see-saw, up-and-down pattern of both blood sugar and insulin levels, and as a result they are always hungry. They can have a huge meal and two hours later, when their blood sugar falls below normal levels, they want to eat again. Many of those who are obese today suffer from just this very problem. This also presents another vicious cycle. Insulin resistance makes one eat and then causes storage of excessive fat, and weight gain causes even more insulin resistance. Furthermore there is something different about the obesity of such individuals. It is centrally located. It's in the gut, what is commonly referred to as a beer belly, and in the chest, with very little fat being deposited subcutaneously or in the arms or legs.

"Now here is where things begin to get interesting. This type of obesity seen in type2 diabetics and those with Metabolic Syndrome, is referred to as the apple shape, being rounded in the middle, as opposed to those who carry their fat in the hips and behind, or the pear-shaped folks. Now for those of you who have fallen asleep, this is a good time to wake up, because what I have to say next is extremely important and necessary to understand what is going on in the aging process.

"Scientists found that there was a significantly higher degree of heart disease and cardiac deaths in the apple shapes as opposed to the pears. Furthermore, they found that those with the central pattern of obesity had higher levels of a substance in the blood known as C-reactive protein or CRP. If these patients had liposuction around the mid-section, which only removes the subcutaneous fat just below the skin, as opposed to the deeper visceral fat lying between the loops of bowels within the peritoneal cavity, it did nothing to lower their CRP or decrease their risk of heart disease.

"CRP has been well known to physicians for some time. It is what they refer to as an acute phase reactant. In other words, it is a protein found in the blood, which becomes elevated during any non-specific inflammation or infection anywhere in the body. A better name for C-reactive protein would be non-specific-inflammation marker. Historically, it was used by physicians to support the diagnosis of rheumatoid arthritis, which is not a joint disease but a systemic disease that can involve every organ in the body; the joints merely being the recipient of the inflammatory complexes. Most patients who suffered from rheumatoid arthritis, an inflammatory disorder, had elevated levels of CRP as expected. CRP levels in the body correlate with the degree of inflammation present. Studies have shown that in cases of acute appendicitis, the greater the inflammation in the appendix, the higher the level of CRP, reaching its maximum at the time of perforation. Furthermore, as the degree of inflammation in these patients progressed, the total antioxidant levels in the body fell, therefore showing that inflammation resulted in the generation of more free radicals and the free radicals were absorbed by the antioxidants. You may be asking why are patients with metabolic syndrome and central obesity having elevated levels of CRP? Heart disease and metabolic syndrome are not inflammatory disorders. Or are they?

"Well, believe it or not, heart disease, as well as diabetes, has everything to do with inflammation, and so does aging! As it turns out, the deep fat cells found in those with central obesity are involved in releasing certain inflammatory markers into the blood stream. These substances initiate a host of reactions within the blood stream. In other words, they cause oxidative stress, which in lay terms is simply known as rust. As we go on you will learn that the process that causes rust outside of our bodies is identical to that formed inside of our bodies. Well, let's take a break here and get a bite to eat? Do we have any hotdogs and fries around or something like that?"

25

Alex Stein intuitively believed that aging was related to inflammation years ahead of his time. In a matter similar to which Albert Einstein, his idol, was able to determine the size of the Universe, without the help of a telescope, Alex too, used the logic of his mind. Einstein, utilizing his *Theory of Relativity,* believed that light was both a wave and a particle, and as a particle it would be subject to the laws of gravity, and therefore would bend as it passed through space. After many very complex equations, he believed that if two parallel lights were sent up into space, when they came back to form a circle upon itself, that would define the size of the Universe. Those estimates are valid to this very day.

Alex always recognized that he was wired differently from most individuals. When he was 7 years old, he had still not mastered fluidity of speech and his parents began to wonder if he was retarded. Later in life, Alex learned that Einstein shared the same disability. In fact, Einstein had delayed speech development until age nine. Ever since then, Alex had developed a sense of kinship towards Einstein. Both men, as most other Asperger's, had poor social skills and difficulty with interpersonal relationships, and poor coordination and often showed selective mutism, whereby they would speak not at all to many and speak excessively to some, whom they felt comfortable with or liked. *Aspies,* as some refer to them, demonstrate unusual sensitivity to sound, light, or other external stimuli, and have difficulty in expressing emotions.

Many of history's overachievers have been suspected of having Asperger's or displaying Asperger traits. Bill Gates and Warren Buffet are amongst them. When Gates and Buffet met, Buffet impressed Gates by saying that his formula for success was his ability to focus. Buffet admits to spending the bulk of his time doing just one single thing: reading financial reports.

Aspies rely on rigid rules and routines, which when interrupted often lead to sensory processing difficulties, anxiety and depression. "You have to remind them that for every criticism it can take upwards of a hundred compliments to undo the embarrassment and humiliation." (Caton, 2007) Asperger's is often seen in engineers and has been referred to by some as the *engineer's syndrome or geek syndrome*. It is believed to be genetic and if one identical twin has Asperger's there is a ninety percent chance of affecting the other. Many famous individuals and overachievers of history are suspected of having had Asperger's. The list includes: Louis IV, Catherine the Great, Cleopatra, James Garfield, Vincent van Gogh, Beethoven, Leonardo de Vinci, Charles Dickens, and William Shakespeare.

Alex was well aware of both his strengths and his weaknesses. By isolating himself in Africa he was able to minimize human contact and avoid distracting social engagements. His preference was to work with animals, such as his chimps, which he found to be appreciative, caring, and loyal.

As Alex began testing his theories on altering the aging process, he became impressed with the results of his experiments. The treated chimps were now better fit, more energetic, younger in appearance, and finally living longer than the controlled counterparts. Before long, some of the natives asked to participate in the studies, and as they too had positive results, the volunteers grew exponentially. Over the next few decades, the results became more and more evident, as the population of male natives reaching the age of 65 had now tripled in the village of Bongele.

Alex was in his glory. And would have remained so, if he had not overlooked one simple event: the two census workers who happened to drift into Bongele one afternoon. The updated survival statistics gathered by them would trigger alarms that reached all the way to Sally Fields' printer back in Washington, DC.

26

As Carlton drove up to Abigail Stein's farm, the first one to greet him was a four-legged, four-year-old, male Golden Retriever. He ran up to Carlton with his tail in overdrive, whining as if he just saw a long-lost friend, and then peed all over him. As Abby exited the barn, she said, "I see that you have already been introduced to Moses. I apologize for him peeing on you, but he only does that to folks he really likes."

"Thanks for the compliment Moses. Hi, I'm *Chad*, and you must be Abigail."

"Yes, I've been expecting you. Please call me Abby."

As Abby introduced herself, Carlton realized that he was right about one thing. Abigail Stein looked nothing like the photo from her Syracuse yearbook. Not even close. She was gorgeous. She was approximately 5' 8", 135 pounds, and had long blond hair and piercing bright blue eyes, to go along with high cheek bones and a slightly turned up nose. Her hair was in a ponytail tucked behind a white straw western hat. A checked red and white blouse was knotted just above her navel and she had cut off jeans which came to the middle of her long well-toned thighs. She wore brown leather Frye boots.

It was obvious that she was not allergic to manual work as revealed by her well-developed *cut* deltoids. The only jewelry that she wore was a leather band around her left wrist. If she wore any fragrance, it was well concealed from the smell given off by the barn animals. Carlton thought to himself, what a paradox! *"An estrogen pie, in shit-kicking boots."*

Carlton attempted to make casual conversation to disguise his instant feelings of arousal.

"Is everyone out here as friendly as Moses?"

"Moses just loves people and everyone loves him."

"Why did you name him Moses? Is he Jewish?"

"No, it's because he is always leading the way, just like Moses did. He is the foreman around here. He is in charge of the grounds, the barn, and all of the horses; he keeps them all in line."

"You talk of him as if he were human."

"In a lot of respects, he is superior to a human. Can you do this for instance?" Abby rested a ball on Moses' nose and the dog immediately snatched it up into his mouth.

"Wow, I have got to try that tonight!"

Abby went on, "Have you ever watched a human try to drink out of a bowl just using a tongue? It's a riot. Moses can run faster and smell and hear better than any human. And I bet that you never caught a fly with your mouth. And as far as loyalty goes, forget it. A dog will never lie to you, never divorce you, and no matter what you do to them, they will always love you. For example, lock your dog and your spouse in the closet and after an hour, let them out, and then see which one is going to kiss you. Do you know of any humans that can pass that test? Moses also has a 300-word vocabulary."

At this point, Carlton was beginning to wonder if Abby was a fruitcake, just like her grandfather.

"We communicate with each other all day and we know what each of us wants. He has one whine for hunger, another if he wants to go out, and another when he has lost his ball. It's just like an infant before they can speak, whereby the mom understands everything. If I say, 'Moses, go upstairs and bring me down your blankie,' it's done. And just look at those adorable eyes." As Abby went on bragging about the wonders of dogs, Carlton thought of one more thing that dogs could do much better than man, and it was regarding where they can lick themselves, but he decided to keep that to himself.

As Carlton looked around, he couldn't help but notice what an eye pleaser Abby's barn was. She and her dad had built it themselves and it was bright red with black trim, and had a magnificent high gambrel roof, capable of storing over a thousand bales of hay. There were six stalls and each one had an occupant. Three of the stalls led directly into a 60 by 60 foot coral. The barn had one other thing that Carlton had never previously seen in a barn; a framed poem written by Rudyard Kipling entitled *The Power of the Dog*. It read:

There is sorrow enough in the natural way
From men and women to fill our day;
And when we are certain of sorrow in store,
Why do we always arrange for more?
Brothers and Sisters I bid you beware
Of giving your hearts to a dog to tear.

Buy a pup and your money will buy
Love unflinching that cannot lie—
Perfect passion and worship fed
By a kick in the ribs or a pat on the head
Nevertheless it is hardly fair
To risk your heart for a dog to tear

When the fourteen years that Nature permits
Are closing in asthma or tumour or fits,
And the vet's unspoken prescription runs
To lethal chambers, or the loaded guns,
Then you will find—it's your own affair
But . . . you've given your heart to a dog to tear.

When the body that lived at your single will,
With its whimper of welcome, is stilled (how still!);
When the spirit that answered your every mood
Is gone—wherever it goes—for good,
You will discover how much you care,
And will give your heart for the dog to tear.

We've sorrow enough in the natural way
When it comes to burying Christian clay.
Our loves are not given, but only lent,
At compound interest of cent per cent.
Though it is not always the case, I believe
,That the longer we've kept 'em the more do we grieve;

For when debts are payable, right or wrong,
A short time loan is as bad as long—
So why in Heaven (before we are there)
Should we give our hearts to a dog to tear?

When Carlton finished reading the poem, he immediately felt vibrations that Abby was going to be a very special lady. *Have any of Kipling's works ever been displayed in a barn before?* Carlton wondered.

    Carlton then went on to explain why he needed riding lessons and that he wanted to begin as soon as possible. They both agreed to a fee of $400 for lessons over five consecutive days, and Abby next gave Carlton a tour of the barn.

"Let me introduce you to your new pals," Abby said. "This here is Hunter; he's my baby. He is an eight-year-old retired gelded thoroughbred with the most perfect confirmation, and we love each other. Next is Candy, a six-year-old mare who is just a beautiful animal, with a mild disposition. She stands fourteen hands and has a smooth lope. This beauty is Stardust. She is a ten-year-old mare, white as snow, part Arab, part Albino, and she can run like the wind. The only problem with Stardust is that once she gets into a full gallop, she doesn't want to stop, so I'm reluctant to use her for beginners. Next is Lefty. She is going on fifteen and a bit of a plug, but she has a very smooth ride, and is a good follower, so she is perfect for younger riders. She is also a good packhorse if need be. And this is Splash, an eight-year-old Appaloosa who has the gentlest mannerisms. And finally this is Splash's one-year-old foal, called Puddles. Isn't she adorable?"

"They are all adorable, and I can see that you take great care of them."

"Thanks, but I would say we take care of each other."

Next, Abby reviewed the basics of horseback riding with Carlton. She taught Western riding and started from scratch. "Okay Chad, shall we begin?"

"I'm ready, Abby."

"Rule number one, safety first. Never walk behind a horse. The hind leg kick of a horse can kill a man, and you can never know when a horse is going to get spooked. Also, don't raise your hand suddenly above a horse's head since that may also spook him. It is important to let the horse know that you are the one who is in charge. A horse can sense this, and if you fail, then the horse will start thinking for himself. If the horse is standing on your foot the temptation is to try and pull your foot out. Don't try it. The horse weighs a good 1400 pounds and it wouldn't work. As painful as it may be, simply throw the full weight of your body into the horse's shoulder and hope that he backs off.

"Always mount the horse from the left side. When you are in the saddle, place the balls of your feet only in the stirrups, and not the arch of your foot. If you fall off, you don't want to be dragged. Then press your heels down as far as you can, and always keep them down. Your thighs need to be firmly pressed against the body of the horse. Next grab the reins with one hand, such that the bit makes a slight resistance in the horse's mouth.

"Keep your hand a few inches in front of the horn of the saddle. The bit against the horse's mouth acts like your brake, and when pressure is applied the horse will slow down and stop. When you want the horse to go forward, simply slide your hand forward releasing the pressure on the bit. Do not raise or elevate your hand, as this will cause the horse's head to jerk. If you want the horse to go to the left or right, simply move your hand in that direction, placing pressure on the opposite side of the horse's neck. Again, do not raise your hand, and always keep that hand level regardless of the command. It's just like a gear box; forward, reverse, left, and right.

"Also, try not to grab on to the horn of the saddle, or everyone will know that you're a tenderfoot. When you want the horse to go faster, release the pressure on the bit and kick the horse with your heels and say, *giddy up*. A horse has a real tough hide, so don't worry about hurting him, *don't pet him, kick him*. Eventually, he will respond just to your verbal cues.

"If you ever get lost, don't worry, the horse knows his way back to the barn. When you are done riding, always get off the horse and walk him until he cools down. Never place a sweaty horse back in the stall. Finally, brush the horse down, and if he performed well, give him a treat. Got all that, Tex?"

"Don't walk behind the horse, don't raise my hand, if he steps on my foot it will really hurt, I'm the boss until we get lost, then he is!"

"Wow, you are a fast learner."

"One more little thing; actually it's not that little, but we can get to that later in the week," as she glanced over at the shovel. "I don't want you to miss out on a thing. Let's save some of the fun stuff for another time. So that's enough talk for one day, Tex. Why don't you just hop up in the saddle and let's give it a ride?"

27

Carlton thought he would never have a bigger pain in the ass after riding the rails to and from Wasilla, but he was wrong. After his first riding lesson he headed directly for the bathtub in his hotel room, as he gobbled down a handful of Advil. Other than his rear end, the first session with Abby went well. He avoided probing into any deep personal matters other than what she volunteered on her own. She seemed very bright and Carlton was cautious not to raise any red flags that might initiate her suspicions. After his bath, Carlton got on his BlackBerry and sent a message. *Contact made, plan to probe more deeply.*

On their second day together, Carlton could sense that Abby was warming up to his charm, and he was beyond just warm himself. "Chad, because you have been such a baby complaining about your butt, I have a treat for you today."

"How kind of you Abby. Do I get a free massage?"

"No, unfortunately, massages are reserved only for those who sign up for a minimum of a week." At lunchtime, however, Abby tied the horses to a tree next to a fast moving stream. She opened her saddlebags and took out some rolls, cheese, fruit, and a leather canteen of Merlot and rolled out a blanket. "You do get a free picnic today." After lunch they drank their wine as they simply relaxed on the blanket. The sun and wine had warmed their faces, in spite of the nippy temperature, and Carlton began to get the feeling that things were about to heat up even more, as he began probing into Abby's personal affairs.

"So why does a sharp girl like you not have a guy?"

"Because I dumped him, if you must know."

"May I ask why?"

"Because he thought he was Superman."

"Was he delusional?"

"No, just thought he could handle two women at once."

"How did he take the news?"

"I'm not sure; he is still in the hospital. He fell off his horse and broke his ankle. Loose saddle girth."

"Whose fault was that?"

"I guess you can say it was his riding instructor's"

"And who was that?"

"Well, it used to be me."

"Wow, when you dump a guy, you really mean it."

"Is that the first time you ever manhandled a guy like that?"

"Funny that you should ask. At Syracuse, I went on a date with this guy from the wrestling team, named Freddie. He didn't seem to comprehend the word *NO*. Before I knew it, he was sitting on me and opening his pants, and wouldn't get off of me."

"What did you do?"

"I used the information that I was taught in my karate class on *self-defense for women*. I took the base of my palm and jammed his nose up toward the base of his brain. I heard his nose break, and then it began to bleed as his eyes teared, and he was unable to see. He rolled off of me and got up swinging blindly, so I gave him my best sidekick and took out his knee. Next he was lying there in the fetal position cursing and screaming, saying he was going to kill me, so I gave him a good kick in the nuts."

"Sounds like you gave Freddie, *a real Heady*. Did you report it to the police?"

"No, I never heard from him again. He was probably too ashamed to let his wrestling buddies know that some girl had kicked the shit out of him. However, after that I did buy myself one of those portable Tasers—the 669, six times more powerful than the ones the police use. I take it along whenever I go out on a date. It's much easier than going through all those gyrations again."

Carlton asked, "Were all the girls at Syracuse like you?"

"Of course not. Only the ones from my sorority."

"How did you wind up as a riding instructor?" Carlton asked.

"After I graduated from Syracuse I landed a very good job in the media field. Within four years I was made a vice president of the company."

"Exactly what did you do?"

"You know all those annoying pop-ups that appear on your computer screen?"

"Yeah, aren't they a real bitch?"

"Well, you can thank me for them! Let's assume that you are interested in going on a cruise and you go online. I would then sell your email address to all of the cruise lines that are our customers. Before you know it, everyone is sending you pop-ups about cruise options."

"So why did you leave?"

"Business was slow and I was told that I had to let 50 employees go, many of whom had worked for the company for years, and had families to support."

"What did you do?"

"I told them that they would only need to fire 49. I quit. My heart wasn't really into it anyways. I'd rather be around animals. In fact, the more I know about people, the more I love my animals."

After lunch they trotted back to the stable.

"Thanks for a terrific lunch, Abby. Next time it's on me."

"I hope you learned something today," said Abby.

"Sure did. A guy should always check his own girth, especially if he's dating you."

28

That evening Deputy Johnson called to update Carlton on the Hinden murder. "We located Hinden's body, or what was left of it. He was placed in a fish chopper that is used by the commercial fisherman down at the docks. Maintenance people found some suspicious bone fragments and called it in. The DNA is a match. We checked criminal records against the local fisherman and came up with a hit, a Tony DiMiceli; he has priors for drugs and smuggling. He is nowhere to be found. Quit his job a few days ago. We did a check on his cell records though and found some interesting stuff. Hinden apparently contacted him, and then DiMiceli made some calls to a Boris Yaspur, Russian mafia, real bad dude. Our best theory right now is that Hinden felt he had information to sell, notified DeMiceli, who called in Yaspur. I suspect that Hinden didn't do as well in his negotiations as he did with you. The only positives here are that we notified the bank and we're canceling Hinden's check. He really doesn't need it right now, and besides, something tells me he didn't live up to the terms of our agreement. Sounds like the Russians are going after Stein. We have taken your advice and have our special ops people in to pick him up. By the way, have you gotten anything out of the granddaughter?"

"I'm working on it, but not close enough to getting a hand on things."

"I'm sending the transcript from Professor Rothberg's comments to your BlackBerry. There is some very helpful info there, so you better get up to date with it. Keep me posted."

29

After receiving the call from General Salagi, Alex came to the realization that his days in CAR were numbered. He not only drew the attention of the local officials but those in Washington as well. He had many anxieties racing through his head. He would need to answer questions about a visa that expired 25 years ago, his practicing medicine without a license, and most importantly, discuss his research with those whom he did not trust. He also recognized that his research had progressed to the point where he was going to need a more sophisticated laboratory. Furthermore, other than Kiros, there was only one other person in the world that Alex trusted, and that was his granddaughter, Abigail. Alex decided to be proactive; he would run.

Over the years he had trained several of the natives, including the medicine man, to care for a wide variety of ailments, and so he felt that the natives would get by. However, his experiments to prolong aging would be no longer. He decided to burn and destroy all of the data, supplies, and materials concerned with his work, other than his precious little black box which he could slip into his pocket.

He felt that the hardest part would be to leave behind his companion, Kiros, who was now like a son to him. Alex lacked social skills and he was very anxious about saying goodbye. When Alex told Kiros of his plan, Kiros said, "I will not allow you to go into the jungle alone. It is far too dangerous for you, Atta Jeune." Alex tried unsuccessfully to convince Kiros to remain behind. The plan was for Kiros to carry the rubber Army surplus raft that his uncle had found in the Ugandi River years back. They would trek 15 miles through the jungle and then use the raft to navigate the Ugandi, which was one of the major tributaries of the Congo River that the natives called the Zaire River.

Once they reached the river, they believed it was unlikely that the local authorities would ever find them. The Congo has hundreds of tributaries, a very circuitous course, and with all of its tributaries it accounts for over 9,000 miles across Africa. The Congo River is the fifth longest in the world, spanning 2,720 miles, the longest in Africa, with the exception of the Nile.

The Congo starts in the southern portion of the Democratic Republic of the Congo and then flows to Stanley Falls near Kisangani, at a point just above the equator, before taking a counterclockwise course. It then loops to the northeast, then west, and finally south, where it can deposit up to 1.2 million cubic feet of water per second into the Atlantic Ocean. Everyone knows that the Nile flows from South to North, but when you ask Africans which way the Congo flows, they will say, *the Congo flows where it wants to flow.*

30

Carlton and Abby continued the riding lessons, and stopping for a casual picnic lunch became a tradition. As it was approaching the end of April, the temperature was still only forty-eight degrees "Does it ever warm up around here?" asked Carlton.

"Oh sure, we have two seasons."

"And they are?"

"Winter and Fourth of July, and the Fourth of July isn't always that nice."

"It is officially spring now, so let's hope things start to warm up soon," said Carlton.

"I don't know who set the dates for the seasons, but one thing is for sure, he wasn't from New Hampshire. In these parts, spring begins on Memorial Day. Summer starts on July 4, and ends abruptly on or before Labor Day. No one is going to be inviting you to a pool party in the middle of September. Fall goes from Labor Day to Thanksgiving. And winter begins on Thanksgiving Day when Santa shows his face, and goes all the way to Memorial Day."

"That's a pretty long winter, isn't it Abby?"

"Tell me about it! And Chad, tomorrow, bring a jacket along."

By day four, Abby was chatting like a ten-year-old at her first trip to Disney Land. She was revealing all the details of her life. "You mentioned that you have a grand-father in Africa; what does he do?"

"Grandpa Alex is a strange dude. I never actually got to meet him, since he left for Africa before I was born. At the beginning we wrote to each other a lot, but then I guess we just stopped when he didn't answer my last letter. We always spoke of getting together, but never quite made it." At that point Carlton was almost about to say that Alex never received the letter, but he caught himself, realizing that *Chad Jay* would have no way of knowing that.

"He did mention that he was doing some research on how to prolong life. Another dreamer in search of that ever-elusive Fountain of Youth. Never ends, does it? How about you, Chad? What's your opinion about this search for immortality, the belief in an afterlife, and the belief in a soul?"

Abby's question turned a relaxing casual lunch into an intellectual philosophical discussion. "When you ask the question about the search for immortality and the belief in a soul in the very same sentence, you are asking a very profound question. I do believe that there is a strong link between these two subjects. Humans are the only species on earth that are aware of the fact that they will die someday. The thought is so unpleasant that we want to believe that death does not mean the end of our conscious awareness. This realization that we are mortal rather than immortal provides the impetus for man to accept the concept of a soul. The concept of a soul enables one to continue conscious feelings and thoughts after death. If man could extend life indefinitely, there would be little interest in believing in a soul.

"If there is a loving and benevolent God, then why do so many good people die young and innocent children become inflicted with fatal diseases? One might say that life is unfair, if the best and worst of mankind come to the same ultimate end without differentiating between the two. The seventeenth-century French philosopher René Descartes rejected the concept of a soul. Descartes said 'If life was fair, there would be no need for an afterlife (or soul), and if life was unfair, than why should one expect to find fairness in an afterlife.' So to answer your question, Abby, I do see a relationship between the desire to significantly extend our lives on earth and the promotion of the concept of an afterlife by religious teachings.

"As for myself, my folks were Catholic, and once a week in elementary school we were sent out for religious instruction. I always had some doubts about the validity of the Bible. Let's face it, how could anyone get all those animals on just one boat? Furthermore, it was necessary to get one of each sex. Have you ever tried to determine the sex of a chipmunk? However, I didn't start to ask the big questions until I got to college. That is when I began to look at the pros and cons for believing in God. The most obvious fact that disturbed me is that it seemed as if no one was thinking for himself. I asked, 'Why do 99.9% of folks have the same religious views as their parents? And why were the other guy's parents the ones who were wrong?' The main pros for believing seemed to be the hope of everlasting life via the soul, a belief in blind faith that someone else told you to accept."

Although Abby was finding Chad's discussion to be quite thought provoking it was not exactly how she hoped the picnic would unfold. Attempting to alter the mood, she poured some more wine, unfastened the top two buttons of her blouse, and stretched her long sexy legs along the length of the blanket.

In spite of the apparent distractions he continued on without missing a beat. "We can go back 3,000 years to ancient Greece. If a bolt of lightning came from the sky, it was assumed that Zeus was pissed off about something. Man has always had the need to provide answers, especially when he doesn't know them. Wouldn't our knowledge have advanced at a faster pace if we were simply able to say, 'I don't know?' Every civilization since has yielded to the same temptation, the denial of the finality of death, regardless of the logic involved.

"Take the Emperor Constantine for example. He was basically a pagan, but also a good politician who understood the popularity and rise of Christianity, and he needed the support of the Christians in his upcoming battle to consolidate his power. In 325 A.D., he called for the Council of Nicea. Prior to that, the principles and doctrines of Christianity varied widely. It was the duty of the Council to reconcile all of these differences and essentially rewrite the Bible, and subsequently all previous editions of the Bible were to be destroyed. The council successfully agreed on the dates for holidays and most other matters, except for the big question: Was Jesus to be considered a prophet or a divinity? It has been said that the discussion became so heated that it erupted into physical violence. In the end, the matter was settled by a single vote: Jesus was divinity, the true son of God. Can you imagine how different the world would be today, if the vote had gone the other way?

"Moslems adhere to the belief that Mohamed was a prophet rather than a deity. They reject the Christian notion that Jesus is the son of God and this belief serves as a major source of anger and hostility between the two sects. Talk about a tight election! Just imagine how many wars and deaths could have been avoided if the vote proclaiming Jesus as a divinity had gone the other way. Shall I continue, or have you had enough of my philosophy for one day?"

"No, please go on."

"With the coming of the Renaissance came a new sense of awareness for creative, artistic and scientific thinking. Prior to this, man turned to the church for the answers to complex questions concerning his origin and his destiny. These are the same two questions which man has been fixated on since the beginning of time. Where did I come from? And where am I going?

"As scientific information emerged it became apparent that much of the newly acquired science was at odds with religious doctrine. The findings of those, such as Galileo, that the earth was not the center of our universe, did not stand well with the church, so he was imprisoned for refusing to recant his views.

"A great debate then ensued between the forces of faith versus the forces of science and reason. Initially, scientists were persecuted for their unorthodox views, but subsequently religious leaders hoped to reach a compromise that perhaps the two might coexist. And yet, as a plethora of scientific data accumulated that contradicted the position of the church, it became evident that a compromise would not hold.

"And then along came a priest, Thomas Aquinas. In 1270, he wrote, *The Treatise De Unitati Intellectus Contra Averroistas or The Trinity of the Unity of the Intellect,* which gave the church a defendable position on which to stand. Aquinas stated that the truth of both faith and experience are fully compatible and complementary. Some truths, such as the mystery of the incarnation can be known only through revelation, and others such as that of knowledge of material can only be obtained through experience. Still others, such as that of the existence of God, are known equally through both. In order to reach the highest truths and those that religion is concerned with, the aid of revelation is necessary.

In essence, Aquinas stated that faith was more powerful than reason, and man did not possess the knowledge, wisdom, or foresight to question God's ways or his supremacy. Furthermore, if God is omnipotent and reason is not, surely He has the ability to alter perceptions of what man thinks is actually so. The true believer therefore needs to accept God on faith alone and not debate the logic of God's wisdom or existence. This position still stands today and by its very nature is one that cannot be proven wrong. Quoting Ayn Rand, 'Reason is not automatic. Those who deny it cannot be conquered by it.' As Stuart Chase said, 'For those who believe, no proof is necessary. For those who don't believe, no proof is possible.'

"Why is it that everyone believes that his religious beliefs are the correct ones and thus superior to the views of others? Not only has this been the basis of most wars, it is also the fuel that ignites prejudice. It is the basis for why one group of folks consider themselves superior to others. And it can also serve as the root of hatred. Until man begins to look at his race and religion as no better than the next, there will be no peace and harmony on this earth.

"The South African policy of Apartheid, the exploitation of the natives of India by the British, as illustrated by Rudyard Kipling in his poem 'Gunga Din,' the obliteration of the Incas by Pizarro and the Spaniards, the enslavement of the African Negro by the White Europeans and Americans, the exploitation of the American Natives by the White colonial settlers, the ongoing struggle between the Jews and the Arabs, are just a few of thousands of examples of such atrocities. When is it going to end? Will it ever end?"

Abby was now beginning to feel that Chad was really hooked on this gal back in town, being that he began to resemble her history professor back in Syracuse. "Wow, I can see why you are an instructor at Dartmouth. I should earn three college credits for just listening to that. Although you still haven't expressed your own opinion on the subject and that was my original question."

"I am a fan of John Keats, and as he stated in his poem, 'Ode on a Grecian Urn,' 'Beauty is Truth, and Truth is Beauty' Carlton replied.

"The church does a lot of terrific things for the community. Organized religion provides a focal point for teaching a code of moral decency, gives people a sense of belonging, feeds the poor, assists the needy, encourages brotherly love, and gives people a sense of hope and optimism, wouldn't you agree?" Abby asked.

"There's no question that the church plays a very significant role in the lives of many, and no one should be denied that right. The only question that is being asked is: could many of these same roles by served by secular groups as well?" he responded. "For example, when I was growing up there was a family in the neighborhood of a mixed marriage; one was Christian and the other was Jewish, and they had two pre-teenage boys. They didn't attend any church services in the community but each week they held what they referred to as *Sunday Sermon*. The entire family gathered in the dining room for breakfast and a moral issue was discussed, with everyone participating.

"One such discussion that I recall was the issue of a trimmed baseball card that the older son had purchased. The frayed edges of the card had been trimmed off in order to make the value of the card appear higher, when in reality it reduced the value significantly. When the boy discovered his error in purchasing the card he was confronted with the option of either pretending he was unaware of the trimming, or to sell the card as a trimmed card at a considerable loss. The concluding moral of all of these discussions was always the same: *The Golden Rule; do unto others as you would have others do unto you.*

"During a parent-teacher conference one of the boy's teachers commented, 'I see that you folks don't attend any church services in the community, so how may I ask, do you intend to teach your children about morality?' The implication was that without God's help, how could anyone comprehend and display morality? The father replied, 'We believe in the principles of Christianity, Judaism, and the Golden Rule and if our children follow those guidelines they will have all the morality that is necessary.' Needless to say, both of these boys have grown up to be honest, hardworking, decent people with the highest moral values, in spite of the fact that one cannot describe them as God-fearing.

"Does mankind need any better guideline for gauging moral behavior other than that of the Golden Rule? I always got a real charge when listening to Carl Reiner and Mel Brooks doing their gig on the *2000 Year Old Man*. Reiner asks Brooks, who is the 2000-year old man, how God was discovered? 'There was this big guy named Phil, a real bully, carried a very big club, and everyone assumed that he was God. Then one day a bolt of lightning came out of the sky, and zapped Phil directly in the head and he dropped dead. We all looked up to the sky and said, *"There's something bigger than Phil!"*'

"Apparently God had a very simple message in those days, it was to zap bullies; they called it *karma.* So why has man found it necessary to keep changing who God is, and what he expects of us? All these different viewpoints not only make it very confusing, but regardless of whom is right, the majority of us will still be wrong. I'm not knocking what anyone believes. If religion makes one feel more fulfilled and allows one to act morally then that is beneficial.

"Our country was founded by those seeking religious freedom. What I do object to, is when others try to deny that very same right to someone else, because they have different views. I believe everyone should have the right to believe or not believe.""What is your opinion about families getting together on religious holidays such as Christmas and Easter?" Abby asked.

"I think it's great, but the purpose doesn't necessarily need to be for religion. To me, this is about family. It is about respect. It is about tradition. It is our way to show that we have not forgotten about the traditions of our loved ones before we came along. Thanksgiving, Santa, the Easter Bunny, the Tooth Fairy—these are all American traditions that are a part of our culture.

"Another concept that I find difficult to grasp is that of prayer. How can God possibly have the time and energy to listen to and respond to the hundreds of millions of prayers that are directed to him on a daily basis? It reminds me of the scene in the movies, where Jim Carrey was God, and each of the two million people who purchased a lottery ticket that day prayed to be a winner. Jim, being a very benevolent God, granted all of them their wishes. Unfortunately, since everyone was a winner, each of the two million ticket holders won only one dollar each.

"Haven't more people been killed in the name of religion, with one group trying to impose their beliefs upon others, than for any other reason?

In ten thousand years of recorded history, there has been less than two hundred years when someone on the planet wasn't at war, and the vast majority of those wars have been over whose God is right. Just look at what has been done in the name of God during the Crusades. Here was a series of wars consuming almost two hundred years (1096-1291), between the cross and the crescent.

"The end of the eleventh century was marked by chaotic times. In the East, Alexios I, Emperor of the Byzantine Empire, and Greek Orthodox Church, was under siege from the Moslem Seljuq Turks, who already had seized most of Asia Minor from him, and were now threatening to attack to the North and advance on Istanbul. In Western Europe, at this time, there was a multitude of regional conflicts among various lords, and the influence of the Church appeared to also be in disarray. So when Alexios I requested the help of Pope Urban II in Rome in combating the armies of Islam, it gave the Pope the impetus he needed to consolidate his own power.

"The Turks had taken control of Jerusalem from the Christians four hundred years earlier, and Urban wanted it returned to Christian hands. At the Council of Clement in 1095, he requested support for the Christians in the East, and called for expulsion of the infidels from Jerusalem. How was he able to convince men to leave their homes and families and travel up to 3,000 miles over a three-year period, to a land that they had never seen? He proclaimed, 'Deus *lo volt*' (God wills it!). He then decreed anyone who would take up arms against the Godless infidels and join the journey to Jerusalem, would be given a remission of all previous sins and their souls would be sent directly to heaven. The Moslems countered with their own call for Holy War, or Jihad. How could either side lose, with both claiming to have God on their side?

"The pope's words instigated the slaughtering of thousands of non-Christian people throughout Europe, as many Jews and pagans were mercilessly murdered. Three years after the call for the first Crusade, the Christians successfully conquered Jerusalem, and slaughtered most of the 30,000 inhabitants of the city, including Muslims, Jews, and even other Christians. And after nine such Crusades, over a two hundred year period, leading to countless deaths, beheadings, torture, rape, and even cannibalism, what, if anything, was accomplished? Nothing but more hate than ever, for all those concerned.

"The theme never ends. Look at all of the wars in Europe between the Catholics and the Protestants, and the Spanish Inquisition, which burned, tortured and stoned to death those that they suspected were not true believers; these are but a few of countless examples.

"Here is an interesting point about the Inquisition regarding the Jews that were in Spain at this time. They were the money-lenders, since Christians were forbidden to participate in *usury,* as it was considered a sin. During this period in history, Spain was ruled by a number of competing lords, each one trying to build a bigger castle than the next. The Jews naturally became their bankers. However, during the Inquisition, the Pope issued an ultimatum to all non-Christians in Spain, predominantly the Jews and the Moors: convert to Christianity, flee the country, or be burned at the stake. Some fled over the Pyrenees, others converted, and many more were simply murdered. Since there were no Jews remaining, the lords had lost their bankers and their ability to raise funds. Therefore, they petitioned the Pope and presented him with their dilemma; the Pope rescinded the decree, by forbidding Jews from converting to Christianity. By the process of elimination, Jews dominated the banking industry, an issue for which many still criticize them today.

"These religious conflicts go on today: the Mid-East, Iraq, Afghanistan, Pakistan, India, Serbia, Croatia, and many other places throughout the world. When, if ever, will it end?"

"That sure is a lot to think about Chad." Abby also thought about another thing, "Why is it that every time I meet a handsome, intelligent, and sensitive man, he already has a girl friend?"

Her discouragement however was short lived as Chad unexpectedly said, "Nice legs, Abby."

"Thanks Chad, I didn't think you noticed."

Abby's track record with men was nothing to brag about. She recognized that she had trust issues. She never had the opportunity to know her grandparents. Her parents passed away at a relatively young age. Her idealistic hopes for a professional career revealed the work place for what it really was: *dog eat dog.* Her dating experiences also left her with a sense of disillusionment as she never sustained a relationship longer than a year.

At Syracuse, she was dating Vincent. He was tall, handsome, intelligent and athletic. His speaking voice simply resonated across the room. Vincent was a wide receiver on the Syracuse U. football team and every woman would have been thrilled to date him. Abby and Vincent's relationship didn't last very long—three dates to be exact. On their first dinner date Vincent told stories about his childhood. He spoke of his parents and his siblings. He mentioned his major and recited all of the courses he was taking. He spoke about his football experience. Dates two and three were more of the same. At the end of the evening Abby said, "Vincent, it was nice *listening* to you."

"Don't you mean it was nice talking with you?"

"No, I meant what I said. I know everything about you, your family and the events of your life. What, if anything, do you know about me?"

Abby had accomplished the one thing that no woman had ever managed: Vincent was speechless. It was their last date.

Abby dated many men since then but her overall conclusion hadn't changed much; most men are two-timing lying scoundrels. If she yearned for a genuine true loving long-standing relationship that would never disappoint her, her best bet was to find it in animals. And yet, there was something about Chad that seemed different. Sure he was handsome and intelligent, but he also gave the impression of being sincere. Abby recognized her errors in the past that made her question her own judgment. And besides, her thoughts were all simply imaginary since Chad already had a girlfriend. *Nevertheless, if this one turns out to be another lying scoundrel, God help both of us.*

Abby now quickly changed the subject. "I'm still worried about Grandpa Alex; what if dementia may be starting to settle in? He doesn't have any family in Africa to care for him. After all, he must be getting close to seventy by now. Chad, did you know that there is a type of Alzheimer's that is hereditary, and involves up to 25% of those who contract the disease? Apparently it began with some Volga German immigrants who initially settled in Pennsylvania and then migrated across the country. Bad set of genes; perhaps Grandpa Alex has them as well."

"No, I didn't know that."

"Great, at least I can now say that I taught you something today as well. I'm getting thirsty from all this talking, Chad, why don't we just have bit more Merlot?"

"Why not?"

As they lay on the blanket, sipping the wine, Carlton asked Abby for her thoughts on religion. Abby replied, "I guess that I have more questions than answers. I don't believe in heaven and hell, and all that, or that God made man in his image, and I'm quite certain that we women didn't come from one of your ribs. I think the Bible has some great moral lessons, but I don't believe one can take it literally, and I believe it was written by mortal men. I believe in evolution as opposed to creationism, but I adhere to the belief that there is a greater force in the Universe which we cannot comprehend."

"What do you envision such a force to be?"

"I don't know. Isn't that an impressive answer? After all, you said that you would have been impressed if the Greeks had simply given that for an answer. There are so many questions for which no one seems to have the answers. How did it all get started, and if you say the Big Bang, then where did the stuff come from that got banged? And what in the world was going on before all of that got started? I can go on and on."

"Can you give me another example?"

"Sure, what was happening before, before, the Big Bang?"

"I would ask for one more example but I'm pretty sure that I know what you would say?"

"Is it possible that this unknown force can simply represent science? Not only for what we know, but for what we still don't know? Did you know that in 1970, it was estimated that every bit of knowledge in the field of biochemistry, was doubling at a rate of every five years, and that was before we had the kind of computers that we have today. Perhaps in time, some of today's mysteries will be as easy to understand as what causes *lightning*."

"Well that was a most interesting and enjoyable discussion, Chad, although I felt like I was back as Syracuse U. As a matter of fact it wasn't anything like I had expected."

"What were you expecting, Abby?"

Abby simply shrugged her shoulders as she thought, *"Perhaps something a bit more romantic?"*

"Other than the Freddie Heady and the cut girth strap, have you had any other meaningful relationships?"

"It's really difficult nowadays to successfully sustain a happy long-term relationship. The statistics also bear that out. It's very unfortunate."

"Why do you think that is so, Abby?"

"First, I believe that many folks are expecting to find someone who will make *them* happy. The first step towards happiness is to like *yourself*. If you don't like who you are, another person can't do that for you. Secondly, couples need to share similar values. That doesn't mean that they have to have everything in common. Interests can vary, but values need to be in tune with what your partner respects.

"As for myself, there are certain beliefs that are important to me. Integrity is one of them. Are you truthful with yourself and with others? Are you a member of society that contributes to the overall good, or simply a taker?"

As Abby mentioned the word integrity, a bead of sweat began to form near Carlton's temple followed by a flushing of his face. Carlton recognized that his relationship with Abby was based on a series of lies, lies that she would eventually discover, and that would place him in the same category as her last boyfriend.

Abby went on, "I dated an attorney for a brief period. One day I asked him the question, 'if two parties with opposing views asked you to represent them, how would you decide which one to represent?' I was expecting him to say that this would be an opportunity to select the one with the high moral ground. Instead he said it would be decided by the one who offered him the higher fee. I broke up with him the following day.

Another essential trait important for me is a good sense of humor, which includes someone who has enough self-confidence to be able to laugh at himself."

"What about religion?"

"I already mentioned that I don't adhere to any specific religious doctrine, but I don't need to have a partner who shares those views, provided that he isn't consumed by such beliefs and doesn't force his views on me. Another area that I have strong beliefs about is the treatment of animals. I have no use for anyone who mistreats an animal. My animals mean a great deal to me. They are loving, gentle, devoted and intelligent. They are great company and we depend on one another.

"One of the reasons so many relationships fail is because people really don't know that much about one another. People's lives cross at a point in time when they appear to have something in common, and then they are expected to be compatible from that point on. It doesn't work that way, because our interests change. That is why values are important. There is a greater probability that your interests will change before your values will.

"For example, we had a dozen or so friends who all went to the same dude ranch on summer vacations. Each year several of them married off and dropped out of the group. One summer, the only ones to show up were Bill and Judy. They stood there for a moment looking at each other and then said, 'Why not? Let's get married!' Bill was a Methodist from England who majored in English literature. He was a big burly guy who loved to bellow out poetry, and he was fifteen years older than Judy. She was a shy Jewish girl from Brooklyn with a high school education who worked as a beautician. Their sole common interest had crossed at a single point in time. Other than their love of horses, they had almost nothing in common. Two years later, they divorced.

"Here's one final example of love gone wrong. I had a friend at Syracuse named Heather, who married a carpenter named Tom. From day one, all they would talk about was designing and building their own home. During the construction period they were busy drawing floor plans, purchasing appliances and furnishings. They drew pictures of what they envisioned, including a white picket fence. When the home was completed, they invited my friend and me for a lovely dinner. They had finally successfully accomplished their goal! A month later, Heather and Tom announced they were getting a divorce.

"It was a classic example of Adler's *As-if theory*. Alfred Adler was a contemporary psychologist of Sigmund Freud, and was born in Vienna in 1870. His *as- if* theory stated that folks formulate a goal, as if attaining that goal is synonymous with happiness. Heather and Tom believed that once they had their home along with the white picket fence that all would be well. During the construction phase, they believed that happiness was just around the corner. However, when the house was completed, nothing really changed. A house was not the substantive thing that was missing from their lives. It goes back to where I began. One cannot rely on another person or a house to provide a sense of fulfillment within oneself."

"Have you found anyone who comes close to being an ideal match for you? Carlton asked.

"Not yet, Chad, not yet."

"Have you given any thought to trying those on-line dating services?"

"I have given it some thought, but haven't pursued it. With my luck, my perfect mate would be somewhere in Oregon. So what do you think, Chad? How compatible a match do you think the two of us would be from the point of view of a profile dating service?"

As Carlton reflected on the fact that his relationship with Abby to date was based on one big lie, he responded, "Actually, I only found one item that you mentioned that I'm currently a bit weak on, but perhaps we can discuss that on some other day." Carlton reflected*," Wait until she finds out what a liar I am?"*

31

After Dr. Rothberg devoured three hot dogs and a large portion of fries, along with a diet soda, he continued his lecture to the CIA committee. "Some of you may be wondering why I am going into such detail in my discussion on diabetes, inflammation, free radicals and oxidation. However, I assure you that if you stay with me a bit longer, it will all begin to make sense. Let us now discuss free radicals and oxidative stress.

"Exactly what is a free radical? I believe it was Ann who asked that in her email. A free radical is any atom or molecule that has a single unpaired electron in its outer orbit. Such substances are unstable and highly reactive and therefore they are associated with oxidative damage to the cells.

"The oxygen free radical is particularly toxic and has been associated with the aging process. A free radical is missing an electron from its orbit and so it has a propensity to want to pair with another electron and restore neutrality and stabilize its orbit. Therefore, it is looking for an electron to steal in order to stabilize the orbit. When an electron is successfully stolen, the donating organ or victim has now been oxidized, or as we say in the vernacular, it has been rusted. When a molecule loses an electron, we refer to that process as oxidation. When a molecule gains an electron, we say that that molecule has undergone reduction and it has been reduced. Another way to state this is to say that the oxidized molecule has been subject to oxidative stress.

"The process of oxidation occurs outside the body exactly the same way as within the body. Elemental iron in the form of ferrous oxide has a valence, or charge, of plus two, meaning that it has two fewer negatively charged particles or electrons than the positively charged protons. When ferrous iron is exposed to oxygen and the elements for a period of time, it becomes converted to ferric oxide with a valence of plus three, by giving up yet another one of its electrons. We now say that the iron has become oxidized. In essence the iron has rusted; **to oxidize is to rust.** The same chemical reaction occurs in our bodies, contributing to the aging process.

"For example, every leukocyte (or neutrophil white blood cell) in the body, contains small amounts of hydrogen peroxide stored in tiny packets inside the cell known as lysosomes. When the body is faced with infection or inflammation, the leukocytes migrate into the area of stress, and break open the lysosome to release the hydrogen peroxide and thus kill or oxidize the offending element.

"We call substances such as hydrogen peroxide, which are capable of stealing an electron from another substance, *free radicals*. If the free radicals attack one of our own proteins and steal one of their electrons, then that protein has been oxidized. When our cellular proteins are damaged in such a way, they now cause our cells to swell and leak fluids and may eventually lead to cell death.

"When inflammation occurs in the body, many reactions within the body contribute to the activation of oxidative stress, thus releasing a host of chemicals. The clotting system is just one example. The normal endothelial, or inner, lining of the blood vessels have a texture similar to that of the inside of your cheek, and when that surface is injured, or roughened, the platelets will stick to it. The first step is that the platelets release ATP (adenosine triphosphate), which causes them to aggregate and clump together. Now, this roughening or any damage on the inside lining of the blood vessel is called a nidus."

"What is a nidus?" Steve asked.

"A nidus is the first step in the forming of a scab. The platelets in the blood begin to clump and stick together and other substances begin to attach to the complex at the wound site, and a clot is formed. If this failed to occur, then one could bleed to death after sustaining any cut. Unfortunately, the platelets are unable to distinguish between a cut and a roughening or damage to the blood vessel initiated through the inflammatory process, or as we like to refer to it, as oxidative stress.

"As the platelets are summoned into action, and they release their ATP (adenosine triphosphate), a series of reactions and chemical inflammatory processes are initiated, so that a plug can form, to either stop the bleeding or in the case of inflammation, adhere to any nidus or roughening already present.

"Now if we examine individuals with high blood pressure or elevated blood cholesterol, or both, we find something very interesting. These individuals have a much higher incidence of damage or roughening to their intimal, or inner, lining of their blood vessels. High blood pressure increases the shearing forces on the inner lining of the blood vessels and roughens or damages the surfaces. This roughened area now allows platelets and fatty deposits to adhere to the vessels at a rate much greater than normal individuals.

"This first became apparent when autopsies were conducted during the Korean War. The blood vessels of many of the nineteen-year-old American soldiers already displayed these signs of aging, with the presence of these diseased plaques, whereas the Korean soldiers showed no such evidence. Furthermore, the distribution of these fatty plaques were not symmetrically located, but rather found in areas of high turbulence or pressure within the vessels. Similar to the manner in which a meandering river will erode its banks in areas of the most forceful flow, such as at its branches or bifurcations, the blood vessels revealed the same pattern. For example, at the site where the internal carotid and external carotid branch off from the common carotid artery was an area of predilection for plaque formation. Why were these changes found predominantly in the Americans? The answer was the differences in life style and diet. Our diet was high in saturated fats, trans fats, and refined simple carbohydrates, as compared to the Koreans."

"Exactly what are Trans fats?" Ann asked.

"Trans fats are made when manufacturers add hydrogen to vegetable oil in a process known as hydrogenation. This increases the shelf life of these foods and also increases flavor and taste since it allows the fats to adhere to the tongue longer. The reason that trans fats have a longer shelf life is because bacteria have difficulty in dissolving these substances. Trans fats are found in vegetable shortening, some margarines, crackers, cookies, snack foods, or other foods made with or fried in partially hydrogenated oils. If manufacturers did not use these substances they would need to replace foods on a more frequent basis to prevent spoilage. The majority of these fats are formed when manufacturers turn liquid oils into solid fats like shortening and hard margarine. Have you ever noticed that one can store an open can of shortening in your home for a year without it spoiling? The reason is that bacteria have difficulty in breaking down trans fats. Guess who else cannot break down trans fats? That is correct, Steve. The answer is humans! These are the fats that raise your bad cholesterol, LDL, and become deposited on the inner lining of your blood vessels, predisposing one to heart disease, as well as accelerated aging.

"Poor dietary choices such as these lead to elevated levels of cholesterol in the blood. When such levels reach a supersaturated state, the liver is unable to clear the fat from the blood and so it attaches to the intimal, or inside, lining of the blood vessel. Now, if the individual has a roughening of that blood vessel, due to excessive pressure on the vessel from high blood pressure, that area of the vessel will act as a nidus for platelets to attach to, and subsequently the fatty deposits will adhere to this site as well. The entire process involves release of inflammatory reactions and causes oxidative stress. Essentially this is what most of us die from. Our blood vessels oxidize, our pipes simply rust out.

"Most lay people would say that the individual had a heart attack, but in reality it wasn't the heart tissue that gave out, but the arteries that deliver blood to the heart. Twenty-five percent of all the blood that the heart pumps out goes directly back to feed the heart through the three coronary arteries, each of which has a diameter less than the thickness of a pencil. It is in these arteries where the disease occurs that causes a heart attack. The problem does not begin with the heart muscle, but with its plumbing. When the pipes become clogged, blood and oxygen cannot be delivered to the heart muscle and a heart attack is the result.

"Now this process, which we commonly refer to as *hardening of the arteries*, occurs in just about everyone, the difference being the rate at which it occurs. In diabetics the rate is accelerated, since the inflammatory process has been activated earlier. Many diabetics are aging approximately ten years faster than others. If you are currently fortunate enough to die in your nineties, then we say you died of *natural causes* instead. It's all the same—it's all part of the aging process; only the rate at which things occur is variable. The big question is, can this rate by modified, and can it be slowed?"

"Scientists have found that the life span of organisms is inversely proportional to the organism's metabolic rate, which is also proportional to its oxygen consumption. It is the same way that radiation toxicity or hyperbaric oxygen toxicity could be explained by oxygen free radicals. Excessive radiation causes cancer, mutation, and aging by the same mechanism as oxygen free radicals cause oxidative damage and loss of functionality to the organism.

"When a molecule gives up its electron to a free radical, that molecule now seeks to steal an electron from a neighboring molecule, and so a chain reaction occurs. Now, if these free radicals rob their electrons from the damaged lung tissue of a smoker, then lung cancer may be the eventual outcome. If the attack occurs in the colon, then colon cancer could be the outcome. If the insult is to the brain, it may hasten the formation of Alzheimer's. Did you know that scientists have found a link between those with excess belly fat and early onset of dementia? Now you can understand the mechanism; belly fat means excessive inflammation and oxidative stress.

"When cholesterol is deposited on the inside of the blood vessel, it is a soft fatty substance. This is not what kills us. However, when the soft cholesterol is attacked by free radicals and gives up its electron to become oxidized, the cholesterol plaque now becomes hard and brittle. We refer to this as hard cholesterol, which can block the flow of blood or even break loose, causing a fatal embolus or heart attack.

"Free radicals have been implicated in many human diseases and there are many more to come: cancer, rheumatoid arthritis, arteriosclerosis, Alzheimer's disease, diabetes, Parkinson's, amyotrophic lateral sclerosis, (Lou Gehrig's disease), kwashiorkor, cataract formation, as well as many forms of toxicity."

Sheldon Rothberg went on to cite a recent British study published in the *Canadian Medical Association Journal* that revealed that individuals who were vaccinated for influenza, had twenty percent lower incidence of heart attacks. Once again, you may be asking, what does the flu have to do with heart disease? One possible explanation is that respiratory illness causes inflammation, which generates free radicals and damages our proteins, leading to plaque buildup and rupture in the blood vessels of the heart.

"So allow me to summarize. When a substance gives up an electron to another, such as oxygen, we say that substance has now been oxidized. Rust is simply the process by which iron combines with oxygen in the presence of water. It is an electrochemical reaction that transfers electrons from iron to the oxygen molecule. The same process is going on within our bodies, as free radicals in search of their missing electron seek out a target organ to oxidize. Rust takes place faster in the presence of water and salt, which provides a conducting media. You may recall that all higher forms of life, including humans, initially evolved from the sea, and our plasma is very similar to the composition of salt water, and the majority of our blood consists of water. Therefore, our blood provides the ideal conditions for rust and oxidation to occur."

"This friends, is what aging is all about. Aging is the result of the free radical process. You may have never thought about this before, but we are slowly oxidizing to death. In other words, we are rusting to death. Whether it be the rusted iron pipe, the blood vessels, the lung, or the brain, the underlying process is the same. It's all the same. It's simply rust."

"Professor Rothberg that was an electrifying discussion," Deputy Johnson said. "I wish that I had you for a Professor when I was in college. You have given us a great deal of material to digest, so let's stop here, and reconvene on Friday, same time, same place. Is that okay with you Professor?"

"Sure, but do you think we can have some coffee and donuts brought in for our next session? I can think better with a bit of sugar in my system."

"I'm sure that can be arranged Professor, but are they good for you?"

Shelly Rothberg stood up, turned and left the room, pretending he hadn't heard the question.

After the Professor left the room, Steve turned to Deputy Johnson and remarked, "The guy is absolutely brilliant, but how can he be asking for donuts when he is so overweight?"

"That's the difference between knowledge and wisdom," replied Deputy Johnson. "Knowledge is knowing what to do, and wisdom is being able to do it."

32

Discussions of life and its meaning became a daily tradition on Abby and Carlton's luncheon breaks. Carlton now felt safe to gently probe into the topic of aging, hoping to find out if Abby had any recent contact with or information about her grandfather. Abby stated, "The big question for me isn't how long one is going to live, but the quality of life. You hear so many folks say, if I wind up in a nursing home, toothless, speechless, and in diapers, where someone needs to feed me and take me to the bathroom, please just shoot me."

Carlton jumped in, "Isn't it interesting that we all start out in life, toothless, speechless, in diapers, with someone having to feed us, and no one would ever say anything such as that about an infant, other than commenting how adorable and cute they are? Let's face it, life is a cycle, and we pass through many stages. Each has its own pleasures, rewards, challenges, and hardships. The poet William Wordsworth reminds us of this in his universal theme: the passing from infancy to adolescence to adulthood, with the gain of experience and the loss of innocence.

"Simply observe a routine discussion in a doctor's office. A mother says to her child, 'Take off your sweater and open your mouth for the doctor.' Three score later, that very same child now says to her mother, 'Take off your sweater and open your mouth for the doctor.'"

"As children, we were all fascinated by the merry-go-round; as teenagers no one had any interest in it. Next you have kids of your own and just can't wait to go to the fair and watch their excitement from the merry-go-round. Later in life, you get to take your grandchildren to the fair and spoil them rotten, and then hand them back to their parents to unspoil them while you go home to relax.

"This is life, Abby. And as we pass through these critical periods, someday we may be in need of a nursing home. Your days of golf, dancing, and going to the gym are over. Is there anything left to live for? Well, guess what? A survey was conducted on residents in nursing homes, and they were asked if they would rather live than die. And over 85% chose life.

"Sure it isn't the same as you knew it when you were young, but there are still many pleasures to enjoy: listening to music, watching your favorite shows, enjoying meals, taking a nice nap, joining activities, and participating in discussions with those in your age group, learning about the accomplishments of your grandchildren, and simply having the awareness that your DNA is being passed on to propagate future generations of life.

"If on the other hand, you have the misfortune to contract an incurable disease with intractable pain, then that is a completely different scenario. In that case I would hope that I would be given the same consideration and kindness that one would make available to their family pet."

Abby jumped in to say, "Amen to that."

"With that as the exception, given the choice, I select life, and I suspect someday that you will as well."

"Chad, are you implying that the day may come when a good bowel movement will be the highlight of my day?"

"You never know what the future will hold Abby."

33

Alex and Kiros were both in excellent shape; they moved quickly through the jungle. Kiros carried the raft on his back, along with the rations and mess kits. Alex had his medical kit, black box, machete, maps, insect repellent, and the paddles. It was a slow and rough passage as they had to hack away brush, watch out for snakes, and fight off the bugs.

They were halfway to the river when a leopard suddenly emerged from the brush and leaped onto Kiros's back. It is unusual for a leopard to attack a grown man during daylight, but perhaps the chicken that Kiros was carrying in his pack had excited the leopard. The animal was clawing Kiros's chest while sinking its teeth into his neck. Alex pulled his *bill hook* machete from his belt and began hacking away at the animal. The leopard leaped off Kiros and onto Alex, knocking him to the ground. The animal was on top of him, its front paw ripping into his neck just below the left ear. Alex let out a painful scream as blood began flowed from his own wound. Again, he swung his machete the way a boxer would throw a right hook, and caught the leopard in the left eye with the hook portion of the weapon. A burst of blood, as well as vitreous fluid, spouted from the beast's eye as it made a high pitched whimpering cry and dashed off into the jungle.

Both Kiros and Alex were bleeding profusely from their necks, and Alex realized that he needed to act decisively to save their lives. He feared that if he tried to close Kiros' wounds first, that he might lose too much blood in the process to be successful. His own laceration was not in a location where it would be possible for him to suture it. Alex grabbed his pack and dumped it onto the ground. He placed several 4 by 4 gauze pads over Kiros's neck and used his own knee to apply pressure to the wound. He now reached for a tube of super glue that he used to close lacerations that were difficult to suture. He applied the glue to a 4 by 4, and pressed it on his neck and applied an ace bandage tightly.

The tightness of the dressing made it difficult for him to breath; he shifted his position such that the back of his head pressed against Kiros's wound, while simultaneously hyperextending his head in order to further open his own airway. With hands pressing on his own neck, he remained in that position for a good minute. When he could no longer feel the blood flow from the wound, he then attended to Kiros.

Kiros believed that he was going to bleed to death, and began reciting his prayers. Alex reached for his suture material, gauze, and a hemostat. So much blood flowed from the right side of Kiros' neck that Alex was unable to locate the site of the bleed. The good news was that the wound wasn't pulsating and the blood wasn't bright red, indicating that the source was not from the carotid artery, but more likely from the jugular vein. Alex's hope to pinch the lacerated vessel with his hemostat did not go as intended. Each time he removed pressure the area immediately filled with another pool of blood, preventing him from seeing the exact site of the laceration.

Such a wound would have provided a challenge for two vascular surgeons in a modern operating room with excellent lighting; Alex was working alone on the ground in the shade of dense foliage. Alex realized that if he was unsuccessful in the next minute or two that Kiros would bleed out and exsanguinate. He also did not want to panic and clamp the area blindly in fear of inadvertently clamping off the carotid artery leading to the brain. After five unsuccessful attempts, he was fortunate to catch the edges of the slit made in the jugular vein by the leopard's canine. He then slipped the 3-0 nylon suture material over the hemostat and tied off the wound. In order to be sure that the sutures would hold, he placed two additional suture ligatures into the outer wall of the vessel and then washed the wound thoroughly with antiseptic before closing the skin.

Three of the six chest wounds were also quite deep, but fortunately no major vessels were involved. Alex sutured the four deepest ones before running out of suture material, and used the remaining super glue to close the rest, before finally dressing the wounds and administering a shot of morphine. Kiros had sustained significant blood loss, and was in no shape to travel, but his wounds were no longer life threatening. For the second time, Alex had saved Kiros' life.

Now Kiros insisted that Alex go on without him. Alex made a fire to scare off any other wild beasts, and provided Kiros with another amp of morphine for later. Their parting was highly emotional, particularly for a man like Alex, who was not very good at displaying emotion. He felt as if he was saying farewell to a son, one that he probably would never see again. He kissed Kiros on the forehead and headed into the jungle as tears streamed down from his cheeks. Alex now had to carry the raft, as well as his own pack, but he managed to reach the Ugandi River before nightfall. He could rest now, before undertaking his journey through the meandering tributaries of the Congo River.

34

It was time for Carleton Terry's daily briefing with Deputy Johnson, and he hoped the news would be better this time. His hope lasted as long as it took for Johnson to open his mouth. "More bad news. Very bad. Our Special OPS people made it up to Bongele. Everything is gone."

"What do mean?"

"I mean everything: Stein, the lab, the IV bottles, his equipment. No notes, no computers, no chemicals, nada, zippo. We are still searching for a black box about which the natives spoke. Perhaps it was in the fire, or he took it with him."

"Where did he go?"

One of the natives said that after the government threatened to come after him, and mentioned that we also wanted to speak with him, that he just destroyed everything. He then planned to hike fifteen miles into the jungle, to catch the river downstream. Apparently he kept an old army surplus raft up there, just in case this day came along. He had a good week head start on us, so I doubt that we are going to find him anywhere around those parts."

"Can't we just follow his route downstream and head him off?"

"This is the Congo, Terry, not the Mississippi; there are hundreds of different tributaries. There's no way we're going to find him."

"At least some good news comes out of that," said Carlton.

"That being?"

"He's not in the hands of the Russian mafia, at least not yet. We also have him on the *no fly list*, so if he tries to fly into the States, we can pick him up."

"What did we find out from the natives about his research?"

"As we suspected, he was doing some kind of experiments on them. He started out by experimenting on chimpanzees. His treated chimps lived 50% longer than the placebo group. After that he started experimenting on himself. Next, he was able to recruit a few native volunteers, when they all claimed to be feeling great and looking younger, they began enlisting by the hundreds. Some of those we interviewed claimed they were close to

120 years old. Our folks were quite confused. They said that some of them didn't look old enough for Medicare."

"What exactly did he do to them?"

"Well, that's the 64 million dollar question, isn't it? We don't know. They all had to have a heparin lock inserted into the forearm."

"What exactly is a heparin lock?"

"It's just a small butterfly needle that is used in every hospital to administer IV's. Between treatments the needle is left in place and a tiny bit of the anti-coagulant heparin is run through the tubing, preventing it from clotting up so that the site can be used over and over without starting another IV. It saves time and money and if you're one doc and several thousand patients it makes a lot of sense."

"What type of treatment did he give them?"

"You're asking good questions, Carlton, wish we know the answers. Isn't this what Field Agents such as *you*, should be telling *me*? All we know is that they were first given an injection into the skin, then three times a week, at bedtime they were given something in the tubing from the IV bottles hanging near their beds, which was connected it to the heparin locks allowing the medicine to run through. All he had to do was use the same IV bottle and simply have each patient use his or her own heparin lock. They also said that they had some kind of a small black box at the bedside, and during the treatments they felt a humming or buzzing sensation. The box was kept on for only a few minutes and then transferred to another patient. That's it! That's all we know. We are trying to get some residue samples from the fire for analysis, but we're not very hopeful. You need to keep pumping the granddaughter, squeeze her a bit harder if need be. Looks like we may be getting some competition in our search for Mr. Stein.

"Roger on that."

"By the way Terry, do you still feel we gave you a boring assignment?"

Rust

35

The tributaries of the Congo River were not only the primary means of transportation for the folks of central Africa, it also served as the lifeline for the area's wildlife as well. As Alex followed the river downstream he observed hippos, crocodiles, wildebeests, zebras, gorillas, and some very, very, large snakes. At times he needed to navigate around sand bars, other times run the rapids: but nothing handles rapids better than a flexible rubber raft. After the first day of travel, Alex pulled his raft on to shore, turned it upside down to convert it into a mattress, and got some sleep.

He was suddenly awakened by a constricting sensation around his left thigh. His initial reaction was that he had developed a cramp from his arduous journey, but when he looked down, he let go a horrific scream. A twenty-foot python was wrapping himself around his leg. Their forked tongues contain sensors that enable them to smell their prey and capture them by ambush, and a sleeping human could offer little resistance as pythons can strike with lightning speed. The python is a non-poisonous snake that kills by constricting its victim to death.

The girth of the snake appeared as wide as Alex's thigh. Its head was down by his ankles and the tail end of the fifteen-foot giant was approaching his neck. Alex had gone to sleep with his machete in hand; he began to hack away next to his own thigh where the snake was constricting. After his first swing with the weapon there was so much blood, he was unable to differentiate the position of the snake from that of his thigh. The snake didn't give up easily, tightening the grip even further, sapping Alex of his strength. After two more vicious blows the snake had been transected and surrendered its grip; the upper portion headed back into the jungle and the lower portion slithered around in circles for a minute or so before coming to rest. It took a while before Alex realized that the vast majority of blood was not his. When he regained his composure, he decided to tie the raft to an overhanging branch on the river and sleep afloat on the raft. The experience did solve one problem. He now knew what he would be having for dinner tomorrow: *python steak*.

When he came to branches in the river, its circuitous nature made it difficult to be certain which way to proceed; he would select the one that he felt would lead him east in the direction of the Atlantic, but couldn't be sure it wouldn't reverse direction farther on. His immediate goal, however, was simply to get the hell out of CAR. After two days of travel, he found himself in Cameroon.

Alex realized that his voyage back to the States would also need to follow a very circuitous path. Although he managed to get out of CAR, he still had the U.S. authorities looking for him. He didn't have a valid passport, and he was in an area inundated with bandits and murderers with no one he could trust. He did have one important thing, the thing anyone in Africa in need of assistance needed the most, and that was money. And better yet, he had American dollars: $5,200 of them.

When he came across several natives gathered at the river's edge, Alex asked to be taken to their medicine man. Alex hoped that this might be someone he could relate to and trust. Trust was not something that came easy to him. He tried to use his method of binary reasoning; however, when Alex became anxious, he couldn't always think as logically as he would like. There was only one person he felt he could count on and she was back in New Hampshire. *"I have got to make it back to Abigail."*

The medicine man and Alex communicated through a combination of French, several African dialects, and *charades*. He learned that a banana truck would be at the village tomorrow, and, for a fee, perhaps he could hitch a ride to the nearest city.

Twenty four hours later, and $500 poorer, Alex reached the Boumba Bek National Park. Next he was able to charter a seaplane to fly him to the Atlantic coast at Equitorial Guinea for $700. His next challenge was to get back to North America without using commercial aviation, just in case he was placed on the *no fly list*.

Alex found a fishing boat that was headed up the Atlantic coast toward Cairo. Alex volunteered to work as a deckhand for free passage. He assisted with the setting of the nets, cleaned fish, and swabbed the decks. Alex wasn't known for his sea legs and the chum he provided from his own vomitus served as a bonus in attracting the fish. When they reached Cairo, Alex jumped ship. His next plan was to get on one of the cruise lines crossing the Atlantic. A cruise would provide the perfect cover, since tourist passengers were not a priority for Customs officials, especially when several thousand arrived simultaneously. He could also get a private cabin for some much-needed rest, the ship would provide him with security, and all ships had Internet access.

Alex located a Trans-Atlantic ship that was scheduled to make its first stop in Newfoundland. A local travel agent confirmed that the ship had vacancies. He was reluctant to attempt to buy passage, his lack of a valid passport once again a hindrance. He arrived at the port four hours before the other passengers, as the crew was loading supplies on board. When he noticed a crew member's hat near a rack of towels, he quickly placed the hat on his head and picked up the largest bundle of towels he could carry and walked up the boarding platform adjacent to other staff, and directly past the security guard.

He made himself look busy until the ship pulled away from the dock. Then he sat next to the Registration desk and observed. There were many passengers complaining about a wide range of issues: "the room is too small" "why didn't I get a window?" "I want to be on the other side of the ship" and the best one was,"how do you expect my wife to fit her fat ass into that shower?" Alex was dazzled by the nature of some of the questions asked by the guests, such as: "does the ship make its own electricity?" *"No ma'am, we have a 3000-mile extension cord."* Another question was, "Does the staff sleep on the ship*?"* *"No, we have helicopters take them back to the mainland every night."*

Alex observed the staff members at the desk, searching to find the ones who were accommodating after being tipped, as opposed to the ones who were less obsequious. He now approached his target, a young Egyptian in his early twenties. "Sir, may I have a moment of your time in private please?" Alex asked, slipping him a bill with Benjamin Franklin's picture.

"Certainly, Sir. Please step into the office," he responded, palming the bill. Alex stepped into the office and sat down. "Those are some tough questions that you are being asked," Alex said.

"You haven't heard the best ones my friend. Here are my four favorites: 'Does the elevator go to the front of the ship?' 'Do these stairs go down as well as up?' 'What time is the midnight buffet?' And 'How far is it to the end of the horizon?'"

"Well I can see that you have important issues to deal with, so I will make this fast. There is someone on this ship, who may have recognized me, and if so, it would be very embarrassing, needless to say. I believe he saw me enter my room. It would be worth a great deal of money to me if you could provide me with one of your unused rooms."

"That is a very unusual request, Sir. Just how much money do you consider *a great deal of money*

"I consider $1,000 American dollars*, a great deal of money*. Don't you?"

"Sir, what you are asking me to do could cost me my job. It is a very unorthodox request. Why not make it $1,500 and I will upgrade your cabin and throw in a balcony?"

"Forget the balcony, but I am going to need a photo ID!" Alex exclaimed.

"That can be arranged. Now, what is your old room number?"

Alex slipped $1500 across the desk and said, "No more questions!"

When activating his ID card, he was given the choice of presenting a credit card or making a cash deposit. He chose the latter. Alex spent the majority of his cruise time in his room. After hanging a *Do Not Disturb* sign on his door, he took a long hot shower, followed by twelve hours of deep sleep. He did make one trip to the ship's library, where he checked out half a dozen books, and checked the ferry and train schedules before returning to his room. He wanted to email Abigail, but was afraid to do so until he was back safely in the States.

He spent most of the day reading and catching up on the news throughout the world. He used room service for all of his meals. After two days aboard the ship, Alex was well-rested and filled with news of the world. He was becoming restless in his cabin, and after midnight he decided to check out the ship's casino.

Earlier that day he had purchased a western style hat and a pair of shades that would help to minimize both his social contact with the other passengers as well as those annoying bright lights. Alex was always fascinated with numbers and the laws of probability. In Black Jack he possessed an uncanny ability to count cards. He was so good at it that he was able to reduce the house's edge from the standard 2.2% to less than a half of one percent. He also was aware that the casinos knew how to spot card counters, since a card counter would bet the minimum amount until the remaining deck was loaded with face cards, and then suddenly and dramatically increase the wager. Although this technique of betting was not illegal in many casinos, it was one that surely would attract the attention of the casino, and Alex could not afford that. His only other option of play in order to minimize the casino's edge was to utilize his knowledge of the Fibonacci method of betting.

Fibonacci number sequences are not only prevalent in nature, but are also widely used in making business decisions, buying stocks, and gambling. Here the player makes his bets using the following progression: starting with one unit, the series is 1, 2, 3, 5, 5, 5, and 5. If at any time in the sequence the player has a loss, he reverts back to a one-unit bet. In this manner, whenever the player has a large wager, it is his winnings at stake, and whenever the player has a loss, it is simply one unit of his own money. According to the *Law of Similarities,* an even odds bet will reveal long streaks of either wins or losses. To illustrate this point, Alex knew that if one flipped a coin one hundred times, deciding in advance to call a head a win and a tail a loss, that one would see a long run, perhaps seven in a row, of either heads or tails. When the player loses seven bets in a row, his total loses are seven units. However, when the player wins seven units in a row, his winnings are 26 units (1, 2, 3, 5, 5, 5, 5). Of interest is that you can re-examine the same sequence and now consider a tail as a winner and a head as a loss, and you may still come out on top. Using this method and starting with a $10 bet as one unit, Alex was able to win back the amount he paid for his cabin. Unfortunately for Alex, a crowd began to gather behind him observing his methods, which made him uncomfortable, and so he decided to move on to the craps tables.

In craps the player has the option of betting with the shooter or against the shooter by betting with the house. The odds are close to even either way, but slightly better when betting against the shooter and with the house. In spite of this, over 99% of players will bet in favor of the person throwing the dice. Why? Because that's the way the house wants you to bet. Your next question probably is: Who cares what the casino wants? Don't underestimate the persuasive powers of the casino. Bear in mind that nothing that happens in a casino is fortuitous. Alex was well aware of the fact that a casino is a well-planned, highly orchestrated, and tightly regulated setting where the players drift in and out like minor characters in a play as the show goes on. The casino serves the role of master psychologist, with the players fulfilling the part of Pavlovian subjects.

Rarely will anyone ever find a window or a clock in a casino. No need to concern yourself, be it night or day. One could always tell their spouse, *"I had no idea what time it was."* Take note that there are no chairs for lounging in the casino. If you're not part of the action, best be on your way. Want to relax? Have a seat and pull out your wallet. The lingo, as well, is no accident. Dealers are trained to call a five-dollar bill a nickel and twenty-five bucks a quarter, and before long the players are lulled into the conspiracy, throwing around nickels and quarters here and there as if they were Monopoly money.

Have you ever noticed the discrepancy between the mild-mannered nature displayed at the Black Jack tables versus the wild enthusiasm and shouting that goes on the craps tables? This too, is part of the orchestrated plot. In Black Jack there is no benefit to the casino in having the players raise a ruckus, since each patron is playing his own hand. However, in craps, the verbal interaction among the players encourages them to favor the shooter and bet against the house. Since the casino wants everyone betting in favor of the shooter, it does everything to encourage and reward that behavior. If you bet with the shooter and against the house, you are called a *right player* and you place your money on the *pass line*. If you bet against the shooter, where your odds are better, you are called a *wrong player* and need to place your chips on the *don't pass line*. If the *right player* wins, he may continue to roll the dice. However, if the wrong player wins, he forfeits his turn to shot again. The right player can place his bets in a large area which is easily accessible to reach from anywhere on the table, whereas the wrong player has to find the tiny box which is found only in the corner of the table. Casinos will often *comp* high rollers who bet with the player, but will do so rarely with a player who bets with the house. The very nature of the shape of the table in craps, whereby players stand side by side or face each other, sharing congratulations and high-fives during a hot roll, places social pressure on the players to join in the party and bet *right*.

    Alex was a man who understood the odds and he was oblivious to social norms. He would be the sole player at the table wagering against the shooter. He stood in the corner of the table, pulled the brim of his cowboy hat down covering the upper third of his face, while his shades covered the middle third. His chin was pressed deeply into his chest; he looked down at the dice and made eye contact with no one. If the shooter's first roll revealed an eight, for the shooter to win an eight had to reappear before a seven. All of the other players at the table would be shouting: *"numbers, throw numbers! 4, 5, 6, 8, 9, or 10."* Any number, but that unspeakable dreadful **seven**. Not Alex! He would bet that a seven would be rolled before the shooter could repeat his point, and when that inevitable event occurred, he would rack in the chips while the other players at the table would moan, groan or curse.

    The casino managers would groan as well with each seven, pretending to be sympathetic, as they raked in the chips. This night, they were not alone, as Alex was raking it in with them. Initially, no one paid much attention to Alex, but after half a dozen players *sevened out* and Alex was the only winner at the table, the dirty looks headed his way. Uncomfortable with the attention, Alex cashed in his chips and headed back to his cabin where he would remain for the balance of the journey. Alex made no new friends that evening, although he left the casino $1,200 richer.

    Thereafter he again spent most of his time reading and sleeping. He remained apprehensive about seasickness, especially after his recent experience as a *professional fisherman*, but to his good fortune, the seas were quite calm.

    When the ship finally pulled into port in Newfoundland five days later, Alex signed up for the first shore excursion, but instead of getting on the tour bus, he grabbed the next ferry back to the mainland. Alex's initial elation to learn that the Neufies spoke English quickly dissipated after he heard the first local speak. The dialect had a ring of backwards Appalachia, Mississippi valley, the Australian outback, and Brooklyn, all rolled into one. *"Was this a newly discovered language?"* Alex wondered. When he asked a local on the ferry what kind of work he did, the response from the not too overly ambitious native was, *"Work, what work? Works all done!"* After a twelve-hour ferry ride he had reached the mainland, and was now safe in Canada. From this point on, the coast was clear. He took Via Rail in Canada from Campbelton, New Brunswick to Montreal and then onto New Hampshire His next goal was to make contact with his granddaughter, Abigail. He had successfully traveled from the Central Africa Republic all the way to New Hampshire without ever having to show a credit card or a valid passport.

36

It was the day for Carlton's last riding lesson, and although his ass was happy about that, the rest of him had ambivalent feelings. First, he felt guilty about Hinden, whose death obviously had something to do with his visit. Secondly, his attraction toward Abby was intensifying by the day, and he had guilt feelings about lying to her. He also knew that when she found out the truth, he really better watch his ass and there would be little chance of them ever having any meaningful relationship. He found it difficult to avoid thinking about Abby as he found her both attractive and intelligent He was also under pressure to obtain more information from her, and he knew that after he squeezed her dry, as Johnson had suggested, he wouldn't be seeing her again. Furthermore, he wondered just what Hinden had tried to sell to the Russians that got him killed. He narrowed it down to only two possibilities: Either Hinden knew that the information he was seeking was important and worth something, or he knew more about Stein than he let on. If that were the case, then Carlton did not do a very good job with his interrogation. Finally, he still had no idea as to what Stein had discovered, or more importantly, what he intended to do with it.

Carlton felt that he was getting good vibes from Abby, and he decided to try and go one step further today. As he entered the barn, Abby had his horse, Candy, already saddled. Carlton thought he had never seen a woman who looked so sexy and so attractive in jeans with shit all over her boots. As she was brushing Candy down, Abby noticed that she had developed a red spot a few inches above the left stirrup site. "How did you get this, Candy?" she said, sympathetically addressing the horse. When Candy failed to respond she turned towards Carlton. "You're not wearing stirrups, Chad, are you?"

"Of course not!"

"Well, what do you suppose gave Candy this sore?" Carlton just shrugged his shoulders. "Let me have a look at your left ankle, Chad."

"No way Abby, I know what you're up to. You just want to undress me, and before long you will have me in bed."

"No, really, let me take a look, perhaps you have some ringworm and gave it to Candy?" Carlton tried to turn it into a joke by running away, but

Abby leaped at his ankle and tackled him, pulling up his jeans. "Those aren't stirrups Chad, that's a .45. *Chad,* what else have you been keeping from me?"

Carlton had just sent up his first red flag and it was on a forty-foot flag pool to boot. "Chad, if you have been lying to me you had better do more than just check your girth, because the last guy that wasn't straight with me is still in the hospital."

Carlton seemed at a loss for words as Abby went on ranting. "Furthermore, I'm not buying this bull about this chick in town that you're trying to impress. You haven't talked about her once, and if she is so hot, why do I catch you starring at my ass every time I turn around?" Carlton was now totally speechless. He couldn't decide if he should pile it on higher and deeper by adding more lies or just come clean. He decided to do neither, so he just stood there.

"Today being your last day, I'm going to teach you the most valuable lesson of all if you plan on spending any time around horses. It should take you about an hour or so. When you're done, just leave the shovel by the door. This is something that you should be really good at. You may let yourself out when you're finished." As Abby stormed out of the barn, her final comment was "And I hope those blisters on your butt last forever so that you can have something to remember me by." Carlton picked up the shovel and started to shovel shit. Somehow, it felt not only good, but well deserved.

37

Boris Yaspur sat in his office, which just happened to be the cabin beneath the deck of his fishing trawler off the coast of Yemen in the Arabian Sea. Boris despised fishing, but the one thing he despised more were intruders into his business affairs. The sea offered him the reassurances that he sought. This boat was not only his office, but it came with a free security force. The Somali pirates controlled these waters, and after one fatal mistake, they knew well enough not to mess with Boris Yaspur and his comrades.

Boris descended from a family of thieves, and he was proud of it. His Great-grandfather, Alexi, was a *vor* back in the days of the Czar. The *vors* were a loosely organized group of thieves who banded together as *thieves-in-law*. In order to be accepted to the group, one had to be voted in by fellow members. Such men adhered to a strict code of conduct among themselves, with the key pledge to refrain from cooperating with authorities. Alexi had a successful career until he botched one job at the age of 48, and was then hanged by the Czar.

Boris's grandfather, Pavlushka, was a thief as well. He participated in the Bolshevik Revolution, as did many professional criminals. One might say that the *Russkaya Mafiya* or Russian Mafia began with the formation of the Communist Party, as criminals and government officials began to intermingle.

Pavlushka had become a mid-level bureaucrat in the Communist Party, and when his son, Borya, who was Boris's father, became 18, he too was brought into the Party. In their capacity as government officials, they were able to pursue a life of crime; they were considered to be *above the law.* They had access to the finest markets in Moscow, where they could find quality beef, fine Vodka, and caviar, either to consume personally or for resale on the black market. Bribes for living quarters, jobs, licenses, as well as kickbacks, and money laundering, were all part of an average day for them in Communist Russia.

Boris knew that he too was destined for a life of crime, but he would choose a different path from his predecessors. During World War II many Russian prisoners were offered lighter sentences in exchange for joining the armed forces. After returning to prison, these individuals were killed by their fellow prisoners for violating the *thieves' code of conduct* by cooperating with the authorities. With this in mind, Boris rejected any affiliation with the Party and strictly adhered to the 18 principles of the thieves' code of conduct.

At the age of 29, he was arrested for credit card theft and spent seven years in the gulag. When asked about his prison time, Boris would say, "It's not how many years you spend in prison that's important, but how you maintain your honor and dignity." Within five years of his release from prison, Boris earned his blue star tattoo on his right shoulder, indicating that he was *a made man* in the most elite of the hundred or so organized crime syndicates in Russia.

Boris's group initially concentrated on money laundering, high jacking, and credit card theft, and then diamond smuggling and weapon sales. As competing mobs began to encroach on their territory, extortion, kidnapping, bombings, and gangland murders became regular occurrences. His colleagues recognized him as a man of *honor and dignity*, and, at the age of 42, Boris had risen to be the top man in his organization.

When private investment was legalized in the Soviet Union in 1988, followed by a collapse of the Union in 1991, one might have thought that bribery, corruption, and organized crime might diminish. The opposite was true. Laws to regulate free markets did not exist. Many former government officials who were now out of work—former KGB, police officials, as well as many others who distrusted the system—now turned to a career of crime. By 1993, almost all banks in Russia were owned and operated by organized crime and 80% of all businesses were being extorted to pay for protection. Many who refused to pay really needed protection, as there were over 1,400 murders in Moscow in 1993. The Russian mob had successfully infiltrated over 50,000 companies in Russia.

According to Jeffrey Robinson, an expert on the Russian mob, and author of *The Merger*, the Russian Mafia is present and operating in over 50 countries and in almost every major city. The FBI states that over one million cases of credit card fraud can be traced to Eastern European organized crime syndicates. Cyberspace is now becoming the newest hot spot for their activities.

Five of Boris's business associates accompanied him this evening as he conducted the meeting with his associates. "This Hinden fellow, he may not have looked it, but he was no dummy. A bit too greedy perhaps, but he was on to something. The American CIA doesn't send an agent to Alaska for two weeks for a reference check. This is big, and Hinden knew it. He believed his old college buddy has actually had a breakthrough in retarding the aging process. Just think of the money that this could bring in on the black market. These women in the U.S. are spending billions injecting poison just to get the wrinkles out of their faces. Imagine what we could do for the rest of their bodies? If this Stein fellow didn't have anything to hide, then why did he run from the authorities? And why is Langley spending all these resources just to find him, as our agents have reported? I feel we should get Stein before the Americans get to him. It's not going to cost us that much to hunt him down and the potential upside is enormous. What do you think, Ivan?" Ivan Vishner was a major player. He owned a major bank in Russia and bank rolled many of the Russian expeditions, as they liked to call them, and if Ivan didn't like the odds and said "Nyet," the deal was usually off the table. Vishner spoke, "I'm in and I'll tell you why. Let's learn from history, because they say it repeats itself. The American Cosa Nostra was doing great. Not only did they have the people behind them, they had the bootleggers, the hookers, and even this guy Hoover of the FBI was supporting them. You want to know where they screwed up? I'll tell you—drugs. Drugs kill kids. Drugs lead to mob rubouts, and drugs lead to poor public relations. Drugs lead to pissed-off people; that leads to pissed-off politicians and then everyone starts pissing on us. If it wasn't for drugs, do you think the Kennedys would have come after them? Joe Kennedy was in with Costello. They were all bootleggers, but alcohol made people happy. No kids got killed. Now, don't think I'm going soft on you folks, I'm not one of these Charlie's Angels. I am however, a businessman, and I want to remain a businessman and I can't do that very well from the gulag or the bottom of the ocean. We have a chance to make billions on this aging gig. If someone is to get it, why shouldn't it be us? We can be the good guys and like the Americans say, laugh all the way to the bank."

"I like the way you think Ivan. Anyone disagree? Ok then, we're all in. Let's get our people out there and bring in Stein and contact our mole at Langley. This Stein fellow can't get too far; he is almost seventy." One of Boris's associates reached into the large fishing net in the bow of the boat and pulled up a sealed bag containing dozens of disposable, non-traceable phones. After calling their contacts in Boston and Washington and relaying their instructions, he proceeded to file the phone at the bottom of the Arabian Sea.

38

As Abby was getting ready for dinner, her phone rang. "Hello Abigail, I don't know how much you remember about me; I'm Alex, your grandfather. I know we have never met, but I'm in trouble and couldn't think of anyone else to call. If you decide not to get involved I will completely understand. If you care to help me, please listen very carefully, and for the time being, don't ask any questions because your phone could be tapped. I'm on an untraceable cell but will need to hang up within twenty seconds. Can you please shoot into town and call me back at this number? And Abigail, if you have a weapon, perhaps you want to bring it along."

"Listen here, Gramps, I have had enough of men for one day, so whatever you're selling, I don't want any," she said, as she abruptly hung up. With that, Abby grabbed her Taser and rushed out to the barn where Carlton was just about finishing his chores. "I can't believe you are still here. I said that you only had to shovel for an hour. Were you planning on spending the night?"

"Actually, I was hoping to get lucky tonight, but I didn't think it was going to be with Candy."

"I'm glad to see that you haven't lost your sense of humor, Chad, or whatever your name really is."

"Actually it's Carlton, but I am growing quite fond of Chad."

"Listen here, Carlton; I have got an emergency call to make in town. Since you follow orders so well, I want you to stay here until I get back. I may not be finished with you just yet." But you can stop shoveling now. Why don't you go inside the house, clean up, and wait for me."

"Whatever you say."

39

"Hello. Who is this?"

"It's me, Grandpa. Who did you think it was?"

"But I thought you told me to take a hike?"

"I just said that in case anyone was listening in and considered following me. What's going on Grandpa? You sound as if you're in trouble."

"I am, Abigail, and I hate to drag you into this but I don't know who else I can turn to. People are looking for me because I have something that they want."

"Good people, or bad people?"

"I'm not even sure about that, so I'm going to assume *bad* until I can trust them, and right now you are the only person I can trust."

"What do you want me to do Grandpa?"

"Again, I need to be very careful what I say on the phone. Can't be too cautious. I don't want to come to the farm. It may be too dangerous for you. Can you come to me?"

"Where are you Grandpa?"

"Over the fireplace there used to be a picture of the family. Is it still there?"

"Yes, I haven't touched any of the old photos."

"I know your dad would take you to that spot when you were a little girl. He mentioned the photo hanging in the living room. He used to write me and say just how much you enjoyed it. You need to meet me there. I'm hoping you can find it from memory, but if not, call back. I will need supplies: food, kerosene lanterns, and all the things that a good scout would need. Also, memorize this phone number and then destroy the paper. I came in by motorbike and couldn't bring very many supplies along." Alex then read off the complete list of supplies he needed.

"Grandpa, in order to bring that many supplies into where I believe you are talking about, I may need help."

"Well, do you have anyone you can trust?"

"Grandpa, this is a real bad day to ask me that. I don't really know."

"Abigail, I'm not the best judge of character, but your dad always said that you had good judgment, so I guess I'm just going to have to rely on it."

40

Abby knew just the place to which Alex was referring. It was a camp that the family had used at Cannon Mountain in New Hampshire. Her dad would write Alex and describe the trips that the family enjoyed there during the summers when she was a child. It was rough mountain terrain, best accessible by horseback, and a good twenty-five miles away from the farm at Grafton.

Abby reflected on this sudden strange twist of fate. Moments ago on the first phone call from her grandfather, she had told him to *go take a hike*, now he was returning the favor. An hour ago she was asking Chad to *take a hike* as well. Now she wished she hadn't. She wanted to trust him, but didn't know if it was safe. She even thought about calling her one-legged useless ex for help, but she knew for sure that he couldn't be trusted. These were the thoughts that were rushing through her head as she headed back to the farm. "Men, can't live with them, can't live without them. Pick one and pray."

41

Carlton had taken a shower, put on some clean jeans and took the liberty to open a bottle of Merlot and set it on the table with two glasses. "I thought this might help in our talks, you did seem a bit flustered back there," said Carlton.

Abby jumped in, "Okay, so let's talk. Perhaps we should start by you putting your gun on the table, and I my girth knife." The good laugh that followed helped to break the ice. "Let me begin," said Abby. "I don't know who you are or what you want from me. The fact that you're still here, makes me think you either care about me or you haven't got what you came for yet. I do know that you have been lying to me, and you know how I feel about that. What I don't know is why? I also know that something big has come up and I really need someone that I can trust. And to be perfectly honest with you, if that scene in the barn didn't happen and you got that bottle of Merlot in me, I was thinking about asking you to stay for the night, which would have come pretty close to being a disaster." Carlton listened attentively as Abby went on. "So here is what I am going to propose to you . . ."

"A proposal so soon? I'm shocked," Carlton said.

"Stop your kidding and listen. I have two options for you: One, we say good-bye now and just walk away, with no explanations. Two, no more aliases, lies, hidden weapons. You just come clean and tell me everything. And I mean everything."

"I'm not sure that I can do that, and even if I tell you the truth you still may not trust me."

"I can't make any promises other than to say, if you ever lie to me again, we're through."

"How about some more wine before I choose which door I want?"

"Sure, take your time; you have thirty seconds to decide."

Carlton filled his glass, and sipped on his wine. He realized that he had an important and possible life-altering decision to make. At the thirty-second deadline approached, he spoke. "My name is Carlton Terry. I am a CIA field operative. I was assigned here by my boss to keep an eye . . . no, that's not completely accurate. I don't want to break my promise in the first sentence. I was sent here to spy on you. Now, before you start handing me the shovel again, let me add some good news. You are right! There is no girlfriend, or a wife for that matter, and even if there was one, that wouldn't have stopped me from staring at your ass."

"Oh, how very sweet of you; please continue."

"I might add that until this assignment I really loved my job, but I hated having to lie to you. We have an interest in your grandfather, Alex. We need to know about his experiments and what he plans to do with an important discovery he has made. Also, we believe he may be in some danger. Some bad people, not us, we wear the white hats, may be trying to harm him. We don't want to see that happen."

"And if you find him first what do you expect to do with him?"

"Basically just talk and find out what he is up to and understand his plans."

"Has he broken any laws?"

"Not that I know of, at least not in this country."

"So why were you sent to spy on me?"

"Your grandfather doesn't have a lot of friends in America. The only one we know of was murdered last week by the Russian mob. Furthermore, he left Africa in a hurry. We had a feeling that he would try and contact you, so I came to keep a close eye on things. Actually, it wasn't turning out to be too bad of an assignment, until Candy had to get herself a rash."

Carlton went on for an hour or so revealing every detail he had learned in the course of the investigation. He also realized that the decision he had made in thirty seconds could bounce him from the agency, not to lose sight of what had happened to the last chap that broke a CIA agreement, poor Mr. Hinden. If need be, he could always find another job, but a woman like Abigail Stein just didn't grow on trees.

"So am I to assume that everything between us was *just part of the job?*" she asked.

"I was instructed to pump you for information. However, I have really enjoyed our time together and the ass-watching was strictly personal time."

When Carlton finished telling all, he concluded by saying that this was why we need to find your grandfather. Abby chimed in and said," And I know just where to find him, and since he needs my help, I will be going to see him tomorrow. Since I owe you one more riding lesson, I am willing to take you along, if you're interested and promise to behave."

"If I come along, will you be civil?"

"Maybe, although you're still on probation."

"Okay, I guess I'll take my chances."

"And that's not all big guy, you're staying here tonight." Suddenly, Carlton felt that this just might be his lucky day, but then Abby tossed him a blanket and pointed towards the couch.

"Better get some sleep, we have a long day ahead of us, cowboy. You can consider this your final exam." She kissed him on the forehead and headed for the bedroom. Carlton thought to himself, "At least I'm making progress; an hour ago I was shoveling shit in the barn."

42

Abby woke Carlton at 5 a.m. sharp. "Listen up, Tex. Before we get started let's go over the rules. I'm the one giving the orders. I'm making you in charge of security. In fact, since you strike me as the ambitious type, I'm making you the Chief of Security. Your duties in descending order are to protect my grandfather, then me, then the horses, and finally, yourself.

"Now here's the plan. You need to drive into town and check out of your motel. Let everyone overhear that you're moving back home. Ask directions on how to get to 93 South to pick up 90. Then drive about 20 miles and pick up the supplies we will need. Make sure you're not being followed. Here is the list. If you think of anything else, use your judgment. You might want to pick up some more ammo for that pea shooter of yours. Also, you might want to buy a rubber pillow for your saddle to protect that rookie ass of yours. We are going to be in the saddle for two days, for over twelve miles per day over rough terrain. And here is the final rule, I'm already taking a big chance in trusting you, but that's my limit. I don't want anyone else involved, not even your boss. After you check in with him today, I hold your BlackBerry; besides where we are going you can't get a signal anyway. Agreed?"

"Yes, ma'am."

"Let's hope you can take orders as well as you can shovel shit."

Carlton called Johnson to admit that his cover had been blown and tried to rationalize why. He explained that this was his only way of reaching Stein and he had to play by his granddaughter's rules. Johnson mentioned that Homeland had picked up a lot of chatter from the Russians, and he believed that they had joined the chase. Carlton pointed out that Abby not only controlled his BlackBerry but she had turned it off as well. So Carlton picked up a small Dictaphone and promised to record everything that he learned from Stein. "It could be a while before we speak again, so just sit tight," said Carlton.

"Be careful," replied Johnson.

When Carlton returned several hours later, the four horses were all saddled up and ready to go and they started to pack the gear onto the two packhorses, Lefty and Splash. The equipment included a generator, kerosene, lanterns, several miner hats with attached lights, an ax, a lighter, a twelve-gauge shotgun, sleeping bags, grain for the horses, mess kits, blankets, insulated clothing and boots, flower, sugar, potatoes, cooking oil, ammo, batteries, fishing line, a map of Cannon Mountain, and a bicycle pump.

"Why in the world does he need a bicycle pump?" asked Carlton.

"I have no idea, but it's on his list."

"I also brought these along," as he handed Abby a pack of Trojans. Abby glared at Carlton with a look that could kill.

"Didn't you say I should pick up some rubbers?"

"You keep this up, smarty pants, and I'm going to give you three choices."

"Those being?"

"The shovel, the girth knife, or the Freddie Heady."

"I hope you're not losing your sense of humor so early into our trip. However, I did bring along the rubber pillow as well, just for backup." When they finished packing, Abby said, "Candy said that you can ride her, provided you put your pea shooter in your shoulder holster instead."

Carlton stared at Candy, and then whispered one word into her ear. "Squealer!"

43

Abby made arrangements for the neighbor's son to care for the remaining animals while they were gone. Abby told Moses that he would not be able to join them on the journey and when he heard the word *stay*, he began to cry; since he refused to listen to the command, he was placed in the barn. Carlton mounted Candy, and with Abby on Hunter, they headed toward Cannon Mountain, the remote area where her family went camping and fishing when she was just a child. Moses continued to howl and cry until he could no longer detect Abby's scent. After merely two hours in the saddle, Carlton reported, "My ass is killing me, and now that we have gone beyond the five-day lesson period, do I get my back rub later?"

"If I don't hear another word about your ass for the rest of the day, perhaps I will consider it."

The trail up to Cannon Mountain was narrow, steep and rocky, and their progress was slow. The sun was out and it was a beautiful spring day in spite of a nip in the air. They meandered their way up the mountain until sundown and set up camp for the night. Next they had to unload the supplies from the packhorses, water them down and feed them, and then start to take care of themselves. For dinner they had smoked turkey and cheese on French bread, and then Abby took out a leather canteen of wine from her saddlebag. It felt good to just lie down and spread out on the blanket and relax.

Abby now said to Carlton, "Now that I know your real name, why don't you tell me a little about yourself? What about your folks? What are they like?"

"Abby, if I start talking about this, we may not get to your grandfather for another week. However, if you want to hear it, I will go into it, but not tonight, since I'm just too tired."

However, Carlton wasn't too tired to fail to remind Abby that he didn't complain about his ass all day. After they drank the wine, Abby said, "Okay Tex, I guess you earned yourself one free back rub."

As Abby sat on Carlton and gave him a back rub, Carlton felt as if he had slipped into heaven. However, being on probation, he felt it best not to try and push his recent good luck any further. With the cool evening air, the wine, the long day in the saddle and now the back rub, Carlton slipped into a deep sleep. Abby rested her head on his shoulder and joined him.

44

At the break of daylight, they were back in the saddle and continued the climb up the mountain. An hour into the trip, they heard a loud rustling in the bushes in front of them. Without hesitation Carlton dismounted and pulled out his pistol. Emerging from the brush was a 1,600 pound giant bull moose, which managed to scare the crap out of him. Carlton had never seen a moose up close and couldn't believe the enormous size of the animal. Once the moose realized that none of the horses was a cow looking for a mate, he disappointedly shuffled back into the brush.

"We must have crossed into his mating area," Abby said.

"You mean to say that they have their own area staked out and reserved?"

"Precisely!"

"Wow, I didn't realize that they accepted reservations way up here? Next time I'll phone ahead."

"Didn't you notice the long bunch of hair hanging from his chin? That's called the bell. A bull will urinate, and then he will soak his bell in his urine. Then using his bell, he will brush his urine scent on the trees along his area, and so he stakes out his mating territory as being his exclusively."

"I really learned something Abby; I'll have to try that someday."

It took a good 28 hours of traveling before passing through Franconia Notch and past Profile Lake where Alex was hiding out on Cannon Mountain. They came across only a few hikers along the way, since the weather was quite nippy and the camping season had not yet begun. The last five miles up Cannon Mountain were particularly slow going, but the views were breathtaking. The horses had to navigate up steep meandering rocky pathways into the wooded mountains. Abby finally spotted the old abandoned cabin that her family frequented in the past. Standing in front of it, she saw a man chopping wood, but no evidence of her grandfather. She cautiously approached the man who appeared to be middle-aged, perhaps fiftyish.

"Can you help me? We are looking for Alex Stein."

Alex was initially guarded, but he quickly noticed the resemblance of the woman to his former wife Rose.

"I most definitely can, young lady; I am Alex Stein."

Abby was astonished. The man looked similar to the way she had remembered her father, but even younger and fitter. "And you must be my granddaughter Abigail?" Alex extended his hand, offering to shake with Abby, but instead she embraced Alex as the two hugged for the first time ever.

"Grandpa this is . . . Carlton Terry. I'm not quite sure how to introduce him since his role has been changing on a daily basis. So far he has been a student, a philosopher, a professor, a liar, a jerk, a security guard, a friend, and let me not forget a spy for the CIA." Abby also wondered to herself, *"So who knows what tomorrow will bring?"*

"So how long have you two known each other?"

"Tomorrow is our anniversary: it will be a week!"

"Wow! You folks surely do move fast."

"It's nice to meet you, Carlton. Any friend of Abigail is a friend of mine. As for those other roles you provide for her, I think I'll just pass on those for the time being. Well folks, you guys must be exhausted, so come inside and wash up while I unpack the supplies, and then we have a lot of catching up to do."

"How did you get access to the cabin?" Abby asked Alex. "It's owned by the farmer at the base of the mountain. He doesn't use it any longer so for $100, he said I can have it for a month. You can't even get a place in Africa for that price anymore."

The cabin was nothing more than a rundown, single-room shack, 24 by 24 feet. A potbellied wood stove and a pine table were the outstanding furnishings, along with several chairs. On the East side were the kitchen utensils. On the West end stood a double bed and two bunk beds. The door was along the South wall, which had two windows, as well as two facing windows on the North end. Pegs along the walls served as closets. There was no electricity, but several kerosene lanterns were present. The exterior was replaced with T-111 siding, and the roof consisted of tin metal strips. An outhouse rounded out the facilities. Carlton thought, *"One hundred dollars a month. I think he overpaid."*

45

Abby and her grandfather spent the next day just chatting away about everything; the Arctic, Africa, her dad, the farm. She particularly wanted to hear stories about her grandmother, Rose, from the Arctic. She didn't feel it was her place to bring up his work, and decided to leave that for her Chief of Security. She still couldn't get over not only how young her grandfather looked, but what great shape he was in as well. He was chopping, splitting and stacking wood, carrying two forty pound bags of feed simultaneously, hauling crates of water, and he didn't seem to ever sit down.

"Did you get the bicycle pump, Abby?"

"Yes it's right here."

Alex opened a duffle bag and pulled out a heavy yellow rubber object. He then attached the pump and started pumping away. Ten minutes later, there was a four-man army surplus raft along with two foldable aluminum oars. "I brought this along just in case we need to make a speedy get away down the river. A raft just like this one has already saved my life once. I would never have gotten out of Africa without it. You should have seen the rapids I had to negotiate. Nothing handles fast water better than one of these babies."

46

Carlton was anxious to start questioning Alex, but he realized that Alex and Abby had to first do some bonding. Secondly, he had to take his assignment seriously. Not the one given to him by the CIA, but his job as Chief of Security. He didn't know if, or when, they might be getting visitors, and so his first order of business was to develop an escape plan. He spent the first few hours just canvassing the area. The cabin was in a small clearing. Directly behind that stood another hundred yards of trees and beyond that stood the steep cliffs that ran down to the river forty feet below. Anyone coming in would have to come by one of four methods: air, water, horse or all-terrain vehicles. Air wasn't very practical, even for a chopper, in this densely wooded forest. If one came by the river, first they would need to navigate the rapids, and then find a way up the steep cliffs between them and the river. He doubted very much if anyone else would favor coming in on horseback. Not only was it time consuming, but one needed a certain amount of expertise and durability for the trip. As he thought about this he began to rub his own sore ass again. He then concluded that the most likely means of invasion would be by all-terrain vehicle.

He had to set up an effective early warning alert system to detect intruders. It needed to be placed far enough from their camp to give them time to initiate an escape, yet close enough that it could be heard. He also needed to take into consideration the possibility of a nighttime attack. He walked to the edge of the high sharp peaks jutting up like palisades from the river below. He knew it would take them at least an hour to negotiate their way down to the water. Carlton surveyed the grounds, searching for materials that could be used to implement a plan. The grounds had a sizeable area where campers had abandoned goods and waste. There were empty bottles and cans, broken metal tent poles, used diapers and all sorts of other goodies. Carlton also noticed a huge stack of corrugated sheet metal roofing panels, each measuring eight by four feet. Apparently they came off an old camper and were discarded when the roof had been replaced at some time in the past. Carlton now formulated his plan.

47

After several days, Alex began feeling more relaxed around Carlton. Even more so, he trusted his granddaughter and sensed that she was developing a fondness for him as well. After dinner Alex decided to open up. "Abigail tells me that your boss sent you to discover what I was doing in Bongele?"

"That's true, but also to be assured that you and Abby wouldn't fall into harm's way. We know that you have discovered something extraordinary and some bad people would like to get their hands on you."

"As I am sure you know by now, my work concerns itself with the prolongation of human life. It is not a new subject, in fact, ever since the beginning of time, man has refused to accept the finality of death." Alex went on as if reading from a textbook. "One can go back to the seventh century b.c., *The Epic of Gilgamesh*, the Sumero-Babylonian hero who was in search of immortality. The Egyptians, the Greeks, the Romans were all seeking immortality. Alexander the Great was searching for immortality. The very word immortality comes from the Greek word athanasis, which means deathlessness.

"The illusive search to find the *Holy Grail*, and the *Fountain of Youth*, are simply more examples of searching for eternal life. In the days of Augustine (354–430 a.d.), Christians were taught that between the period of death and resurrection existed an intermediate state, called Purgatory, where the soul remained before Judgment Day, when it would be sent to heaven or hell. The very concept of the existence of a soul expresses the belief that there exists a conscious existence after death. In Genesis 3:4 the statement *'You will not die,'* implies the survival of the soul after death, a concept that lives on today. The Protestant Reformation started as a protest against the Catholic Church's policies of selling indulgences to reduce the time the soul had to spend in Purgatory.

"Since then the publication, *The Coming Race*, released in 1871 by Edward Bulwer-Lytton, revived the interest in communicating with the soul and this led to séances, such as those held by the Fox sisters of Hydesville, NY. In an article published in the New York World newspaper on October 21, 1888, Margaret admitted that her sister Katie and she perpetrated fraud as opposed to spiritualism. Later, under the leadership of Henry Sidgwick the Society for Psychic Research (SPR) was formed. An offshoot of this came about in 1930 by Joseph Banks Rhine, a biologist from the University of Chicago who went on to teach at Harvard University. His interest in communicating with the dead was galvanized after hearing a lecture from Arthur Conan Doyle, the creator of Sherlock Holmes. Subsequently Rhine coined the term ESP or Extra Sensory Perception. Many other notables in history have adhered to other bizarre beliefs. Mary Todd Lincoln held séances in the White House to communicate with her dead son. Nancy Reagan consulted psychics to plan the daily schedule of the President and relied on astrologer Joan Quigley. Richard Nixon consulted Jeane Dixon, as her warnings started our counter-terrorism efforts.

"Man has always been fascinated with a need to explain the unexplainable. There are all those folks out there who insist they have seen flying saucers and creatures from outer space. How about applying a bit of common sense? Would you travel many light years to finally reach the destiny of another planet and then spend your time by hiding out in the swamps of New Jersey?"

Carlton was trying to encourage Alex to start speaking of his experiments, but Alex simply went on with his own agenda as he avoided eye contact and spoke in a manner reminiscent of a college professor giving a lecture. "Take the story of the *"clever"* horse Hans. In the late 1880's a German high school teacher, named Wilhelm von Osten, believed he could teach a horse how to solve mathematical problems. He started by writing numbers on a black board, and the horse would be able to tap out the number he had written. He then went on to more complicated problems. If he asked the horse the square root of 16, the horse would correctly tap his hoof four times. Starting in 1891, von Osten began taking *"Clever Hans"* on the road throughout Germany. There were many skeptics and so in 1904 the Hans Commission was established with a team of prominent scientists. It was the conclusion of the committee that Hans' talents were real and that no trickery was involved.

"The investigation was subsequently passed on to a psychologist named Oskar Pfungst. Pfungst solved the mystery by placing a curtain between von Osten and Hans. When the horse could no longer see his master, he was unable to give any correct answers. von Osten was unaware that he was inadvertently signaling the horse. As Hans began tapping out the answer, von Osten watched his hoofs, but as soon as he arrived at the correct response, his master would look up. This told the horse to stop tapping. Mankind will always be reaching out to find miracles were there were none. The hope to find life after death, the desire to have a soul, are just more examples."

"Perhaps Hans couldn't really do arithmetic but I know that Moses can," Abby chimed in.

"Be serious, Abby!" said Carlton.

"Really, I can prove it. I will tell Moses that I have three milk bones for him, but then I give him only two, and put the third in my closed fist. He will claw at my hand and cry until he gets the third one."

"Wow, Abby, Perhaps you should take that act on the road the way Hans did!" Abby and Carlton laughed but Alex simply went on. "So as you can see, the story goes on and on. Man's quest to defy death is the very basis and foundation of all religious beliefs. This eternal hope provides the impetus to defy all rational thinking. Where do I fit into all of this, as an atheist scientist? I am not trying to defy death; I am just attempting to extend life out to its natural limits."

48

"It's true that I have discovered something important and something very powerful that has the potential to alter much of life as we know it today. I'm also hesitant about releasing this information. First, my work is not yet complete. Secondly, I need to reason out in my own mind, using my binary method, to determine that this knowledge will add more good to mankind than harm."

"I don't understand how any harm can come out of you helping people to live longer."

"Then I assume you are unfamiliar with the writings of the British scholar Thomas Robert Malthus, who in 1798, wrote in *An Essay on the Principle of Population* that the world's food supply was growing at a geometric progression, while the population was growing at an exponential progression, and therefore, mankind faced the risk of mass starvation without any intervention to the current status.

"In addition, a gentleman named Dave Holaway, of Eager, Arizona, wouldn't agree with your position either. He wrote a letter to the editor of *National Geographic* that was published in June, 2010, and I quote, "Exploding population on this planet far overshadows any other problem that we face.

"I'm not the only one to have doubts about the benefits of my work.

"Did you know that Einstein had serious doubts about sending that letter to FDR making him aware of the process of fission and the bomb? He feared that in the long run, the world would be a better and safer place without nuclear weapons. In fact, if he didn't fear that Hitler might get the bomb before us, he may never have sent that letter. Similarly, I too, now fear that the information may fall into the wrong hands. I am not a very trusting man Mr. Terry. However, I do trust my granddaughter, and I believe she trusts you."

Abby now jumped in, "I didn't say that I trusted him completely Alex, after all he was sent here to pump me, and I only said that he seems to be moving in the right direction."

"I understand, however, time maybe running short, so I have decided to tell both of you what I discovered at Bongele." Alex then reached into his pocket and pulled out a small black box with a plastic cover, which was just about the size of one of those radar detectors. "I know a lot of folks would love to get their hands on this right now, but that's only a part of the story, which I will get into later."

"I don't want to miss any of this Alex, so I'm going to turn on my Dictaphone if you don't mind?"

"Well, I hope you brought lots of tapes because this is going to take a while. What I have discovered is actually quite logical, and I'm going to start from the beginning and try to simplify the information such that if you pay attention closely, you will be able to not only understand what it is that I have discovered, but be able to predict what it is as well."

"This is not going to be the first lecture of yours that I have heard," stated Carlton. "Your old friend Steve Hinden gave me your talk about Pharmacology when I went to see him in Alaska. Quite impressive, I must say."

"How is ol' Steve doing these days?"

"I'm very sorry to have to tell you this, but Steve Hinden is dead. He was murdered by the Russian mob shortly after speaking to me about you."

"And you asked how any harm can come from my work? How very naïve of you! I'm so sorry to hear about that. It also shows that we may not have much time at all. So after dinner tonight, if you will be kind enough to turn down those distracting lanterns, I will discuss my work with the two of you."

49

As Abby was preparing dinner, Carlton began to set his exit strategy into place. On the horse trail, approximately a half mile from the camp, he strung a tripwire across the path. The wire in turn set off a series of clattering cans that would wake the dead. One hundred yards closer to the camp, he inserted the metal tent poles into the ground along the path with about ten inches of metal protruding, hoping this would present another obstacle to delay the arrival of visitors. Additional contraptions were added; glass, cans, and boards with nails. Next, he assembled all of the metal roofing strips, curved each one into a semicircle and wired them together into one long 40-foot chute. When he ran short, he took several off of the cabin they were using. He assembled them with the uphill side always overlapping the one below, so that anyone sliding down the chute would not confront the edges. He then tied stones to the end of the chute in order to stabilize it and slid the chute down toward the water. Finally, he fastened the top of his *slide* to the tree at the top of the cliffs. He had now created an evacuation slide similar to those used on commercial aircraft. Next to the door of the cabin, he placed the three mining hats, if needed for nighttime flight, the 12-guage shotgun, and a pack with enough rations for two days. He also had all of the horses tied to a single hitch nearby, so they could be freed quickly if need be, to seek their way home, as he recalled Abby's comment that the horses could always find their way back home. Carlton's plan was complete; he was now prepared for an assault by land with escape by water. Now he had to present the plan to his boss.

Carlton led Abby to the edge of the cliffs. "Abby, when you were a kid did you ever go to the playground and go down the slide?"

"Probably, but I can't say I specifically remember when."

"Didn't it sound like fun though?"

"I suppose so."

"Well, look what I built for you, dear."

"You have got to be kidding; if you think that I'm ever going down that, then you are out of your cotton-picking mind!"

"That went well," thought Carlton.

Carlton next decided to share his emergency escape plan with Alex, who seemed much more accepting. They then tied a rope to Alex's raft and lowered it down to the water in preparation for a possible hasty retreat.

50

That night after dinner, the topic of Alex's work to alter the aging process was raised by Abby. "Before you get into the details of your work, can I ask you a question, Alex? Haven't we already made great strides in improving longevity? After all, the life expectancy has gone up dramatically in the past fifty years."

"Most definitely," responded Alex, "but we are not even close to reaching our potential. In a landmark study by Hayflick and Moorhead, it was demonstrated that human cells cultivated in a test tube, or in vitro, could replicate only a limited number of times before the chromosomes begin to mutate, and so, many gerontologists believe that the doubling capacity of cells imposes limits on human life span. In humans the doubling capacity before mutation set in was limited to approximately fifty reproductions. According to this theory, in the absence of disease, and excluding futuristic prosthetic transplants, nanotechnology, and gene manipulation, the maximum life expectancy of human beings is approximately 120 years old. Although the assumption that the maximum human life span is fixed has been shown to be invalid in a number of animal models and may be invalid in humans as well.

"The longest living human as verified by the *Guinness Book of World Records* was Jeanne Calment, a French woman who lived to 122. Yes, we are making progress, but we are still not close to reaching our potential. Maximum life span is usually longer for species that are larger. The maximum life span for mice is 4 years, for dogs 29, for chimpanzees 59, and for Indian elephants 86. Some sharks, whales and tortoises live up to 200 years. A bivalve mollusk has been found that is 400 years old, and the jellyfish, Turritopsis natricula, is considered biologically immortal and has no natural maximum life span. In plant life, a giant sequoia tree is alive well into its third millennium, and the oldest known plant is a creosote bush in the Mojave Desert, called King Clone; it's about 11,700 years old.

"Our scientific and technological advancements are enabling many of us to live longer. Anti-platelet drugs such as aspirin and Plavix have given us the ability to interfere with platelet stickiness and agglutination, which is the first step in nidus formation. Anti-hypertensive agents have helped keep blood pressure under control, thus limiting those shearing forces to the vessels. The ACE inhibitors, in particular, seem to not only control blood pressure, and minimize the work of the heart, but there is some evidence that they also contribute to stabilizing the inner lining of the vessels, where as you know, where all the trouble begins.

"The statin drugs, such as Lipitor, should not only prolong life but improve the quality of life as well. By lowering LDL cholesterol, they have been able to considerably reduce fatty plaques in the blood vessels. Furthermore, there is some evidence that they, too, have an additional independent effect on stabilizing the intimal layer of the blood vessels, and reducing oxidative stress even more. In addition, our understanding of the role of antioxidants, better nutrition, and the role of exercise have all contributed to the increase in life expectancy.

"Even though we can now appreciate the positive role exercise plays in maintaining good heath, there are still many common misconceptions about it. Some forms of exercise are much more productive than others. One can attain the maximum benefit utilizing a balance of resistance training and aerobic conditioning. It is common to see folks doing one or the other exclusively. Many body builders are obsessed with resistance training, but may never step on a treadmill. Folks tend to work at what they are good at, as opposed to what they need, which is what they do poorly or not at all. Some folks work out in the gym on a daily basis and yet they never seem to change their appearance or their state of conditioning because they never vary their workout. The body responds to change.

"Metabolism is the sum energy expenditure of all body functions, and it can be either aerobic or anaerobic metabolism. Aerobic metabolism refers to a series of chemical reactions that require the presence of oxygen. In contrast, anaerobic metabolism means just the opposite—a series of chemical reactions that do not require oxygen. The maximum benefit to an individual is attained when changing exercise from purely aerobic, to adding short bouts of anaerobic metabolism.

"For example, assume you are running at level 7 on the treadmill, a level which you are capable of sustaining for an hour. Now you decide to go to level 12, a degree which you cannot sustain for more than a minute. At this level, the body is now temporarily consuming more oxygen than it is capable of generating, and you are in anaerobic metabolism. Now the body will call upon its reserves and actually increase the number of mitochondria in the cytoplasm, which are the energy turbines of the body. Repeated episodes of pushing your effort to the maximum, such as this, will now increase your exercise tolerance in the future.

"Another misconception regarding exercise is the issue of *spot reduction*, or the belief that you can burn fat in the particular area of the body that you prefer. There is no such thing as *spot reduction*. One has no control where fat is going to be deposited or removed—that is determined by your genes. Fat is not an active tissue such as muscle, it simply lies around in storage and does not do any work. Often you will see someone in the gym who wants to lose belly fat and what are they doing? Sit ups. That's wrong; in fact, it will actually make one's belly look larger by adding muscle to the abs. If one wants to lose belly fat, the best exercise is to jump on the treadmill and burn calories. Fat will dissolve first where it tends to be deposited first, and that varies from individual to individual, and is genetically determined.

"The final misconception to be discussed is that most gym goers are preoccupied with body weight. As one exercises over time, more body fat will be converted into muscle. Fat is relatively metabolically inactive when compared to muscle, which is performing work. For every pound of muscle one adds, an additional fifty calories a day will be consumed. Therefore, if one added ten pounds of muscle, and lost the same weight in fat, such an individual would burn an additional 500 calories per day. For the same volume, muscle is much denser than fat, and so one who has added muscle will not only *appear* more fit but will *be* more fit as well. The scale does not provide that information.

"Let's talk about oxygen. The human body is composed of approximately 75% water and water is 89% oxygen by weight. Therefore oxygen composes almost 70% of the body and it is the most vital and abundant element. Humans can survive weeks to months without food, many days without water, but only minutes without oxygen.

"There is one paradox I should point out to you about oxygen. We can't live without it, as it provides us with energy and allows us to function and yet it is also the thing that helps to kill us since the body cannot oxidize or produce rust without it. Once again, it is a matter of degree. Although exercise has been shown to assist in slowing the aging process, it, in itself, can lead to the production of excessive free radical formation when overdone. One would expect that marathon runners would have longer life expectancies, and yet this is not the case. That is why exercise physiologists recommend no more than forty five minutes of aerobic exercise at a time and only five or six days per week. Beyond that, the cons may outweigh the pros.

"Can you explain the mechanism of antioxidants to us, Alex?"

"Have you ever played the game of Packman where that cute little guy runs around and gobbles up the bad guys? That is exactly how antioxidants function. In theory, they neutralize the free radicals so that they cannot do damage to the cellular tissues. I say in theory, because free radicals are so highly reactive and unstable that they attack the first target cell available to them and so antioxidants usually don't get there in time to be very effective. Vitamin C, E, A, catalase, superoxide dismutase, fruits and vegetables, especially blueberries and broccoli all have high flavonoid or antioxidants levels. One study suggested that those drinking green tea, lived longer than coffee drinkers. Here too, the story is not that clear. For example, beta carotene is an antioxidant and studies have shown that patients taking it as a supplement did not live as long as others. Also the antioxidant content in foods seems to have more of a beneficial effect than taking antioxidants from pill supplements.

"There have been many other advances that have improved our average survival rates. All of our advances in medical imaging to detect tumors in the early stages, our progress in cancer treatment, and heart disease, and the implementation of cardiac revascularization, avoidance of excessive exposure to the sun, avoidance of smoking, consuming red wine, eating fish, ingesting omega-3 fats, have all contributed to our improved survival rates. A recent study demonstrated a 35% reduction in breast cancer for woman taking fish oil pills, which can be attributed to its anti-inflammatory benefits.

"Prior to my work, there have been only two proven methods known that successfully delay aging. The surest method is called death. The only other proven means has been through caloric reduction. As early as the 1930's, Clive McCay showed that in mice, caloric restriction was shown to reduce oxidative stress along with the generation of free radicals, and thus increase life span by 35%, and as high as 50% with extreme caloric restriction.

"There are many substances being experimented with and studied to see if they can delay aging. Hormone therapy with HGH or human growth hormone is one. It has shown to increase muscle mass and improve the immune system and enhance libido, but if one has an undetected tumor, it will stimulate it to grow faster, and it has been shown to actually decrease longevity in mice.

"DHEA and melatonin have also been shown to improve memory in addition to the other benefits of HGH, but there has been an increase in breast and prostate cancer associated with it. Estrogen therapy has attenuated the symptoms of menopause and decreased heart disease and osteoporosis, but that too has increased the risk of uterine and ovarian cancers.

"The substance Telomerase was able to delay aging in mice cells, but the mice didn't live any longer. It did manage to enhance cell replacement and proliferation; however, brain and heart cells do not proliferate or divide. Finally, there is some controversial work with a substance called klotho, which works by gene manipulation. "Now allow me to explain the mechanism of gene cloning, since much of my findings have been in this area. Gene cloning or genetic engineering is the manipulation and alteration of gene synthesis. In the early 1970s scientists discovered naturally occurring enzymes that could be used to engineer DNA molecules and therefore tamper with the very makeup of life.

"It works in a way similar to the cut and paste function of your computer. Restrictive enzymes, such as those found naturally in bacteria can cut the long stranded DNA into smaller fragments and thus isolate specific genes. Scientists can alter or remove certain genes either within an organism or from one organism to another species. Some bacteria-made enzymes have the ability to cut DNA chains, which are abnormal, at specific sites and replace them with the correct messenger to synthesize normal substances. A fellow named Tom Johnson has been able to increase the life span of round worms by 50% through gene therapy.

"Through this type of genetic engineering one can now produce bacteria capable of breaking down oil slicks and dissolving industrial waste. This technology enabled us to dissipate much of the oil spill from the BP well in the Gulf disaster."

"I would think you would need an awful lot of bacteria to suck up all that oil" Abby said.

"How long do you think it takes for bacteria, such as E. coli to reproduce?" Alex asked.

"I don't know; a week or two perhaps."

"Would you believe thirty minutes?" Alex responded.

"Wow, they *are* quite busy," Abby replied.

Alex continued, "The same process is also responsible for synthesizing substances such as human insulin, human growth hormone, and hepatitis B vaccine. Plants can produce their own pesticides, and one can obtain higher yields from fruits and vegetables by having them survive freezing temperatures, and even produce their own nitrogen. Genetic engineering holds the potential to cure many recognized disorders caused by inheritance of defective DNA. Sickle cell disease, Tay-Sachs, Duchene Muscular Dystrophy, Huntington's Chorea, Cystic Fibrosis, and Lesch-Nyhan syndrome are just a few of the over 3,000 diseases which fall into this class. Recently, there have been some experimental trials in treating HIV patients in this manner by removing genes from AIDS patients and replacing them with genes from those who are immune to the virus.

"Physicians will be able to remove some blood from the patient, make a normal copy of the defective gene, insert that into the patient's white blood cells, return the blood to the patient, whereby the gene will now function normally. This isn't science fiction; it has already been done.

"With the aid of computers, we have been successful in mapping the entire human genome, with all of its 3.3 billion base pairs and 30,000 genes, although, as of yet, we still do not understand the function of at least half of them. In time many of today's mysteries of life, as well as the cures for many diseases will be found utilizing this process." He paused, and said, "Let's take a break here, I need to heat up some water and take a shower, it has been three days now. And then I'll tell you folks about Leonard Guarente." Carlton now thought to himself *"Thank God!*

51

After a one-hour break Alex went on, "My initial fascination in this field of gene manipulation was stimulated by a biologist named Leonard Guarente of MIT who made an amazing finding in 2000. He discovered that calorie restriction activated a gene called SIR2 (Silenced Information Regulator Gene), which had the capacity to slow aging. His work was performed on yeast. Yeast calls are fascinating since they can metabolize food by either one of two pathways. They use fermentation when food is readily available, but resort to respiration when food is scarce. When the food supply was scarce, the yeast not only increased its respiratory rate, but the levels of SIR2 increased drastically and behold, the yeast's life expectancy increased as well. On the other hand, excess food supplies decreased survival rates, and lowered SIR2 levels. Perhaps you are saying, that's great news for yeast, but what does it have to do with us? The answer is that round worms, as well as humans, have a gene similar to SIR2.

"Guarente concluded that by shifting the yeast's energy from metabolic oxidative stress, which occurs during the normal breakdown of food into energy, as opposed to shifting its efforts to the role of respiration, which spared calories, the yeast was subjecting itself to a more efficient and healthy process. In other words, the mere process of metabolizing food generated free radicals. He further postulated since it was unlikely to get humans to take in 30% fewer calories, perhaps someday one could trick the body into believing it was in a caloric restriction mode. The challenge then is to utilize gene manipulation to produce SIR2, thereby sending more of its calories towards respiration as opposed to the accumulation of harmful fats associated with oxidative metabolism, and thus slow the generation of harmful free radicals that accelerate aging.

"Perhaps this may also explain some of the benefits of exercise. We know that exercise burns calories and keeps weight in check and it also strengthens the heart's function by raising VO2 max, which is a measurement of the heart's ability to extract oxygen more efficiently. Furthermore, it raises the HDL good cholesterol, which helps bring LDL cholesterol out of the blood vessels and back to the liver where it can be broken down. Perhaps exercise may also benefit the individual by shifting more of its metabolism to the function of increased respiration, as opposed to using the body's metabolic pathways to focus on digestion and the oxidative stress of fat metabolism which leads to the generation of free radicals."

Alex began to explain the aging process in a manner very similar to that which Shelly Rothberg had done for the CIA committee. He reviewed the changes that occur in all of us, including the acceleration of the process in diabetics and the role of inflammation in causing oxidative stress and the generation of free radicals. However, Alex Stein went much further.

"By now, everyone knows that free radicals are toxic to the body, but most folks don't realize that they are also necessary. As our body generates energy from the breakdown of glucose, free radicals are produced as an unavoidable by product. The cell has two key components—the nucleus where our genes, which contain our DNA reside, and the cytoplasm. Within the cytoplasm there are small structures, or organelles, called mitochondria. These are the energy turbines of our cells. It is here that carbohydrates from our diet are broken down and synthesized into our energy-producing substance, ATP (Adenosine triphosphate). However, when ATP consumes oxygen to produce energy, byproducts are formed, which are the free radicals. One cannot eliminate all of the free radicals, since many are the result of normal metabolism.

"Since these free radicals are missing an electron needed to stabilize themselves, they are highly reactive and unstable, and are immediately searching out a target molecule to replenish the missing electron to restore its orbit to neutrality. Therefore, they will attack the first target that they come across, which just happens to be the very same place where they were formed, that being the mitochondria. There have been thirteen different mitochondrial proteins identified in man, and these are now the ones subject to attack. As the protein surrenders its electron to the free radical, it now becomes electrically unstable, being that it is short an electron, and thus it now needs to steal an electron from a neighboring protein. Therefore, a chain reaction is created.

When mitochondrial proteins are damaged in this manner, their membranes begin to leak and the smaller of these proteins can now escape the mitochondria and become released into the body of the cell causing a generalized systemic reaction. This ongoing process causes mitochondrial protein to malfunction, which leads to abnormal protein synthesis, and mitochondrial mutations. The body's metabolic pathways are now disrupted, causing oxidative stress and the loss of equilibrium or homeostasis within the body.

"By analogy, one may compare the body's mitochondria to the turbine of a power plant which has now *rusted,* and therefore is less capable of producing energy. The machinery becomes robbed of energy and toxic wastes accumulate, leading to its ultimate break down.

"When examining comparative biology, it was found that organisms that aged more slowly had less free radical mitochondrial damage and lived longer. Furthermore, mammals that were subject to caloric restriction, which to date still remains the only non-genetic intervention proven to increase life span, have been shown to have less mitochondrial damage.

"Studies in yeast have now been able to *tag* and identify six of the known thirteen mitochondrial proteins. As it turns out, the mitochondrial proteins are capable of self-repair by eliminating damaged or mutant mitochondria and replacing them with new healthy ones. Over time, the mutant mitochondria begin to accumulate in greater numbers, contributing to the aging process, as our essential components simply *rust* and fade away. Speaking of fading away, I am ready to turn in for the night. We can continue in the morning—if you kids are up for it?"

52

As Alex turned in, Abby and Carlton stepped out for some fresh air. There was a distinct nip to the air, so Carlton made a fire as Abby sat on a blanket. "So, what do you think of my grandfather?"

"He is a real character, plus a raving genius, and we need to assure his safety."

"Carlton, I really appreciate you for saying that. In fact, I feel that I owe you an apology. I was a bit too rough on you back in the barn."

"Your apology is accepted. As Confucius would say, 'To take offense adds as much suffering to the world as to offend.'"

"Thanks for being so understanding. Many folks, especially men, have disappointed me in the past. Dad died when I was young. I never met my grandfather until now, and my last two boyfriends have turned out to be two-timing weasels. When I believe that I can trust someone, and then they let me down, I become disappointed in myself for using such poor judgment. In the poem, "It Dropped So Low—in My Regard—," Emily Dickinson captures my feelings.

It dropped so low—in my Regard—I heard it hit the Ground—And go to pieces on the Stones
At bottom of my Mind—
Yet blamed the Fate that flung it—less, Than I denounced Myself,
For entertaining Plated Wares
Upon My Silver Shelf—

"Can you translate that for me Abby?"

"Sure, I can do that for you. I am really glad that you are here with me, Carlton. I consider you to be someone that I trust and hold in high esteem. But if you turn out to be another phony, I will smash your head on the ground like a pumpkin."

"I thought that was what you were trying to say."

As they both had a good belly laugh, Carlton said, "Abby this could be the start of a great relationship."

Carlton then went on, "As far as your unfortunate past experiences, you have my sympathy. Someone told me a long time ago that life is not fair. I, too, had a rough going in my youth." Carlton had previously been reluctant to talk about his past, but he opened up to Abby revealing all.

When he finished, they both looked at each other in silence. Then Abby spoke. "Confucius also said, 'The past is dead, and the future imaginary, so let's focus on making the most of the present.'"

"I agree" Carlton said.

With that, Abby put her right arm around Carlton's shoulder and planted a soft passionate kiss on his lips. It was a kiss that lasted well into the night, as they embraced and stretched out on the blanket in front of the fire. Carlton reflected: *the present is sweet!*

53

<*Author's note*: This chapter encapsulates many of the concepts and findings described in *Ending Aging*, by Aubrey de Grey, Ph.D., and Michael Rae>

After breakfast Abby and Carlton urged Alex to continue his discussion. Alex went on without missing a beat. "The question now becomes, what, if anything can be done to slow down or eliminate mutant mitochondria? Eric Schon, of the Department of Neurology at Columbia University, used gene manipulation to insert six cloned mitochondrial proteins of algae into the nucleus of cells in human patients suffering from neuromuscular disease. The cloned cells were then capable of successfully coding the DNA of the nucleus by inserting the new genetic sequence into its DNA and therefore reproduce itself and replace the abnormal protein with normal mitochondrial DNA. The mutated gene was now capable of producing normal protein synthesis, correcting the underlying defect.

"Aubrey de Grey, Ph.D. and Michael Rae, in their book Ending Aging, discuss how gene manipulation has already altered aging. As our bodies breakdown and metabolize sugar, the byproducts formed bind to proteins and gum them up, by forming undesirable linkages in the proteins, which then predispose the protein to form mutations."

"Excuse me Alex, but can you explain how these cross links gum up the works?""Sure Abby. Imagine the protein as being a bamboo fishing pole. Let's assume you are holding two such poles in your hands, side by side. As you bend both poles simultaneously, you note how flexible they are. Now have the poles attached to each other close to each end with a six-inch piece of wood acting as braces, to form a rectangle. The braces now represent the glucose by-products. Now as you try to bend the poles, you will notice a marked decrease in their flexibility. They have lost considerable suppleness and elasticity. This is what cross-linkages do to your proteins. The result is stiffening and hardening of your blood vessels and arteries, which is exactly what occurs during aging.

"It has been noted that these so-called cross-linked proteins are far more common in diabetics and in the aged. Drs. Anthony Cerami and Peter Ulrich determined that these substances accounted for the complications seen in diabetics. They cause a decrease in the elasticity of blood vessels and the heart, resulting in hardening of the arteries. They also affect the myelin or fatty sheath that insulates nerves and affect the proteins of the lens causing cataracts. These are the agents that lead to diabetic retinopathy and neuropathy, damaging the eye and the nervous system, as well as contributing to kidney disease.

"In 1991, in Manhasset, New York, a company named Alteon was formed with the goal of finding a way to inhibit the formation of these toxic complexes. After 710 unsuccessful attempts, they came across a compound, which they named ALT-711, or algaebrium. Again using gene manipulation, they were able to insert algae proteins into the cell's DNA, which were now capable of catalytically breaking down crosslinks where glucose was attached to proteins. ALT-711 in rodents was not only capable of slowing down complications of hardening of the arteries but it was able to restore suppleness where there was already previously lost flexibility. Unfortunately the results were not as satisfying in man.

"It was further shown that the rate of accumulation of glucose cross links, called Advanced Glycation End products (AGEs) was slower in animals that lived longer. The more quickly we age, the more AGEs that accumulate in the tissues, and the quicker we lose flexibility. Diabetics with poor control of blood sugar, as measured by HgA1c have been shown to have higher levels of AGE links and shorter life spans demonstrating that AGEs play a significant role in aging.

"However, in humans, attempts to decrease the formation of AGEs run the risk of complications, since AGEs are also a result of normal metabolism, and one is fearful of messing with nature. Therefore, instead of trying to prevent formation of AGEs, the focus has turned towards removing them before they can damage proteins and impair tissue function by robbing them of their youthful flexibility and hastening the pathway to death. One such attempt to prevent AGE-link damage was to utilize high dose antioxidants to bring down free radicals, since it is the free radicals that accelerate the formation of many of the AGEs. In rodents such experiments were successful, as the number of crosslinks was diminished. However, similar studies in humans have been much less successful, since rodents have a much higher level of oxidative stress than we do and therefore produce more free radicals, and in humans, some of the AGE formation pathways do not involve free radicals. One drug that initially seemed to offer hope was pimagidine, a member of the aminoguanidine family of drugs, but its side effect profile prevented it from being of clinical benefit.

"Approaches such as these, designed to limit the formation and expedite the removal of AGEs, represent one more hope of correcting many degenerative diseases such as muscular dystrophy, ALS, Huntington's chorea, Parkinson's disease, Alzheimer's, sickle cell disease, as well as cancer, and aging itself.

"In short, the rate of aging appears to be a function of free radical production, their ability to damage mitochondrial proteins, the adequacy of antioxidant defenses, and the efficacy of the body's repair systems. Stop the damage done by free radicals attacking mitochondrial proteins and you will retard aging. In other words, stop **RUST**."

"Up until recently, scientists have been limited in their approach because they have been unable to target specific cells. With the advent of nanotechnology, or engineering performed at the molecular level itself, all of that has now changed. Here is a perfect example of what the future has in store, as so elegantly described, once again, by Aubrey de Grey, in his text on Ending Aging.

"Dendrimeres are microscopic man-made nanoparticles that can be synthesized in a variety of shapes; spherical, rice shaped, star shaped or with a complex series of brush like tentacles arranged to resemble the spokes of a wheel, all of which are designed in such a way as to be capable of binding to a wide range of molecules than can now target a specific cell type, or deliver drugs into a specific target cell.

"Here is a schematic illustration of what a dendrimere particle looks like, and how it functions. The brushes on the surface allow specific molecules to be attached to the particle, which now can deliver these substances directly into the cell.

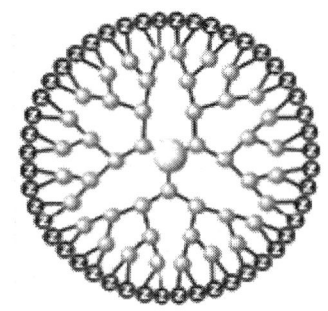

"For example, as de Grey points out, cancer cells need to divide very rapidly and to do so, they need to produce lots of DNA. The vitamin folic acid is needed in the manufacturing of DNA, and so for the cancer cells to thrive, they need to vastly increase the folic acid receptors on their surfaces, so they can mop up more folic acid. Now if we take a nanoparticle dendrimere, we can attach folic acid to it, and then attach the chemotherapy drug methotrexate to the complex. As the cancerous cells now soak up the folic acid, the methotrexate follows as well, and is able to attack the cancer."

"That sounds like what my mom used to do when she mixed my medicine in apple sauce." Abby interjected.

"With this technique, much lower doses of the potentially toxic chemotherapy need to be used, and the body's normal cells are spared. Using similar approaches, we may be able to attack free radicals and defective genes at the very site where they are produced."

54

"Alex, what I don't understand is how you managed to gather all of this information in a small village in Africa?"

"That's the beauty of it. Initially it wasn't possible, but thanks to the Internet, folks from all across the world are now working from their living rooms, basements, attics, garages and even their campers, both amateurs and professionals, including the world's greatest minds, to share ideas, ask questions and retrieve information simply by going to www.DIYbio. I could never have been able to formulate and test many of these hypotheses without the theories and findings of men such as Aubrey de Grey and Ray Kurzwell.

"DIYbio came about in 2000, by Professor Vinjay Pande's group at Stanford Chemistry Department. It was initially designed to perform computationally intensive stimulations to comprehend protein-folding dynamics, and it has now grown to the most powerful distributing computer cluster of scientific knowledge in the world. Anyone, including students, professors, amateurs, professionals, futuristic prognosticators, or simply the curious minded, may go online and contribute or ask questions. Currently there are tens of thousands of participants and it is growing every day.

"The DIT SENS lab is headed by PhD candidate John Schloendorn at Arizona State, who says, 'I want to make a dent into the suffering and death caused by aging.' Alex added, "I believe such men as John Schloendorn, Aubrey de Grey and Ray Kurzweil, have noble and admirable intentions. There are many who may not agree, since their work and findings may seem unorthodox and difficult to comprehend, but history has looked at many of the great minds with a similar skepticism.

"Let's discuss Ray Kurzweil. He was born in 1948 and raised in Queens, New York. Kurzweil is an author, scientist, inventor, entrepreneur, and a futurist. He envisions that the fields of biology and technology will revolutionize technology at exponential rates. He states that if one is capable of surviving for another fifteen years then one's life expectancy will keep rising every year, faster than your age. Utilizing what he refers to as the Law of Accelerating Returns, he envisions the fields of biology and medicine being revolutionized by technology with exponential progress due to nanotechnology and gene sequencing. He points out that it took years to sequence the first 1% of human genes and scientists worried that they would never complete the task, and yet they remained on schedule to meet an exponential curve. If you reach 1%, and keep doubling your growth every year until you reach 100%, you will reach 100% in just seven years.

"Kurzweil has developed too many innovations to begin to discuss. He developed the voice recognition pattern whereby computers can take dictation and transcribe the words spoken. He devised music synthesizers capable of accurately duplicating the sounds of real instruments. In his book, the *Age of Intelligent Machines*, published in 1990, he predicted the demise of the Soviet Union, stating that cell phones, fax machines, and the Internet would make it impossible for totalitarian countries to control the flow of information. Once again his predictions were relevant, as the Mid-East revolutions would not have occurred when they did if not for the Internet and Facebook.

"He stated that computers would be able to defeat any human chess players, and was proven correct in 1997 when the IBM computer, Deep Blue, defeated the world's greatest chess player, Garry Kasparov. His prediction that the silica media of a computer can act and function faster than man's carbon media was demonstrated once again during February 2011 when the IBM computer, Watson outscored mankind on the show *Jeopardy*. He also correctly predicted not only the vast growth of the Internet but the fact that it would be wireless.

"Kurzweil cared little about health until he developed diabetes at the age of 35; at that point he decided to discover the means to reverse aging. His methods were quite unorthodox and could not necessarily be supported by current scientific thinking. He ingested 250 supplements and ten glasses of alkaline water each day, along with ten glasses of green tea and several glasses of red wine. He believed that the water helped to flush out toxins and the alkalinity helped neutralize toxic acid waste products. He also underwent intravenous infusions of a chemical cocktail that he believed would reprogram his biochemistry. He ate only organic foods with low glycemic loads and avoided all foods rich in sugar or carbohydrates. He ate mainly vegetables, lean meats, tofu, and foods high in omega-3 fatty acids such as wild salmon, and used only extra virgin olive oil in cooking.

"He focused on getting sufficient sleep, avoiding stress, caloric restriction, vigorous exercise, regular massages and meditation. Kurzweil joined the Alcor Life Extension Foundation, a cryonics company. In the event of his death, his body is to be chemically preserved, frozen in liquid nitrogen, and stored at an Alcor facility in the hope that future medical technology will be able to revive him."

"Do you believe he is correct regarding all of his theories and predictions?" Abby asked.

"Not everyone is a believer in the theories advocated by Ray Kurzweil. Pulitzer Prize winner Doug Hofstadter has said, of which I tend to believe as well, 'It's as if you took a lot of very good food and some dog excrement and blended it all up so that you can't possibly figure out what's good or bad. It's an intimate mixture of rubbish and good ideas, and it's very hard to disentangle the two.'

"Another very impressive individual that I have previously referred to is the British author, theoretician, gerontologist Aubrey de Grey. He was born in England, in 1963, and is the Chief Science Officer of the SENS Foundation. He cites seven types of metabolic and cellular damage that lead to aging. They are cancer causing nuclear mutations, as well as mitochondrial mutations, which alter the ability of the cell to function properly. **Intracellular aggregates can cause damaged proteins to accumulate in the cells, whereas extracellular aggregates, such as amyloid deposits, are more likely to be the culprit in disorders such as Alzheimer's.** Another type of cell damage is due to cell loss, which is seen in such organs as the heart and brain where cells do not rejuvenate. Other damage to cells is caused by cell senescence; whereby cells lose their ability to divide, but do not yet die and continue to produce harmful substances. The final type of cell damage seen is attributed to the formation of extracellular cross links; which cause proteins to lose their elasticity, leading to such diseases as hardening of the arteries.

"However, what I discovered at Bongele takes everything to a completely new level. Let me begin by saying that I could never have made these discoveries on my own. Men with great insight into the intricacies of our body's metabolic pathways have enabled me to test my hypotheses.

"Now, I said that antioxidants are not very effective in mopping up free radicals, but that's not the entire story. In mice when the anti-oxidant catalase was inserted into the organism's DNA, there was no measurable benefit. If however, the catalase was inserted *directly i*nto the mitochondrial DNA, the life span of the mice increased by 20%. One needs, therefore, to be able to have catalase enter **directly** into the mitochondria, if it is to be an effective clinical agent.

"Catalase is an enzyme present in animals, plants, and yeast. It is a potent antioxidant that breaks down hydrogen peroxide, a harmful byproduct of metabolism, to water and oxygen. It is also believed that low levels of catalase contribute to hair graying, as hydrogen peroxide levels rise which causes the hair to bleach from the inside out.

"In an article published in the Journal of Biological Chemistry in May, 2003, Cheng Cao et al, of Harvard Medical School, demonstrated the *Abl* related gene of the enzyme tyrosine kinase could be directly bound to the antioxidant catalase. So with this as a background, it now brings us up to my work in Bongele.

"As a result of reading Cao's paper, using gene manipulation I was able to isolate catalase from yeast and attach the catalase to a nano particle dendrimere and inject it into the body. The tagged catalase was then able to bind to the enzyme tyrosine kinase, which is normally present in both the nucleus and cytoplasm of cells, and thus deliver high concentrations of the antioxidant catalase to both the nucleus and the **mitochondria** within the cytoplasm, neutralizing many of the toxic effects of the free radicals before they could attack and deform mitochondrial proteins. This paper started me thinking. What if we could slow the rate by which free radicals steal electrons from our mitochondrial proteins by supplying an exogenous source of electrons for the free radicals to attack?

"The second part of my work relates to the experiments performed by my friend, Leonard Guarente. You may recall how Guarente found that yeast that consumed fewer calories, produced more of the gene SIR2, and therefore they lived longer. Since it was felt that humans would not realistically decrease their caloric intake by 30 to 50 % the hope was to be able to trick the body into believing it had consumed fewer calories and therefore produce more SIR2.

"In my work with gene engineering, I was able to isolate and reproduce the activator gene in humans to stimulate and turn on the production of the SIR2 gene. First I was able, through gene manipulation, to discover one of the seven mitochondrial proteins that were not previously isolated. I named it, sSIR2, or stimulator gene of SIR2. Through gene splicing, I was able to have the new gene inserted, which then tricked the body into believing it was in a state of caloric restriction, causing an increase in the production of SIR2, and greatly improving life span.

"My third approach at attempting to delay aging is still untested and that is one of the reasons that I am reluctant to share my findings at this point. I haven't been able to work out all of the details to date, but I believe it holds great promise. The idea came to me when I asked myself, *if a free radical is out to steal an electron . . .* " At that moment, Carlton's security alarm began to explode; unwanted visitors were now headed their way.

55

It was not very difficult for the Russian mob to detect the whereabouts of Alex Stein. Steve Hinden's call to DiMiceli at the fisheries in Wasilla put the mob in touch with Hinden. From him, they learned Abigail's name, as well as the location of the family farm in Grafton, New Hampshire. The bloodhounds did the remainder of the tracking, following the scent to Canyon Mountain.

It was night when their uninvited guests appeared. The time had come to put the escape plan they had rehearsed into effect. They grabbed the three mining helmets and turned on the headlamps. Next they reached for the pack placed by the door; Abby made sure she had her trusty Taser in hand; Carlton picked up the 12-gauge with one hand and freed the horses with the other; Alex held on to his little black box, which he referred to as the Stimulator, and they rushed toward the cliffs. They could now hear the sounds of the all-terrain vehicles approaching their campsite. They were able to make out four vehicles, accompanied by a pair of baying bloodhounds.

As they ran for the cliffs, Alex did two uncalled-for acts. First he did not see any cause to discontinue his lecture. "Are you intrigued by what I have discovered, Abby?" "Sure, Alex, but first I want to be assured that I am going to live long enough to hear the end." Secondly, he fell. In spite of Alex's youthful appearance and overall excellent conditioning, he was still a klutz.

Abby and Carlton stopped to assist Alex just long enough to have the two bloodhounds catch up and corner them. Another minute later, the four Russians with their automatic weapons were on them. There was no escape. Carlton considered a shootout, but decided that the odds were not in his favor. He then grabbed Alex's black box, along with his gun, and tossed them behind a nearby tree.

As they were escorted back to the camper, Abby asked, "What can we do for you fellows today? Just drop by to borrow a cup of sugar?" No one smiled. No one spoke. The Russians contemplated shooting Carlton and Abby on the spot since they weren't being paid any extra for having to cart them along. However, they reconsidered, thinking they might be useful in convincing Alex to talk.

56

When they entered the camper, the obvious leader of the group, pointed to Abby. "You, over there, get on the bed." Abby looked terrified. "Don't worry, we're not rapists; we're simply assassins."

"Wow, you had me worried there for a minute," answered Abby. As she sat on the bed, her hands were cuffed to the headboard and her ankles were duct taped. Next, Alex was placed in a chair in the center of the room and his hands and feet were taped as well. Carlton was then cuffed with hands behind his back to the iron rod attached to the stove, and his feet were also taped.

The leader then began to interrogate Alex. "This is your granddaughter, correct? We followed her here from the family farm." As Alex hesitated, the Russian added, "Don't even begin to think about lying to me, because with every lie someone is going to lose a body part."

With that Abby jumped in, "Yes, I'm his granddaughter."

"And who is this fellow?"

"He is my new boyfriend. Today was supposed to be our anniversary. We have been going together for a week."

"How romantic!" said the Russian.

"He's an instructor at Dartmouth, name is Chad Jay. I asked him to help me up here with the supplies, and what a mistake that turned out to be. It's time for a new boyfriend anyway. Couldn't even sit in the saddle. If you don't believe me check out the blisters on his ass. Also you can check his ID, it's right there on the table. And by the way, may I ask what your name is?" inquired Abby.

"Call me Z, like the last letter in the alphabet and the last person you will ever see, if I don't get what I want." Abby thought that Z was actually a very appropriate name from him, since it looked as if Zorro had taken a sword to his face. Z was wiry, and appeared to be in excellent physical shape. It was apparent from his demeanor that he was a professional and Abby felt that she would be wasting time trying to use her charm on him. Abby was correct in her assessment of Z, whose full name was Zakhur Yuri. He had served as a soldier in Boris's organization for the past six years. He started out as a small-time hood and worked his way up to a position as an enforcer, or what is referred to in the vernacular as a bone breaker, extorting funds from legitimate businessmen or collecting debts from unlucky gamblers. He subsequently earned credibility as an assassin with a specialty of installing car bombs. He was also an excellent marksman and never failed on an assignment.

Z was stationed in the Boston area, but preferred to be in Atlantic City, for when he wasn't executing people his next favorite passion was casino gambling. This assignment was an important one for him. Success would earn him the blue star tattoo that he coveted, along with a placement to his liking. Z had taken down many targets during his career and he wasn't about to let a 70-year-old man become his first failure.

Abby looked Z in the eye and said, "Well, you have already indicated that it's not a cup of sugar that you want. And your buddies here, I suppose they are called W, X, and Y, correct?"

"You're pretty smart young lady; let's hope that your grandfather is as talkative as you."

"I'll talk, just don't hurt anyone," Alex interrupted.

"Good, very good. Now we have had a long night, so we are first going to have something to eat and then we will get started. And you two, just remember, we really don't need you folks, so any funny business and that will make two less mouths to feed."

Abby decided to see if she could do any better conversing with W and X, as she had now decided to christen them. "So what do you boys do for a living?" she asked.

W replied, or was it X? "We spent a lot of time in college," as they both simultaneously began an annoying snorting laugh. W and X were undoubtedly identical twins, and resembled two Buddha book ends, both being short, stocky, and round faced. Abby got the impression that they never came within ten miles of a college, and so her initial hope was to have these two get into a fight over her, like two dinosaurs competing for a piece of meat, and hopefully kill each other.

She turned towards Y, trying to get a read on him. Y didn't say much. He was built a lot like Z, possibly ten years younger. Their similar facial features of a pointy nose, narrow chin, and beady eyes made Abby believe that W was the younger brother of Z.

57

After their meal, Z started to interrogate Alex about his scientific findings and Alex began to talk. Whether Alex was really crazy may have been a matter for conjecture, but one thing was for sure, he could certainly act that way if needed. He spoke in such a manner that it would have made the *Old Professor*, Casey Stengel, sound like a Rhodes Scholar. When Stengel was called upon to testify before Congress on baseball's anti-trust exemption, he left Congress scratching their heads wondering what he had said. Rarely did he complete a sentence and he jumped from one subject to another. Stengel was no match for Alex. Not only were his thoughts circuitous, but he used mostly scientific and Latin terminology that had no meaning to the Russians, who were also taping his comments. After several hours, Z had regretted his comment that he hoped Alex was as talkative as Abby. After six hours, all of the Russians tapes were depleted and everyone had a headache.

"Tell me where that black box is that I have been hearing about."

"I'm not sure where I put that." said Alex.

Carlton was now quick to jump in. "I believe you dropped it when we were running in the woods. I saw it fall out of your pocket. I'm pretty sure I can find it for you, if you promise to let me go. I don't have anything to do with whatever is going on here," said Carlton.

"Sure, we can do that," said Z. They freed Carlton's legs, and W and X escorted Carlton into the woods. Just before they left, Z instructed them to put two slugs into Carlton as soon as they located the box. Z then left Y guarding Alex and Abby, as he went out to check on the dogs and gather firewood. Carlton stumbled through the woods for a while, acting confused. When he came across his .45, he covered it with his foot and pointed away saying, "There it is!"

As the two Russians turned, he dropped to the ground, picked up his gun, and with his hands still in cuffs, fired one shot into the chest of the twin standing closest to him. As the second twin raised his weapon, Carlton, from his knees, fired once again; the bullet entered directly over the heart of his victim. Both twins died instantly. Carlton thought,

"The alphabet has been shortened by two—W and X were now gone." He then grabbed the keys, uncuffed himself, took W's weapon and headed back to the cabin. When the shots rang out, Z was still gathering firewood. *"That's one less mouth to feed,"* he thought. Actually, it was two!

58

With Z away, Y now decided to help himself to Abby. He started by simply running his hand threw her hair, and then began to rub the back of his hand down her face. "What do you think you're doing?" Abby shouted.

"I'm not the one who claimed not to be a rapist, young lady. So why don't we make some good use of this down time? Besides, it may just be your last thrill in this lifetime. In spite of Abby's swearing, kicking and spitting, Y had managed to cut off all of her clothes. She still had the Taser in her pack, but was unable to reach it. Alex began screaming as well, but Y simply ignored their cries as he removed his pants and sat down on her. As he leaned over and attempted to kiss her, she yanked her head forward and head-butted him in the nose.

Carlton was now approaching the cabin. The dogs were tied and began to bark. Hearing the ruckus, Y started toward the door, but Carlton beat him to it. As he swung the door open it hit Y, delivering him the second smash to his face in the past minute. The struggle began; as neither could reach his weapon, they both dropped to the floor. Y again tried for his weapon, but Carlton managed to kick it away. Y grabbed for a knife; Carlton reached for a chair. Several swipes of the knife narrowly missed Carlton's face, before one pierced his shirt sleeve. As Y attempted another stab, Alex, who was still tied to a chair in the center of the room, was able to kick Y behind the knee, taking him down once more. Carlton smashed his chair over his victim's head, knocking the last bit of fight out of him. He then threw a blanket over Abby and untied her restraints. After Abby dressed, she gave Y a farewell kick in the nuts, and to add insult to injury, she said, "You have to have a lot of guts to take a wiener that small out in public."

Carlton shouted, "Back to plan A. You guys head for the cliffs and I'll be right behind you. And Alex, please concentrate, on one thing only this time: not falling." As they headed back into the woods, Z heard the commotion and started back to the cabin but Carlton had already set out to join Alex and Abby.

Z was furious with his kid brother. "I give you a simple assignment—watch a girl and an old man who are tied up—and you screw it up! Where are the twins?"

"I guess the boyfriend shot them, because he was the one who tied me up. From the way he was fighting. I think he is more than just a boyfriend."

"What about the girl?"

"The way she kicks, I'm not so sure she is just a girl." Z untied his kid brother, swearing at him in Russian the entire time. "I will try to head them off at the cliffs before they make it back to the river, while you get our raft and the motor off the All-Terrain," Z commanded.

This time the dash through the woods was uneventful. As they reached the chute above the cliffs, a shot rang out over their heads. Carlton had stored some cooking oil next to the slide, waiting for just this moment. He now poured the oil down the slide to provide additional lubrication, and gave each of them a sheet of cardboard to sit on. "Are you sure this is going to work?" Abby asked.

As a second shot sounded even closer, she decided not to wait for an answer. Abby yelled, "Later!" As she leapt onto the home made chute, Carlton responded, "Sure it will work, I tried it many times in the playground." As he spoke, he could hear Abby screaming all the way down, as she went flying down alongside the cliffs into the waters below. Alex followed uneventfully, and then Carlton. Midway down Carlton's trip, the strap of the automatic weapon became hooked on one of the metal edges of the slide, causing the weapon to fly out and crash onto the cliffs below, leaving him with only his .45. The trio made it down safely with only a few cuts and scrapes. Now they released the slipknot and pulled down the slide so that no one else could follow, then hopped into the raft and began paddling downstream.

59

"That was fun, can we do that again?" said Abby sarcastically.

"It looks like we have a real good head start on them," said Carlton. "Even if they have a raft, it will take them the better part of an hour to negotiate the cliffs. According to our maps, in about ten miles we will hit some rapids, and after that we should be in the clear," stated Carlton.

"Do you know just how big those rapids are Abby?"

"Now you're asking me that question. Now! This is the Pemigewasset River, and at this time of year it's famous for the best white water rafting around. Eventually it empties into the Gale River and then the Ammonoosuc River about twelve miles from here, but before that there is a three-mile stretch of treacherous Level 5 rapids."

"Just how big are Level 5 rapids?" Carlton asked.

"The scale goes from 1 to 5, no higher."

"That's just great." Carlton said sarcastically.

"Wow, Carlton, another fun ride. You seem to have created your own little amusement park out here in New Hampshire."

After Z fired his erratic shots at the cliffs, he headed back to the cabin. Ropes now had to be fastened to the trees, and the raft and motor needed to be hoisted past the cliffs down to the river. The Russians had a small outboard motor, although their technology was a bit outdated. The engine was a 2.5 horsepower, 1950 Elgin engine. It held a liter of gas, had a pull-cord flywheel, a manual choke, and was able to reach a speed of up to eight miles per hour. They would need all of that in order to catch up, as it took them a half an hour to reach the river below.

An hour into the voyage Abby cried out, "Look, they're coming. They have a raft as well, and their raft is bigger than ours; in fact, they have a motor on the back of theirs."

"What didn't these guys bring along with them?" Carlton asked. The rapids were now only a hundred yards in front of them when Carlton said. "They don't look that bad. It appears as if they are only about three feet in height."

"I can see that in addition to not knowing anything about horses that you have never done any whitewater rafting. When the rapids appear to rise three feet as you view them from the outside, they also descend another three feet once you are inside of them, and so from the crest to the depth there is a six foot difference." Abby rebutted. "Fortunately, we have Alex's rubber raft. A non-flexible boat has no chance of making it through those rapids, but the raft can bob like a caterpillar," Abby added. With those words, the raft entered the whitewater's of the Pemigewasset.

Alex and Carlton each held on to a paddle with one hand as the other hand grasped the nylon rope fixed around the top of the raft. Abby placed herself on the floor of the raft and extended both arms to grip the nylon ropes mounted on the pontoons. The rapids were enormously powerful, and the raft bobbed up and down five to six feet with each gyration, imitating a wild bronco. Carlton and Alex attempted to use their paddles as rudders in the hope of preventing the raft from spinning wildly out of control. "Have I mentioned to you guys that I don't know how to swim?" Alex asked.

"No need to worry. This water is so cold that if you fall in you're sure to be immobilized within a minute." Carlton replied.

"Thanks for the reassurance, I feel so much better now."

Carlton said, "We do have one advantage. I'm assuming they want Alex alive. We don't really matter to them, but they wouldn't be able to just shoot at us indiscriminately." Carlton contemplated using his pistol, but realized that he had only six bullets remaining in his clip. "I'm afraid that I can't get off a shot in these rapids," he said. The raft was bobbing and dipping, as Abby had predicted, like a caterpillar on a bowl of jelly during a tornado.

When the distance between them was a mere fifteen feet, Y tried to throw his anchor hook line towards them, hoping to catch the nylon rope of their raft. The Russians were now directly next to them; Y managed to grab on to Abby's left wrist and tried to extricate her from the raft. Abby reached into her pocket with her right hand, pulled out her Taser and zapped Y on the forearm. He let go a scream as he was thrown into the rushing water, where he immediately disappeared below the churning surface. Carlton shouted out, "I guess we'll never get to know Y."

Even though the rafts continued to bob and spin, Carlton felt he was close enough to risk a shot. He fired at the base of the raft, but his first shot hit nothing but water, as well as his second. His third attempt resulted in a blast of gunpowder, followed by a jet stream of air bursting out of the raft, as Z and his raft were swallowed up by the rapids. The assassin made a futile attempt to swim but within a minute he was the victim of a frontal attack by a protruding boulder that smashed into his forehead. Z was dazed,

Rust

as if a tuning fork had just exploded in his brain. To his good fortune, the frontal bone of the skull being the strongest of the head bones prevented a fracture. His good fortune lasted only seconds as the next boulder confronted the temple just in front of his ear. The weaker temple bone offered considerably less protection, and the sharp boulder penetrated his skull, piercing his brain. Gray and red matter oozed from his head; several deep ghastly gurgles were the last sounds Z made as he went down. This time he did not resurface.

A few moments later, the waters became calm once again, and the exhausted trio spread out on the pontoons of the raft for a well-deserved rest. Several miles downstream from the rapids, and still totally exhausted, they found a clearing in the river and pulled the raft onto the shore. Carlton made a fire that allowed them to dry out and catch a breather.

"That was a hell of a ride!" Abby stated. Now they needed to devise a plan to get back to Langley. The Russians had confiscated Carlton's cell phone and so they had no means of communication. The plan was that Abby would hitch a ride, lease a car, get hold of a cell phone, and come back for them. Abby was somewhat anxious about hitchhiking, although she still had her Taser. It didn't take long for her to get a ride, as the first trucker heading down I-93 picked her up. She used the trucker's cell, which fortunately had one bar, and phoned the number of Johnson's office, which Carlton had given her. When she reached Deputy Johnson, she gave him a brief accounting of their situation, as well as their location, based on the GPS from the cell.

Ten minutes after Abby hung up, Deputy Johnson called her back. "We have an operative nearby who will pick you all up and get you back to safety at Langley. He is a French Canadian, name is Mark Gauthier. He will confront you with an unlit cigar in his mouth, and ask for a light. Your response shall be, 'I don't smoke, but if I did I would try one of those.'"

Meanwhile, Abby was able to rent a Hyundai at Littleton and hurry back to Alex and Carlton. When Abby got back to the raft, they still had time to kill before help arrived, and so Alex went on explaining his discoveries.

60

During the ride through the rapids, Alex was still going about explaining his discoveries although no one was listening. Carlton realized that even if he managed to get Alex back to Langley safely, he would be isolated and engulfed with a plethora of interrogators, and so Carlton wanted to find out for himself exactly what Alex had discovered. Carlton now asked Alex about, "Can you return to where you left off, when you said, *If a free radical needs to steal an electron . . .* "

Alex now resumed his lecture as if nothing had happened. "Sure, but first I need you to understand the relationship between our blood and how rust affects it. Now bear in mind that the makeup of our blood originally came from the seas, and the contents of our plasma is very similar to the makeup of salt water. Early fish had open circulatory systems, whereby seawater simply diffused through their bodies. Evolutionists believe that the species of fish that we evolved from was known as the Rhipidistian crossopterygian. It was approximately 350 to 500 million years ago, during the Devonian period that the first creature climbed out of the sea and came onto land. Tiktaalik roseae resembled a cross between a fish and a crocodile, with primitive jaws, fins, scales, but with a skull, neck, and ribs of a four-legged walking tetrapod. Their circulatory system, similar to ours, was closed but they still retained characteristics very similar to salt water. Also keep in mind that plasma consists mostly of water, therefore our blood provides the ideal milieu for rust formation.

"Now, if one takes a rusty iron bar and performs electrolysis on it by passing an electrical current through it, liberating oxygen and restoring the elemental iron to its non-rusted state. Wouldn't it be great if we could simply do the same thing inside our bodies? Just apply an electrical current as a source of electrons to our blood vessel linings and simply *de-rust* them.

"Once rust has formed inside of our vessels, could it be reversed or is it simply too late to do anything about it? This last question is of great significance. When cholesterol-lowering drugs first came to the market, physicians asked themselves this very same question. In other words, once a fatty plaque formed inside the lumen of the vessel, was in there forever or could the disease process be reversed? The answer to the question carried great significance to those who already showed signs of disease, since there would be no benefit in taking a drug if the lesion was static and irreversible as opposed to dynamic and still able to change or reverse itself.

"To answer this question, physicians studied patients who already had evidence of coronary artery disease and had suffered from a recent heart attack. The lumen or patency of the coronary arteries was measured by injecting dye into these arteries in a procedure known as coronary angiography. The patients were then re-evaluated two and four years later and the procedure was repeated to measure change. The study was double blind, whereby the investigators did not know the treated group from the control placebo group. The results were impressive.

"The group that was treated with the cholesterol lowering drugs had a 40% greater patency, or re-opening, of the vessels than the placebo group. Their blood vessels revealed better flow in the arteries years after the original disease narrowing. This proved that even though a blood vessel is blocked by a fatty plaque, the process is reversible. It is a dynamic, rather than a static, process. In the same manner that the blood vessel becomes obstructed, it is possible to unobstruct it. To phrase it another way, oxidative stress is reversible. **In the same manner as rust outside the body is reversible, rust within our bodies is reversible. And that means that the damage caused by aging is also reversible.**

61

"If a rusted iron bar can be made to *unrust* by passing electricity through it, can a similar approach be used in our bodies to reverse rust? Since the process of oxidation is the same within the body as from without, why not apply the same technique to the body? What if we were capable of sending a harmless low current of electricity to the blood, and therefore provide an indefinite number of externally supplied electrons to the body? Now the free radicals that are circulating and looking to steal electrons can obtain them from the electrons supplied by the current, as opposed to having to steal them from the body's target organs, causing them to oxidize and become victims of oxidative stress. Stop oxidation, stop rust, and delay aging."

"Now this is easier said than done. We know that electricity and water do not mix and our body is made up predominantly of water. Everyone is aware of the danger of death by electrocution from high electrical current, but what about very low electrical current or even electromagnetic energy?

"In fact, the use of electrical current to treat disorders of the body has been around for some time. For over 60 years physicians have applied electrical stimuli to the brain in Electroconvulsive Therapy (ECT) for the treatment of severe depression refractory to medication."

"What do you mean by refractory? Abby asked."

"Those are cases that do not respond to medication." Alex added. "The current induced seizures resulting in a massive neurochemical reaction in the brain. Although the exact mechanism of action is unknown, it is postulated that the current causes the release and discharge of neurotransmitters. Brain cells normally oscillate at different rates, and ECT enables all of the cells to fire at once. It is analogous to shocking a failing heart in ventricular fibrillation and then managing to reset the timer. Patients suffering from depression have insufficient levels of serotonin in their brains, and it is believed that ECT raises the brains sensitivity to this neurotransmitter.

"The concept of sending electrical impulses through the body is not a novel idea. The greatest electrical engineer of all time, Nikola Tesla used this approach. Tesla was born in Croatia in 1856, and discovered alternating current, plus he had over one hundred additional electrical patents. His

AC current proved to be much more efficient than Edison's direct current. Tesla was the electrical engineer who designed the hydroelectric power plant in Niagara Falls, where his statue stands today.

"The Tesla coil is a type of resonant transformer which he invented in 1891. Tesla took two copper coils that resonated at the exact same frequency, both being twenty inches in diameter. One of the coils was attached to the power source, the transmitter, and the other to the receiving device. Since the two coils were operating at the same frequency, they created an electromagnetic field in between them, which can carry current in the same manner as a singer can fracture a wine glass when she hits the resonating note. This coil has the capability of receiving wireless transmissions. Mercury vapor streetlights and radio transmissions are both variations of the Tesla coil. This exchange of energy can occur without having any deleterious effects on the human body. Tesla proved this by often giving demonstrations on how he could safely pass his newly discovered AC current through his own body to cause a lamp to light.

"Radio waves also work by the same principle as Tesla's coil; however, they are too diffuse and therefore do not have enough usable energy. In 1943, at the age of 86, he offered his newly discovered *"death ray"* to the U.S. War Dept., which subsequently became the prototype for today's lasers. Lasers are another example of wireless transmission of energy. However, they need a direct transmission with nothing blocking their path and they are very powerful and dangerous if not properly regulated. Personally, I suspect that his practice of sending electricity through his body on a repeated basis had some bearing on his longevity.

"Give me a minute to mention a few other recent discoveries, and you will be better able to comprehend what I have found. An Israeli company, named NovoCure has effectively treated patients with brain cancer by applying an array of electrodes resembling a tight fitting helmet to bathe the cancer in an electrical field scrambling the tumor cells and preventing them from multiplying. The helmet is powered by a six-volt battery, and the results were at least as good, and possibly better, but without the side effects of vomiting, fatigue, and infection often associated with conventional chemotherapy.

"Utilizing this type of approach, advanced brain tumors progressed slower and sometimes even regressed. The patients lived longer and the median survival rate was up from 30 weeks to 62 weeks. Three out of ten patients were alive after two years, as noted by the National Academy of Science, published by Kirdon in 2007. The FDA has now approved a portable device made by NovoCure, which uses electrical fields to disrupt the division of brain cancer cells without affecting normal cells. The Novo TTF weighs six pounds and patients carry it around in a small bag and the current is sent through four electrodes attached to the patient's shaved head.

"Furthermore, a private company named Ardian in Mountain View, California has developed a methodology of treating uncontrollable hypertension by using low energy radio frequency wave energy to deactivate the kidney sympathetic nerves. The procedure damages certain renal nerve endings, causing the arteries to permanently relax, and has been successfully used in Europe for several years now.

"Recently USC researchers, de la Rosa et al, made some interesting findings using electric pulse therapy. They placed a microchip with aluminum electrodes in a test tube along with the whooping cough bacteria and added a pulsed electrical voltage. They were able to destroy the bacteria by lysing the cell without damaging its DNA. The main factors attributed to destroying the bacteria were the electrical field strength, the number of pulses applied, and the strength of the conduction suspension.

"I then asked myself, what if such a chip could be inserted directly into the body as opposed to experiments performed in a test tube? And guess what? There is now just such a chip. It is called the LP implant, a new kind of technology that operates on a bio frequency, DSP/CPU, 10 Terabytes of nanotube memory. It can send frequencies throughout the body and can communicate with any device that comes in contact with the body. The little black box that I carry with me is attempting to do something very similar. Inserting a chip into the body that can transmit data to a receiver is nothing new. Vets routinely inject identification chips into pets, so they can be located if lost or stolen. The microchip is drawn up into a solution of saline and simply injected into the subcutaneous tissue.

"There is now a company known as WiTricity Corp. founded by MIT physicist Marin Soljacic. They have developed a system of wireless electricity, similar to that used by Tesla's transformers, whereby power jumps across a tiny gap between two coils resonating at the same frequency. The energy traveling between them can reach seven feet, and this form of low frequency magnetic resonance has had no ill effects on humans, provided they do not have a pacemaker.

"These technologies are still experimental, so please don't try this at home. Before they can become commercially available one needs long-term safety studies, and the power needs to be greater so that longer distances can be traversed. It is just one more reason why I conducted my studies in Africa as opposed to the States. If you really want to die of old age, just wait for the FDA to approve your work. Furthermore, if someone has already reached the age of 90 years old and one says to them, 'I may have something that can not only prolong your life and but will also make you feel better.' What are you going to say? Where is the downside? Are you going to worry about a potential side effect ten years down the road?

"The future of all electricity is wireless and it will be commonplace shortly. In a similar manner by which your phone has been freed of wires, your TV and other electrical devices will soon find wires and batteries obsolete as well.

"In 1990, two medical researchers, Drs. William Lyman and Steven Kaali, at Albert Einstein College of Medicine in the Bronx, found that the HIV virus could be deactivated in a test tube by applying a low voltage, small direct current of electricity. Again, I asked myself, if this can be done in a test tube, why not try and attack diseases with electrical current directly in the body?

"Now this is no simple task. To begin with, one cannot simply pass electricity through the entire body for two reasons: First, electricity will take the path of least resistance. This point is well illustrated when one attempts to defibrillate a patient using chest paddles. One needs to place the paddles correctly for the electrical current to pass through the heart. One paddle needs to be placed on the anterior chest at the level of the right second rib; the second paddle needs to be placed at the level of the sixth left rib, not on the anterior chest wall, but in the mid axillary line that runs down from the center of the armpit. If an inexperienced person inadvertently places both paddles next to each other on the anterior chest wall, the current will simply travel along the skin from one paddle to the other, bypassing the heart, and be totally ineffective.

"Secondly, large doses of electricity can be harmful or lethal to the body. A lightning bolt carries as high as 30,000 amps of current and up to a million volts. Keep in mind, it is current that kills, not voltage. When the brain is struck, the blood can coagulate, causing anything from death, to stroke, or amnesia, paralysis, confusion, difficulty in coding, depression, and other abnormalities, including post-traumatic stress disorder. Lightning disrupts the normal electrical impulses of the brain and interferes with multitasking. Each year approximately 1,500 people are struck, with 75% receiving serious injuries and a mortality rate of 30%.

"Stun guns, or Tasers, also affect the body adversely by causing electro muscular disruption. These weapons interfere with the communication system between the brain and the muscles. However, to date, there has not been found any longterm adverse sequella in humans. So we know that high doses of electricity are harmful to the body, but what about very low doses?

"Low intensity currents (LIC), are now gaining popularity in electrotherapy. These units send a direct current, either continuous, or in pulses, into the body to promote healing. Using currents of 200 to 800 micro amps, they have shown to enhance the rate of re-epithialization of skin and shorten wound-healing times. And finally, work is being done so that one may insert a nano microchip into the body, which uses a bio frequency that sends and receives processing information via a high band width."

Once again Alex was abruptly interrupted, as a black Dodge SUV pulled up to where the trio was waiting. Out stepped Mark Gauthier, a handsome, 5'10", well-built gentleman, with designer shades and a small Backwoods cigar hanging from his lip. After the cues were exchanged they all jumped into the SUV and headed down the interstate. Abby then phoned the car dealership telling them where they could pick up the rental, which she claimed had mechanical problems.

Mark Gauthier had been a low-level CIA operative for the past seven years. It took him three years to get his first promotion, but only two months to have it rescinded after a DWI. Gauthier's life was in a state of disarray. He was obsessed with playing Texas Hold 'em poker on the Internet and had amassed massive gambling debts, which contributed to his recent divorce. He was a desperate man who found himself walking a very thin line.

When several well-planned operations had gone south at the last minute, Langley suspected that they had a mole in their midst. In an age of multi-nationalism, cyberspace and the blurring of nationalism, unabashed loyalty was becoming more and more difficulty to attain. For too many, it was the mighty dollar that bought loyalty. The Russian mobsters were well aware of the role of capitalism in this new age, and with operations in every major city, they could not afford to be without up-to-date information from Langley. So when the word went out that Gauthier was to be Stein's pick up, the Russians felt that they had one last opportunity to get their hands on Stein.

After a few minutes of driving, Gauthier pulled off the interstate onto a deserted road. "Why are we stopping here?" asked Carlton.

"Instructions ol' chap, just following instructions." Gauthier had them all exit the van, and then he pointed his .45 directly at Carlton's chest. "Sorry, ol' chap, but this job doesn't pay me nearly enough to pass up a score like this. I'm going to need that little black box in your pocket, young lady." Abby reached into her pocket and pulled out the black box, which was the size of a radar detector, as she looked over to Carlton for guidance.

"Don't be a hero, Abby; just give him the box, the same way you gave it to Freddie." Abby approached Gauthier and held the box out above his hands and then let go of it. As Gauthier reached to grab it, she pivoted and with all of her might and rammed the base of her palm upwards into Gauthier's nose. He screamed as his nose broke and blood gushed; he was blinded. Abby again followed with her sidekick, taking out his ACL. The only variation from the previous attack was that this time it was Carlton who kicked the perpetrator in the nuts. "Yeah, I can see that all you guys wear the white hats," said Abby sarcastically. Carlton then cuffed Gauthier with his own cuffs as they proceeded to deliver him to the Chief of Police at Littleton and then they continued on towards Langley.

62

During the drive, Alex resumed his findings once again. "One of the challenges confronting me, and one still in need of refining, is my goal of being able to send negatively charged particles into the mitochondria, whereby that can neutralize free radicals, rather than have the free radicals attack and deform the mitochondrial proteins. You may be asking yourself, why do we need to worry about this since I have already managed to send the antioxidant catalase into the mitochondria to accomplish the very same purpose? The answer is that catalase can only do so much, since we cannot overwhelm the system with it. Catalase breaks down the free radical, hydrogen peroxide, but blocking it totally can have some side effects with our metabolic pathways. If you recall, hydrogen peroxide is stored in our lysosomes inside our white blood cells and when released it is the substance that attacks and kills foreign invaders such as bacteria. Therefore, we cannot eliminate the formation of *all* hydrogen peroxide, and so a second line of defense to attack the free radicals is desirable.

"The task of delivering an electrical field directly to the cell's DNA and proteins may seem like science fiction to some, but it is now feasible. Nanoparticles can be made of different sizes and shapes. Rice University scientists state that their "rice" shaped particle, (no pun intended), can remain in the circulation ten times longer than its spherical counterpart. Whereas, Duke University researchers believe their star shaped nanoparticle is superior. Many nanoparticles are made with an inner non-conducting iron core, and an outer covering of gold.

"Such particles can amplify and focus light much greater than anything that has come before. They allow *plasmons*, which resemble ripples of waves in an ocean of electrons to constantly flow on the surface of the metals. When light of a specific frequency strikes a *plasmon* that oscillates at a comparable frequency, similar to that of a Tesla coil, then the **energy from the light is converted to *electrical* energy,** which now propagates as *plasmons* throughout the nanoparticle. This allows an electrical field enhancement at the open end of the particle making it more accessible for the cell's DNA and proteins to absorb the particle. This is a major breakthrough since it is harmless electrical energy, which is needed to supply electrons to our proteins. My working theory, therefore, is that **the flow of electrons created by the electrical field can directly neutralize the toxic free radicals which attack our proteins**.

"I have presented both of you with a great deal of information, so let me try to summarize the salient facts.

- Free radicals cause oxidative stress and aging by stealing electrons (oxidation) from our mitochondrial proteins deforming them and making them less functional.
- The anti-oxidant, catalase, has been shown to increase life span in rodents but only when one was able to incorporate it directly into the mitochondrial DNA.
- As sugar is metabolized, complexes are formed which crosslink with proteins, causing them to deform, resulting in the loss of elasticity and vitality to our organs.
- An electrical current passed through an iron bar will not only prevent the bar from rusting, but can reverse rust that has already formed.
- It is now possible to deliver wireless electricity, in the form of electromagnetic energy using low frequency resonating magnetic fields (Tesla coil), through the body without demonstrating any harmful effects to the body.
- Electrical current has been applied to our bodies to treat a variety of ailments, including electroshock treatment for depression, regenerating skin, treating some forms of brain cancer, and shocking the heart back into normal rhythm.
- With the use of dendrimer nanoparticles we can now deliver substances into specific areas of targeted cells.
- Nanoparticles of various shapes can now deliver microscopic substances directly into the DNA and cellular proteins and convert their light energy into electrical energy, serving as a source of electrons to neutralize toxic free radicals.
- Utilizing gene engineering we can now introduce synthetically modified genes into the nuclear DNA, and trick the cell into reproducing the desirable gene.
- The most effective approach to prolonging life in both yeast and humans has been through caloric reduction, which elevates levels of the gene SIR2.

"So what have I been doing in Bongele?

- With the use of a nanoparticle, I have been able to deliver catalase directly into the nucleus and cytoplasm, by capitalizing on its affinity to bind with the tyrosine kinase, an enzyme present in the cell. The mitochondria in the cytoplasm can insulate their proteins from free radical attack as they are neutralized by the anti-oxidant properties of the catalase.
- Utilizing gene engineering, I was able to isolate and reproduce the gene to stimulate production of SIR2, tricking the body to believe that it was in caloric restriction mode and therefore prolong longevity.
- Finally, I am testing various methodologies to supply electrons to the mitochondria through the use of harmless electromagnetic energy, which can be produced by converting light energy reflected off a nanoparticle into electrical energy, so that free radicals can attack the externally applied electrons as opposed to the ones of our mitochondrial proteins.

"In short, the goal is to prevent our bodies from rusting to death.

Abby had only one question, "Did you have to go all the way to the jungle of Africa to figure this out?"

63

Back at Langley there were extensive debriefings. The tapes that Carlton made from Alex's statements as well as Alex's black box were taken into evidence. After Alex was debriefed, he was shipped off to Dr. Rickett and a team of other shrinks to see if he was *in his right mind*. Next on the agenda for Alex was a meeting with a group of prominent scientists, physicians, philosophers, theologians, and Senator Stevens, Chairman of the Senate committee for Health Education and Welfare, and who also served on the Senate Banking Committee. Senator Abe Stevens had been a Southern Baptist Minister prior to becoming a senator. He was under enormous pressure from his constituents to support a balanced budget and he was well aware of the fact that the results of Alex Stein's research would hinder those efforts.

Alex Stein sat at the end of the long conference table as he examined his examiners. His opening comment was, "For some reason you folks remind me of the Hans committee that investigated *Clever Hans*." The committee members all looked at each other, confused, as Stein went on.

"So, you folks want to know what is going on in my mind, so I'll tell you." Alex proceeded to discuss his research with the committee in the same manner as he had previously explained to Abby and Carlton. As he spoke, the committee member's facial expressions ranged from confusion to boredom. "I don't know what you fellows were doing in college, but I was paying attention, and I learned a great deal about the human race, both in terms of how we got here and how we operate."

The Senator now rudely interrupted, "Mr. Stein, we have already read a great deal about your atheistic views, and personally I feel they are both antagonistic and insulting to our divine creator. Furthermore, your research attempts to alter the very essence of life as God had intended it to be."

"Very well, Senator, then allow me to begin to explore just what God has intended. Let's look at a few examples. Let's start discussing the chick embryo, which like the human embryo starts out with gill slits to remind us that our origins started in the seas . . ."

"Excuse me Mr. Stein, but we are not here today to discuss chick embryos," interrupted the Senator.

Stein quickly responded, "You see, that's one of the problems. You people just have no patience. That's why you don't come up with the right answers. If you find what I have to say that boring, why don't you just leave the room and have one of your aides page you when I get to the part that you consider important? Now, as I was saying, the chick and human embryo are almost indistinguishable from each other initially, and yet in humans these gill slits go on to become the bones of the middle ear and the thyroid and parathyroid glands.

"If you studied comparative anatomy, you would realize that the organs and features of any given species became modified to homologous structures in other species so that they could survive in the challenges of their environment, as Charles Darwin so elegantly described in his theories of natural selection and survival of the fittest. One can hold the skull of a deer, and compare each and every bone to its homolog in the skull of an alligator. One final example, and then you may invite the Senator to begin paying attention.

"Let's talk about the Purkinje system and the papillary muscles of the mitral valve, which sits between the left atrium and left ventricle of the heart. When the powerful left ventricle contracts, blood needs to be propelled forward out of the aorta to the rest of the body. In order for it to do that efficiently, the mitral valve first needs to close so that the blood does not regurgitate backwards into the left atrium and the lung, which would be disastrous.

"Fortunately the mitral valve has its own muscle attached to it, the papillary muscle, which enables the valve to close. However, the timing is of paramount importance. The valve needs to remain open long enough for the left atrium to deposit its blood into the ventricle, but then it needs to close before the left ventricle contracts to prevent back flow. The papillary muscle and the left ventricle contractions are timed a few hundredths of a second apart, operating similar to the distributor cap on your car engine, to allow the papillary muscle to contract just before that of the ventricle. This mechanism functions flawlessly, with perfect timing, every second, for the duration of one's life span. And this is only a single example of millions of amazing functions that occur in the body every day.

"Mr. Stein, it is apparent that you have a brilliant scientific mind, but science can only go so far in providing us with the answers to life's mysteries. This country was founded on Judeo-Christian values; we say, *In God we trust*, not, *In science we trust*. Your desire to tamper with, dissect, and invade the very essence of life as bestowed to us by our Divine Creator is unnatural and perhaps even immoral. For some explanations we need to rely on faith." Senator Stevens lectured.

Alex replied, "Many folks on this planet have different opinions and beliefs as to what God is and what he expects of us, and one cannot prove or disprove these beliefs. To quote Stuart Chase, "For those who believe, no proof is necessary, for those who do not believe, no proof is possible."

"Can you prove your theories Mr. Stein?" asked the Senator.

"Some things can be proven."

"Such as," Asked the Senator.

Mathematics! Mathematics can be proven. Math is as close as we can come to an absolute truth. *Mathematics is Beauty*. Take the Pythagorean theory, for example. In a right angle triangle, the sides a square plus b square equals c square. This formula holds true anywhere in the universe and will never change over time. It is an absolute truth.In Plato's *The Republic*, the author attempts to design the ideal society. Plato strongly believed in a strong education. And what do you think Plato considered being the most essential of all disciplines to master? The answer is mathematics. Mathematics dictates the relationships between many forms, shapes and structures throughout nature." *Truth is Beauty and Beauty is Truth, and Mathematics are both."*

"I don't doubt the very important role that mathematics plays in our lives, but what does it have to do with nature?" asked the Senator.

"The answer is *everything* Senator. Let's take *the Golden ratio*."

"Do you mean *the Golden Rule?*"

"No Senator, I mean *the Golden Ratio*. The Golden ratio, also known as Phi (ϕ)."

"The only thing I know about Phi, is that it's on my Phi Beta Kappa key," interrupted the Senator, as the room erupted in laughter.

"Phi is symbolic for the Golden ratio and is equal to 1.618034—- It is defined as an irrational number since it goes out to infinity, just as pi does. It is named after the Greek architect Phidias, who designed the Parthenon employing the ratio. Let me tell you a bit about it, since the ratio is ubiquitous in nature and throughout the universe.

"If you take a line and divide it into two unequal segments, such that the ratio of the larger segment is to the smaller segment, as the whole is to the larger segment, guess what? The ratio is always Phi or the Golden ratio, which equals 1.618. This ratio continues to appear throughout many forms of nature and throughout the universe as well.

```
    A           B              C
────────────────•───────────────
```
AC/AB=AB/BC
which equals 1.618 or PHI (φ)

"This ratio is present throughout human anatomy. If a value of one is assigned to the length of the hand, the combined length of the hand plus the forearm are in a ratio of Phi or 1.618 to each other. Likewise the same holds true for the ratio of the upper arm to the forearm, the distance between the eyes versus the mouth, the top of the head to the navel, the top of the head to the length of the forearm, and many, many more. The nerves, veins, arteries of the body branch in accordance with the golden ratio.

"The realization that Phi played a significant role in nature was first appreciated by Leonardo Fibonacci, the greatest mathematician of the middle ages, who wrote the *Book of Abacus* or *Book of Calculation* in 1202. In the Fibonacci series, each number in the sequence is preceded by the sum of the previous two numbers. Beginning with 0 and 1, the sequence becomes; 1, 1, 2, 3, 5, 8, 13, 21, 34, 55, 89, etc. The ratio of any successive pairs is always equal to Phi or 1.618, and the number more closely reaches Phi as the numbers increase. For example 8/5 = 1.6, 144/89 = 1.618033985, 10946/6765 = 1.618033985.

"Now Senator, perhaps you are thinking, what does this have to do with nature? You didn't appreciate my discussion about fish, so perhaps you may find rabbits more interesting. Let us look at Fibonacci's study of mating rabbit pairs as he examined it back in 1202.

"We begin with a newborn pair of rabbits (assuming each pair has one male and one female). The rabbits are in an enclosed pen and each pair reproduces every month, but it takes two months before a rabbit can become old enough to reproduce. How many rabbits will we have over time?

- After 1 month, you will have **1 pair**
- After 2 months, you will still have **1 pair** (still growing)
- After 3 months, you will have **2 pairs** (gave birth)
- After 4 months, you will have **3 pairs** (older pair gives birth, new pair still growing)
- After 5 months, you will have **5 pairs** (first 2 pair gives birth, third pair still growing).

"Note that with each succeeding month, the number of rabbit pairs follows the Fibonacci sequence; 1, 1, 2, 3, 5, 8, etc. Are you beginning to see a relationship between mathematics and nature, Senator?

"From the golden ratio and the golden rectangle one can construct the golden spiral, which is a logarithmic spiral which gets wider by Phi for every quarter of a turn that it makes.

"The DNA molecule, the template of all life, is based on the golden ratio and the golden spiral. The DNA molecule measures 34 angstroms long and 21 angstroms wide for each double helix spiral. Both 34 and 21 form a ratio of 1.618 or Phi, and both are numbers in the Fibonacci series.

"Fibonacci numbers appear everywhere in nature. From a single cell, to a grain of wheat, to the scales of a pineapple, to the bracts of a pinecone, to the hives of bees, to the horns of animals, to the waves of the ocean, all follow the Fibonacci numbers and the Golden ratio. The bodies of snails, seashells, ants, dolphins, seeds, plants, flowers, all have structures that employ the Golden ratio and Fibonacci numbers. When counting petals, buttercups, lilies, and irises each have 3; buttercups and wild roses, 5; delphiniums have 8, corn and marigolds have 13, asters and Black-eyed Susans have 21, daisies contain 34, 55, or 89, and sunflowers contain 55 or 89. All of which are Fibonacci numbers.

"In addition, the galaxies and the orbits of the planets, as well as the orbits of electrons surrounding the nucleus of cells, follow the Golden spiral. We also see the Golden ratio throughout art and architecture. The Egyptian pyramids, Notre Dame, the Guggenheim Museum as well as the Parthenon, which was designed by the Greek architect Phidias, who Phi is named after, all employ use of this ratio.

"The *Mona Lisa* and the *Last Supper* are created in proportions that utilize Phi. Many shapes used in everyday life, from your credit cards, to the postcard, to the Christian cross follow these proportions. The mask of the perfect human face, the Egyptian Queen Neferiti of 1,400 BC, possesses facial features in these proportions. Why is it that we consider some faces more beautiful than others? It is because those that more closely meet these proportions are seen by us to be in balance with nature and therefore more pleasing to the human eye. Even plastic surgeons performing reconstructive facial surgery attempt to emulate the Golden ratio. So I ask you Senator, do you now see a relationship between mathematics and nature? Or do I need to go on?"

"I believe you have made your point, Mr. Stein."

"Now there are some of you in this room who attribute all of these scientific and mathematical findings to a divine creator and believe nothing short of a miracle can explain these findings. You may say that nothing so intricate could simply come about without the work of a divine creator. The odds are simply against it. To this I say hogwash! To begin with, if the process didn't work, that species would not have survived the test of time. Those that are here today are representative of the very few that have managed to survive. There were millions of other species that just didn't hack it. Next you may ask how could a mechanism as intricate as this, simply come about on its own. And now, I will give you the answer, Senator, as well as to the other distinguished members of this committee. ***The answer is time, lots and lots of time.***

"The alternative explanation, that a divine creator was able to comprehend all of biochemistry, anatomy, physiology, embryology, genetics, mathematics, and determine the sequence of three billion base pairs of DNA and 30,000 genes for each and every individual, is simply incomprehensible and preposterous. Let's not forget about the hundreds of thousands of other animal species, as well as the myriad number of those in the plant kingdom as well as the world of bacterium.

"If scientists do not attempt to comprehend the shapes, dimensions, and characteristics of substances such as DNA, then how will we be able to alter and prevent disease and improve the quality of our lives? It is the loss of elasticity and suppleness of our tissues that bring about accelerated aging and eventually death.

"In a manner similar to that of a coiled spring in an automobile that begins to rust, lose flexibility, and fail to function properly, our mitochondrial proteins experience a similar fate. They rust, lose the ability to effectively recoil, mutate, break down and eventually cease to function.

"Now Senator, you previously stated that is unnatural, and perhaps immoral, for scientists to probe into such matters and attempt to unravel the very *divine* secrets of life. However, in my opinion, nothing is more natural."

Senator Stevens interrupted, "Let me go on record as saying that I take exception with both your methods and your lack of appreciation for the gift that the Almighty God has granted unto us."

"Senator, I adhere to the *atheist's code*, that only by scientific method and reasoning can we hope to learn about the world we live in, and that any other method of gaining knowledge is unreliable and should be considered suspect."

"When it comes to comprehending how the universe was created you simply believe in nothing, Mr. Stein."

"I disagree with that statement as well."

"Okay, then, Mr. Stein tell us what you believe in this regard."

"Well for starters, I believe in **Phi!** So allow me to ask you Senator Stevens, which do you think is more plausible? That all we are and all we have has simply been created by God, or came about through energy, waves of light, matter in motion, chance, chemistry, mathematics, evolution, and lots of time. Why would a loving divine creator insert all of the same blood vessels and its tributaries in a pig as in man? Why in the world would a divine creator want to put the gill slits of a fish in a human embryo? Do you all understand that all of the basic principles of biology, chemistry, and physics apply to everything in the universe, mankind being no exception? We are no different. We are not unique. If an iron bar can be made to rust when it comes into contact with oxygen and water, so can our organs as well.

"It is time that separates the 20-year-old with the start of a fatty plaque in his blood vessel from the 30-year-old pre-diabetic with insulin resistance, from the 50-year-old with premature aging from diabetes, from the 65-year-old with a heart attack, from the 75-year-old with dementia, and from the 95-year-old who we say died of natural causes. How do they differ from each other? What separates them from each other? It's simply a matter of the rate at which this very same aging process occurs in all of us, either slower or faster. Simply time. *It's all the same.* At the end we all rust to death. The only question is when. So gentlemen, you ask what my work has been about. It's really quite simple. My purpose was to see if I could delay the inevitable. *Just buy time!*

"As for my work with gene sequencing, nanoparticles, and electromagnetic energy, that too shall all come out in time." Stein then asked the committee members if they had any questions, in the manner that a professor might address a class of college freshmen. The audience sat in silence as each glanced around the room, looking for anyone with the courage to question Stein's logic. When no one raised a hand, Senator Stevens spoke, "Ladies and gentlemen, this meeting is now adjourned until further notice." He then stormed out of the room without saying another word.

64

Deputy Johnson began by congratulating Carlton for bringing Alex back safely. Then he said, "In spite of some terrific work Carlton, we are still required to place you on administrative leave for breaking your cover. You do understand that the Agency cannot tolerate that from anybody. It's very clearly stated in the Regs."

"What was I supposed to do, just keep lying to the girl?"

"Terry, you're a spy, a member of the CIA, that's what we pay you for. You are a professional liar! If we didn't want liars working here, we would do our recruiting at Eagle Scout meetings or Baptist Church Sunday School sessions. Besides, you're not supposed to care what the girl thinks about your morals. You can never break your cover."

"Just how many people know that you are a CIA Operative?"

"I only told Abby and she only told her Grandfather."

"This reminds me of the time when one of Lincoln's Generals came to him with a secret plan to end the war. Lincoln asked just how many others knew about the plan? The General responded, "me, as he held up one finger; you, holding up a second finger; and I told just one other person; holding up a third finger. Lincoln looked at his three fingers and said, "That looks like 111 to me."

"You just can't break your cover Terry."

"So you're telling me that I'm being suspended?"

"Well, if you insist on calling it that, I guess so. You'll have to go through Internal Affairs, you know—psych evals, lie detectors, all that crap; some pay docking, perhaps a temporary reduction of rank, but I'm confident you will get through it. In three or four weeks, hopefully, you should be back with just a reprimand."

Carlton did not say another word. He simply placed his badge, ID, and gun on the desk, turned and walked away. As he closed the door behind him, he heard Johnson call out, "Any chance you can set up a chess game between Stein and me?"

65

Over the next several weeks a plethora of high-ranking meetings were held in Washington. Members of the Senate, House, officials from the Office of Budget, the Surgeon General, members of the Executive staff, as well as a host of scientists, Board certified Gerontologists, and electrical engineers all met to discuss Alex Stein's findings.

The next committee scheduled to meet were the members of the National Heart Lung and Blood Pressure Institute, known as the NHLBI, a division of the National Institute of Health (NIH). This committee was comprised of one member from five national health organizations: the AMA, the American College of Physicians, the American College of Surgeons, the American College of Cardiology, and the Department of Health and Human Services, the agency that manages Medicare and Medicaid.

When one tends to inquire into the exact makeup of the committee, the response given is a bit circuitous. Upon requesting this information by phone, one is told to inquire by email, and when emailing, the response is that such information can only be given via phone. One of the duties of this quasi-governmental group is to provide guidelines and standards for appropriate treatments. For example, when the statin drugs, such as Lipitor, first appeared, the committee stated that patients should not be treated with these agents beyond age 70, in spite of the fact that it was clearly shown that such agents lowered LDL cholesterol. The MR. FIT study (Multiple Risk Factor Intervention Trial for the prevention of coronary heart disease) clearly revealed that the lower an individual's LDL cholesterol, the greater the longevity for life, regardless of age. Nonetheless, the Committee's position was not to treat those beyond a certain age limit.

Exactly what their motives were, one can only speculate. Was it the fear of a higher risk of side effects, such as myopathy, with potential damage to the muscles from statin therapy, or were there other considerations? Was it the fear of turning just about every senior citizen in America into a patient that would require costly physician visits, blood tests, and expensive medicines? Or was it the fear of prolonging life drastically and suddenly for many Americans, placing an enormous pressure on our resources, especially our financial resources? Many folks wished that their mothers could have access to these drugs, but the real question was, what about the other guy's mother?

One thing was certainly clear; having a significant portion of the population suddenly live longer would place an enormous strain on the government's financial resources. Those in the Office of Budget Management were quick to remind us, that in the first 65 years of life, the government lists us in the asset column. Beyond that, we move to the liability column, whereby the Treasury Department now needs to send us a check. When social security first began during FDR's administration, folks retired at 65, lived a few more years if they were lucky, and then passed away. With the average life expectancy now climbing past the mid-seventies, the situation has changed drastically. Can you imagine the financial straits the government would be in if folks began to live past a hundred, to say nothing about where we would put them?

Furthermore, any time a politician attempts to push back the retirement age, the AARP folks are certain to immediately terminate that individual's political aspirations. So, with this in mind, an ominous gloom hung over Alex Stein as he reflected upon his upcoming meeting with the NHLBI scheduled for later that afternoon.

Although the committee predominantly was to serve as a health care group, it was indeed a quasi-governmental body, and one that couldn't look at the findings in a purely objective manner. When the NHLBI committee met, all of the data and statistics hereto mentioned were available to them.

"Mr. Stein, we have reviewed your findings in great detail and without exception, the committee finds your work to be very impressive," stated Dr. Franklyn Dickson, the Committee Chairman. "However, the findings that you have presented to us have many ramifications. As you are well aware, no living organism on this planet exists in a vacuum. The life cycle of any one species has significant impact on many others. We are all evolving and evolution works best when changes occur gradually over time, enabling time for adaptation. A sudden drastic alteration of the status quo will not only affect other species, but the environment as well. Many such changes may not be readily apparent at first glance. For example, a sudden increase in the world's aged population would lead to severe overpopulation. There would be a need for increased food supplies, increased cattle production, increased harvesting techniques, additional healthcare resources, more nursing homes and hospitals, more medical personnel, additional housing demands, increased fossil fuel production, just to name a few.

"Furthermore, our budget reports show that a sudden increase in the population would have an enormous adverse effect on the budget deficit."

"Let's not forget about Ida May Fuller, who was the first American citizen to receive Social Security benefits, when she received a check for $22.54 on January, 31 1940. Ida resided in Brattleboro, Vermont and retired in 1939 having paid a grand total of $25.75 into the system, and at her death at 100 years old, she had collected $22,888.92 from Social Security. How many more Ida Fullers can this country afford?" Inquired the Director of the Budget.

After weeks of debate the committee issued their conclusions in a resolution:

> "The experimental findings of Alex Stein appear to raise more questions than they provide answers. Is it feasible to even explore prolonging life for a few at the expense of the many in the future? The committee finds that his work is in need of greater study and research, particularly in the arena of public safety. Therefore it is our recommendation that all materials and information gathered on the subject be considered *to be on hold, pending further review,* and thus relegated to the sub-basement of the Science and Technology building of the Smithsonian Institute Building, under lock and key, with the designation, TOP SECRET—FOR CIA EYES ONLY.
>
> *Be it so resolved*, the National Heart Lung and Blood Pressure Institute, a division of the National Institute of Health, by Dr. Franklyn Dickson, M.D., FACP, and Chairman.

66

Two weeks after Carlton walked out of Johnson's office, he received a phone call. "Terry, Chief Brenner here. How's it going?"

"Not bad, Sir, not bad."

"Listen up Terry, the word is that you're contemplating leaving the Agency? We don't want to see that happen. The Agency needs good men like you. Is there anything I can say to make you reconsider?"

"Right now, Sir, I have another very attractive offer, which comes with a fantastic benefit package. I believe some time away from the Agency will do me good, but thanks for the offer."

"Okay Terry, but if there is anything I can do for you, don't hesitate to call."

"Actually, there is something. There is a native in Bongele, CAR, named Kiros . . ."

67

One week later, Alex was sitting on the porch of his granddaughter's farmhouse when Carlton and Abby approached him. "Grandpa, we have hired another hand to help around the farm. He is out in the barn and I would like you to go say hello to him."

"Do we really need any additional help? It seems as if the three of us have everything under control."

"Another hand can't hurt. Besides we're planning on adding another bedroom to the house."

"Whatever you say Abby. What's his name?"

"It's one of those foreign-sounding names."

Alex just shook his head in bewilderment as he shuffled off to the barn. As he opened the door, there stood Kiros. Not a word was said as the two embraced, and for just the second time in Alex's life, tears ran down his cheeks.

68

Alex, Kiros, Abby and Carlton sat in the living room at Abby's farm. "Alex, how do you feel about making these incredible discoveries, knowing that they are now locked in the basement of the Smithsonian?" Abby asked.

"Perhaps it's for the better at this time. The world just isn't ready for anything that abrupt. Change is best when it occurs gradually over time. It will all come out in due time."

"Grandpa, you are so patient and forgiving. You remind me of the line in John Milton's 'Paradise Lost,' *'They also serve, who only stand and wait.'*"

Alex went on to say, "Besides, I have a new idea. Would you kindly shut the lights and allow me to be undisturbed?" Abby and Carlton looked at Alex, and then each other as they both bolted for the door.

As they walked towards the barn Abby said, "Carlton we have been through a lot together in a short period of time and I have learned a great deal from you, but that's not the important thing. After all, there is an infinite amount of knowledge to be learned and one never stops learning. To me the important thing is not how smart someone is or how much wealth they have accumulated, but how they treat others. Some folks are takers and those people never have enough and are never happy with themselves or others. You have sacrificed a great deal for both Alex and me, and I really appreciate that."

"I have learned a great deal from you as well Abby. You have the values, character, and sense of humor that I desire in a friend and lover. My promise to you is that I will never lie to you again. And I do love you, Abby."

"And I love you, too, Carlton. And to show my appreciation, I promise never to ask you to shovel manure again." They saddled up Hunter and Candy, and together they rode up the hill behind the farm as Moses led the way. As Hunter and Candy rode neck and neck, Abby asked, "How does it feel to go from being a spy to a mere farmhand?"

"It feels great, just great." Then they reached out and held hands.

"Yes it does," said Abby, "yes it does! I wonder, do you think we have learned anything from all of this?"

"Sure did. I don't know how long this life will last, but in the meantime, let's just make the most of it," Carlton said as they smiled and rode off, hand in hand.

69

EPILOGUE

Forty-five years later.

Alex sat on the porch of the farmhouse. "Happy birthday Grandpa! I would have put candles on the cake but then there wouldn't have been be any room for the cake. How does it feel to be 115?"

"Actually, I'm more excited about having had the opportunity to spend these past 45 years with my family."

"Thank you for saying that Alex. Now don't forget you promised to finish reading that story to the kids. Caden, Cole, go sit on G-4's lap, and he'll finish that story for you."

"I'm delighted that everyone is using that term today, when they called me Great-Great-Great-Grandpa it made me feel old." As the kids sat on Alex's lap, he began to read the story. "G-4, what are those things." Cole asked.

"Those were called electric and telephone poles. They carried electricity into your home, on wires, so that you could watch Panovision."

"How gross!"

"Excuse me Alex, my apologies for interrupting, but I noticed your tremor. Don't forget about your appointment with the Registered Nurse Assistant today," interjected Carlton. "She called yesterday to say that your APNC (Anti-Parkinson Nano Particle) came in the mail, and she needs to give you the shot. She said it might take up to a week before your tremor is completely gone."

"Abby, did you know that way back in the early 1960's there was a Neurosurgeon at New York Medical College, named Irving Cooper, who was treating Parkinson's surgically. They had to crack open your head and then insert a frozen probe into the substantia nigra portion of the brain and ablate the diseased tissue. Now that's what I call gross!"

"Amazing," Abby said, "Now all it takes is a single shot! Who knows what the future will bring?"

Alex added, "Well it's *about time* that we are managing to conquer some of these dreadful diseases. In fact, it's all just a *matter of time*. I can remember when those *Golden Years* were actually the *Rusting Years*. *Time* is what enabled us to evolve. *Time* allows us to oxidize. *Time* sets the stage for our genes to mutate. *Time* differentiates one individual's rate of decay from another. And in due *time*, man shall unlock even further secrets of aging. *Time* is all we have and *time* is all there is. ***All in due time!***

AUTHOR'S POSTSCRIPT

All of the scientific publications referred to are real and factual. The scientific information presented, (excluding the Epilogue and the experiments and findings of the fictional character of Alex Stein) have all been presented to the best of my knowledge.

ABOUT THE AUTHOR

Glen Joshpe, M.D., FAAFP, CMD, graduated from New York Medical College in 1969. He completed an Internship, Internal Medicine Resident training, and a Clinical Hematology Fellowship at Flower-Fifth Ave. and Metropolitan Hospitals in NYC. He practiced Internal medicine, Family practice, and Geriatrics in Stamford, N.Y. for 35 years before retiring in 2008.

He was a member of the American Society of Geriatrics, Fellow of the American Academy of Family Physicians (FAAFP), a nationally Certified Medical Director (CMD), and in 1990 received certification by the American Board of Family Practice and the American Board of Internal Medicine in Geriatric Medicine.

He has previously published *Joshpe's Journey* and *One Doctor's Life* (www.pubgraphics.com), both collections of autobiographical humorous vignettes, and *Pearls and Pitfalls of Medical Malpractice* (www.avoidmalpractice.us). **Rust** is his first novel, which focuses on his special interest in aging. Glen lives with his wife Vicki, in Bradenton, Florida, and summers in the Catskills. To order *RUST* go to www.amazon.com.

Made in the USA
Charleston, SC
08 January 2012